Hometown Love

Christina Tetreault

For more information on the author and her works, please see www.christinatetreault.com .

DIGITAL ISBN: 9780990651123
PRINT ISBN: 9780990651130

OTHER BOOKS BY CHRISTINA

The Sherbrookes of Newport Series

Loving The Billionaire, a novella

The Teacher's Billionaire, book 1

The Billionaire Playboy, book 2

The Billionaire Princess, book 3

The Billionaire's Best Friend, book 4

Redeeming The Billionaire, book 5

More Than A Billionaire, book 6

Protecting The Billionaire, book 7

Bidding On The Billionaire, book 8

Falling For The Billionaire, book 9

The Billionaire Next Door, book 10

Love On The North Shore Series

The Courage To Love, book1

Hometown Love, book 2

The Playboy Next Door, book 3

In His Kiss, book 4

PROLOGUE

The distinct ringtone he'd set for work calls bounced off the walls of the stairwell. Without pausing, Mack Ellsbury pulled his cell phone from his pocket. "Hello."

"Acker called a squad briefing regarding that Amber Alert," Special Agent Dakota Smith said in lieu of a proper greeting.

He'd gotten the message about the Amber Alert while standing in line at the deli. Rather than stick around to enjoy his late lunch, he'd had them wrap it and headed back to the office. "On my way now." Mack pulled open the door, then headed straight for the squad area where several other agents and the squad supervisor were already gathered.

"Okay, here's what we know. Daniela Batista, age twelve, left North Salem Middle School yesterday with a friend. She has not been seen since. However, her mother Maria Batista didn't report her missing until this afternoon." Duncan Acker, the squad supervisor, said to the other special agents and task force officers around him. "Evidently, she has run away before after an argument, stayed with a friend for the night, and come home the next day. According to the mother, they argued Wednesday night about Daniela moving in with her father. Maria and José Batista divorced nine months ago. Mother and daughter moved to North Salem while the ex-husband stayed in Fall River."

1

Mack's gaze remained focused on the missing girl's school picture. Of all the cases he worked, a child abduction got to him the most. To make matters worse, this one hit so close to home. He'd grown up in North Salem. His family lived there. He had friends there. Kidnappings just didn't happen in North Salem.

"Mrs. Batista called town police and reported Daniela missing this afternoon after her daughter didn't come home from school and all her friends claimed not to know where she is."

"Amber Alert mentions a white sedan," Dakota said.

Duncan nodded. "Daniela's friend told the mom that she saw Daniela get into a white car as they walked home from school."

"Friend give any other details?" Oliver asked.

"She said the car had four doors, but didn't remember anything else about it. She did say the car picked Daniela up on Pleasant Street."

Mack knew every inch of the town. Several stores, the bank, and a restaurant were located on Pleasant Street. "There's a few store fronts on that road. Some may have security cameras that caught something."

"Excellent. You head into town and pull any surveillance video you can," Duncan instructed. "Dakota and Oliver, interview the girl's friends. They may have kept something from the mother." Duncan turned toward Bruce, another agent on the squad. "Track down the father. So far, local LEOS have not had any luck, and Mrs. Batista believes her ex-husband might be involved. It was an ugly divorce and custody battle."

Duncan continued with instructions as Mack pulled out his cell phone. It was already past two o'clock, and he knew this was going to be a long day, which meant he wouldn't be able to pick up Grace before the daycare center closed tonight. He dialed his mother.

After several rings, she answered. "Hi, Mack. Everything okay?"

While he spoke with her on a regular basis, he never called in the middle of the day unless something was up.

"Missing girl case. I expect it to be a long day. Can you pick Grace up after work for me?" He hated asking. It would take his mom a good forty-five minutes to reach Boston and at least another forty-five to get home depending on traffic. He had few options, though, because he might not be calling it a day until midnight or later.

"Of course. I'll head over as soon as my meeting with the principal ends. I didn't plan to stay late today anyway. Grace can spend the night, and you can pick her up tomorrow."

Thank God for his family. He didn't know what he'd do without them. He just wished when things like this happened they didn't have to go so far out of their way. "Thanks, Mom." Mack ended the call, and then phoned the daycare center downstairs. Once he let them know about the change in Grace's day, he grabbed his gear and headed out.

Located on the North Shore, North Salem remained a picturesque New England town, a place that didn't change. In fact, with only a few exceptions, it was the same as when he'd lived there.

Mack turned onto Union Street and past the church, the For Sale sign on the old Kerry house catching his attention. He'd always liked that house. Unlike the cookie-cutter homes built today, it had character. Hopefully, whoever bought the place wouldn't make too many changes.

After passing through the intersection, Mack turned onto Pleasant Street, all thoughts of the Kerry house gone. If the car had picked Daniela up on this street, hopefully, at least one camera had caught it. Despite being a safe town, he assumed at least some of the businesses had security cameras outside. Since the bank would definitely have some, he made that his first stop.

After the bank's video angles proved useless because

they only covered the ATM machine and the front door, Mack headed for Quinn's Hardware. Being a family-owned business, he guessed there was a fifty-fifty chance they had cameras outside.

Giant green shamrocks and a leprechaun near a pot of gold decorated the front window. Pushing open the door, he wondered who had done the artwork. He couldn't picture Robert Quinn, the store's owner, taking the time to draw shamrocks. Perhaps his granddaughter, Jessie, had done it. According to his father, Jessie more or less ran the store these days.

Once inside, Mack headed for the front registers where Patti rang up a customer. About ten years older than him, Patti had grown up in the house next door. When the customer left, Mack stepped forward. "Hi, Patti. Is Mr. Quinn or Jessie around?"

"Jessie is in her office. Do you want me to call her up for you?"

He'd spent two years working here in high school, so he knew where the office was located. "I can find her, thanks."

The office was at the far end of the building, with a large window looking into the store. Through the open door, he spotted Jessie seated at the desk, focused on the computer. Knocking, he said, "Jessie, can I come in?"

She glanced at him, the movement causing her long dark ponytail to slip off her shoulder. Behind her wire-rimmed glasses, she blinked then nodded. "Hi, Mack. Of Course. How are you?"

"Good, but I'm hoping you can help me. A twelve-year-old girl named Daniela Batista is missing. She was last seen getting into a car on this street. Does the store have any security cameras outside?"

Jessie nodded again. "I saw the Amber Alert on the news. I can't believe something like that could happen here."

Part of him felt the same way. "Unfortunately, it can

happen anywhere."

"Gramps had five cameras installed a few years ago. Three are out front and two cover the back parking lot. Do you want to see everything?" She pushed the sleeves of her bulky sweater up to her elbows and scooted her chair back.

"Just the video from out front."

"Anything to help. The girl's mom must be worried sick." She rolled her chair to the back desk where a television sat next to the surveillance equipment. "Why is the Boston police department involved in this? Shouldn't our police department be handling it?"

Mack pulled a chair next to her. "I'm here on behalf of the FBI, but the town police are involved, too."

Jessie stared at him. "You're not with the Boston police anymore?"

"Yes and no," he answered, surprised Jessie didn't already know about his change in jobs. It was no secret—not to mention, his mom and her grandmother were in a quilting club together. "I'm a task force officer with the FBI now, so I'm still employed with the city, but I report to the FBI's Boston field office almost every day and assist them."

"That must be interesting." She looked back at the screen. "This is the view from camera one."

For the most part, the camera only covered the entrance into the store.

"What about the other ones?"

Jessie switched to camera two.

Mounted on the corner of the building, the angle of the camera allowed it to capture a good portion of the street.

"Excellent. Let's see what we got."

"School gets out at two-fifteen. Do you want me to go back to that point in the video?"

"Yeah. I don't know exactly when the girls came by here."

Jessie scrolled through the data. "Do you want coffee

or anything? I can ask Patti to get you one."

"I'm good. Thanks."

Next to him, Jessie fell silent again until she reached the desired spot on the video. Cars drove up and down the street, but none stopped.

After five minutes of tape, they had nothing.

"So how long have you been working with the FBI?"

"Three years now." Mack cracked his knuckles as he continued to watch the screen. "What about you? Has your grandfather handed the reins over to you finally?"

"More or less. He stops in a couple times a week, but he spends his time in the store with the customers." Jessie played with the cuff of her sweater as she spoke. "What kind of car are you looking for?"

"A white sedan with four doors. That was all Daniela's friend remembered."

"I don't think I've met Daniela or her mom."

"They moved to town nine months ago."

Jessie leaned closer to the screen. She must have seen the same thing he had. A white Honda Accord had stopped at the curb.

"Do you think that's it?"

He hoped so. "Could be."

Another four minutes passed before the camera picked up Daniela and her friend. Both girls appeared engrossed in their conversation as they walked. When they approached the car, Daniela stopped, said something to her friend, and then got into the passenger seat of the car. As the vehicle pulled away, Daniela's friend headed in the opposite direction—the way they'd been headed before they'd stopped.

"Oh, my God." Jessie's hand flew to her mouth "Did I really just see that?"

Mack pulled out his phone and dialed the squad supervisor. Now that they had a license plate, they had a solid lead. "I've got video of Daniela getting into a white Honda with New Hampshire license plate 532 RZC. I'll grab a copy of the video and head back in." Mack disconnected the call and then looked at Jessie who'd gone pale. "You okay?"

Jessie shook her head. "I... I just can't believe I saw that. Not here in town anyway."

He understood how she felt. "But now we have a lead to go on. With this, we have a good chance of finding her." He squeezed her shoulder. "I'll need a copy of this video."

She made him one before saying, "Good luck. I hope you find her soon."

"You and me both. Thanks for your help."

Mack returned to the office with the video and soon they tracked down the owner of the car, José Batista's brother. When they questioned him, he'd been so nervous that he slipped up and mentioned he was meeting José later that night at a motel in Manchester.

Now several hours later, Mack, along with other members of the squad and local police department, prepared to descend upon Batista's room. A quick check with the woman working the front desk verified which room he was in and that he planned to check out on Saturday. Not that he'd get the chance.

Mack gripped his holstered Glock as they approached the door. José Batista had no criminal record and no weapons registered to him, but one never knew what might be on the other side of the door. The guy felt desperate enough to kidnap his daughter and book plane tickets to Texas; who knew what else he might be willing to do?

Next to him, Dakota stopped and pounded on the door.

Perhaps assuming it was his brother, Batista opened the door. Dakota restrained him before the guy could even blink. While the other agents secured the room, Mack approached the girl seated on the bed. "Daniela?"

The girl nodded and gripped the remote control she

held. "Please don't hurt my dad." Tears slipped down her face.

Tired but relieved, Mack sat down next to her. "We won't."

CHAPTER 1

Six months later

Perspiration trickled down Jessie's temple as she crossed Main Street. She heard the sound of children in the playground on the Town Common, but she didn't pause to see if she knew anyone there. If she stopped, it was more than likely she'd see someone she knew and that would interrupt her morning run. Already it was taking longer than usual thanks to the four weeks off she'd been forced to take after pulling her hamstring.

She turned onto Union Street as her thoughts went back to the day before. In the five years since she'd ended things with Jeremy Flynn, she hadn't seen or heard from him, despite the fact he lived just ten miles away in Danvers. That wonderful record, however, had come to a screeching halt yesterday—when she'd walked into the coffee shop next to her doctor's office in Salem and saw him sitting with Sharon Pelletier. Jessie had stopped dead in her tracks. When their eyes met, he'd smiled, but she'd turned and walked out.

Ever since then, she'd struggled with the same question. Should she talk to Sharon? A few years younger

9

than her, Sharon lived in North Salem, too. While they were not friends, they knew each other. Depending on how long Jeremy and Sharon had been together, Sharon might not have seen the real Jeremy yet. He hadn't showed Jessie the real him for almost a year. Maybe she could save Sharon from all she'd experienced with Jeremy.

Side-stepping a puddle leftover from the previous night's rain storm, Jessie continued down the sidewalk, passing the well-maintained homes lining the street, her options going back and forth in her mind until she noticed the rented moving truck parked at the old Kerry house. Built in 1796, it was one of the oldest homes in town and had been in the Kerry family for over one hundred years. Earlier that year, Lincoln Kerry had passed away and his son had come home just long enough to clean it out and put it up for sale. If Lincoln were alive, he'd be devastated, but perhaps he'd be glad to know a fellow North Salem resident had purchased it and not some stranger.

She'd known Matthew "Mack" Ellsbury and his younger sister, Erin, all her life. And while Erin and her parents, Rose and Matthew Ellsbury, remained in North Salem, Mack had moved not long after college to be closer to work.

A dull ache in her leg caused Jessie to slow down as she passed by Mrs. Mitchell's house, and she waved at the widow working in her flowerbeds.

Trying not to think about the ache or what to do about Sharon, Jessie pushed on. Maybe she'd started running again too soon. Tomorrow, she'd head over to the gym for a swim before opening the store.

"Hey, Jessie," a familiar voice called out as she approached the Kerry house. "How's it going?"

Jessie stopped, grateful for the distraction as Sean O'Brien came down the front steps on his way back to the moving truck. "Hi, Sean. I was going to call you this afternoon. The bathroom vanity you ordered came in yesterday."

Sean stopped in front of her. "Excellent. If we finish up here early enough, I'll pick it up. Otherwise, I'll get it tomorrow." Sean uncapped the water he'd grabbed on his way over and took a long swallow. "I want the downstairs bathroom finished before Mia comes back for Ma's wedding."

"She won't make it back until then?" She'd become friends with Sean's girlfriend that summer when Mia had stayed at The Victorian Rose. Earlier that month, Mia had returned to California to finish the movie she was staring in.

Sean shook his head. "Doubt it, but I'm flying out to California next weekend."

"Need a break already, O'Brien?" Mack emerged from the house, a backward baseball cap covering his dark hair. "I guess that's what happens when you get old."

For a moment, Jessie spiraled back fourteen years and her tongue went from being a useful organ to a giant bowtie just like it had every time Mack had tutored her in geometry during study hall. A senior, and one of the most popular guys in school, Mack was the number one crush of most of the girls in her freshman class—including her. Not that he ever noticed any of them. Why would he when every cheerleader in North Salem and Danvers was constantly throwing themselves at him?

"Hi, Mack. Congratulations on the new house," Jessie said once the knot in her tongue loosened.

Mack's forehead creased and his eyes searched her face. "Jessie?"

Jessie let Mack's surprise go over her head. After all, he hadn't seen her in a while.

Sure, he visited his family frequently with his daughter, but he didn't make a habit of stopping in at the hardware store. In fact, before today, the last time they'd seen each other had been six months ago when he'd come in for the security videos. Back then, she'd still had long hair and glasses. Not to mention, she'd been wearing her favorite oversized cranberry sweater and a long skirt, a fact she shouldn't remember but did because, well, this was Mack, so he wouldn't have noticed the weight she lost.

"It's nice to see you. Your parents must be happy you're moving back."

"Yeah. Grace, too. She already has plans to spend every weekend at my parents' house. They haven't agreed yet, but she's well on her way to convincing them."

"She does adore your mom," Jessie answered, thinking of all the times she'd seen Mrs. Ellsbury with her granddaughter.

"You've met Grace?" Mack asked with surprise.

"This is North Salem, remember? Your mom brings Grace to my grandmother's every Sunday for quilting club if she has her. And your dad comes in the store with her."

Another look of surprise passed over Mack's features. "I didn't know that, but it makes sense."

"She even started her own quilt. Your niece did, too. Your mom brings her over on Sundays sometimes, too."

Jessie waved at another of Mack's friends as he came down the front steps. "Hi, Tony."

"Hey, Jessie." Tony Bates smiled as he walked toward them. "Unless you ladies want to finish alone, get your asses in gear. I've got things to do this afternoon."

"I gotta go anyway." Jessie took a step backward. "Will I see any of you at the block party tonight?" Once a month, starting in late spring, their community threw a block party on the Town Common, shutting the whole area down to traffic.

"Not me. Too much work at the house, but have fun," Sean answered. "I'll see you later." With that, he went back to the moving truck.

"I might pop in. If I do, I expect you to save me a dance," Tony said.

She rolled her eyes. She never took anything Tony said seriously, especially not lately. Ever since she'd lost the weight and ditched the glasses, he'd been saying things like that, but she knew better than to get into any kind of relationship with Tony. While he was a good guy, he didn't understand the concept of monogamy. He went from one woman to the next much like the way people changed their underwear.

"Bates, get your ass over here and help me with this," Sean called from the truck.

Unable to contain her smile, Jessie glanced at the ground. Whenever Tony flirted with her, Sean went into his protective guardian role. Thanks to her close relationship with his sister, Charlie, Sean treated her a like a baby sister.

"I might take Grace if she's not too tired. I think she'd like it." Mack waved at a car passing by the house.

"She loves it," Jessie answered, looking back up.

"My parents?"

"And your sister."

"I should've known." Mack readjusted his baseball cap, a habit he'd had for as long as she could remember. And she could probably remember every time he'd done it. Yeah, she'd had a big-time unrequited crush. Apparently, that hadn't faded too much because he was still the hottest guy she'd ever seen.

After saying goodbye, Jessie continued down Union much slower than she had been when she'd started her run. Yup, a run tomorrow was out of the question.

As she passed the senior center, she waved at the group doing Tai Chi, one of the many programs the center offered. She spotted Mack's grandparents and a few of her former elementary school teachers there. She'd tried to convince her own grandmother several times to try some of the programs, but Gran insisted that eighty-three wasn't old enough for the senior center.

By the time Jessie turned onto Pleasant Street, she'd stopped running and limped the final distance to her apartment.

"Morning, Jessie," Morgan Lee said, coming out the

door before Jessie could open it.

"Are you going to work?" Although she'd known Morgan for several years and considered her a good friend, Morgan had only recently moved into town.

"Someone called in sick. I doubt I'll make it tonight, sorry."

As a newcomer to North Salem, Morgan had never been to a block party, and Jessie had invited her to join her and her friends tonight. She figured helping Morgan settle into town was the least she could do because if it hadn't been for Morgan, Jessie would never have found the strength to leave Jeremy.

"Next time."

Morgan nodded and started toward the parking lot behind the building. "Have fun tonight."

Upstairs in her apartment, Jessie kicked off her sneakers and tossed them in the bedroom closet next to the boxes she still hadn't unpacked. She'd moved into the apartment the winter before but somehow still hadn't finished unpacking. By now, she wasn't even sure what was in some of the remaining boxes. One of these days, she'd get around to them. Or not. At the beginning of the summer, she'd made a to-do list, which included emptying those boxes. So far, she'd only crossed off half the things on that list.

It wasn't as if the boxes were going anywhere. She went into the bathroom, dismissing the boxes from her mind as she again wondered whether or not she should speak with Sharon.

Forty-five minutes later, dressed in a denim skirt and Quinn's t-shirt, Jessie walked into the hardware store, her home away from home.

***

"Thanks for the help today," Mack said to Sean, Tony, and Striker over the pizzas and beer he'd bought for them when they finished emptying the truck.

"Still surprised you moved back," Striker said as he reached for another extra large slice of meatball pizza.

Part of Mack was surprised, too. Growing up, he'd had a love/hate relationship with North Salem. While he loved the people, it wasn't always easy growing up in a place where everyone knew everyone's business. Thanks to the fabulous grapevine in town, it was highly likely that if he got into trouble at school, his parents would know about it before he even handed them the note from his teacher. If he made out with a girl in the park by the river, the girl's parents would most likely know before he brought her home.

Yeah, as a teenager, he'd looked forward to getting out of North Salem. Watertown had been a perfect spot for him. It was close enough to his family, but far enough away that the entire town didn't know his business. Or at least it had been a perfect place before Grace.

The older his daughter became, the more he recognized the benefits of a small town. Here, she was closer to her grandparents, and she'd grow up in a place where people cared about each other. For all their quirks, residents in North Salem took care of their own.

"Changed my mind about the town."

"Change seems to be a theme around here these days," Striker said beside him.

From all he'd heard and seen, he couldn't argue. "How's the Victorian Rose doing without your mom and you in charge?" The bed and breakfast Sean and his mom ran for years had become part of Sherbrooke Enterprises a month ago.

"Seems to be doing well. The place is always booked solid. Ma couldn't stay away, though. She pops in one day a week and helps in the kitchen."

"Talking about change, what do you think about Jessie?" Tony asked, his beer halfway to his mouth.

"Almost didn't recognize her," Mack admitted. She didn't look at all like the woman he remembered from his last visit to the hardware store, and she definitely didn't look anything like the skinny girl who'd played soccer with his sister and attended her slumber parties. "She looks good."

"Good? She's hot. Don't know how it happened. Thinking about asking her to the baseball game in Boston next weekend."

Mack laughed. To hear anyone refer to Jessica Quinn as hot struck him as crazy, but Tony was right. She had changed. He hadn't missed her cute ass or toned legs when she'd jogged away. In fact, he'd stared at her until Striker called him over to the truck.

"Find someone else, Tony." Sean reached for his beer.

"Evidently, O'Brien's the only one allowed to have fun." Any humor in Tony's voice was overshadowed by his sarcasm. "You know he's dating Mia Troy, right? The movie star."

"Christ, Tony, you know Jessie's not your type. All you're looking to do is score. If you'd stop and think with your brain and not your dick, you'd realize she's the kind you bring home to meet your mother. She'd be better off going out with Mack or Striker," Sean said, sarcastically.

Tony chugged the rest of his beer. "Have you met Striker's last two girlfriends?"

Sean shrugged. "Okay, she'd be better off with Mack, then."

"There wasn't anything wrong with Charlene." Striker finished his pizza.

Tony laughed before opening another beer. "Did you forget the Fourth of July already? I thought Mrs. Mitchell would have a heart attack when Charlene showed up on the Common wearing that dress and with the little peep show she gave Father Perkins when she bent over to pick up her purse."

Grace had gotten sick while waiting for the fireworks, so they'd left early—a fact Mack hadn't been happy about until just this minute. "Sounds like I missed quite the show that night."

"Forgot about that." Striker shrugged. "Guess that only leaves you suitable material, Mack."

Right now, Mack wasn't sure he wanted any woman in his life. He had his hands full with a growing daughter. "All set. You'll have to find someone else to play matchmaker with."

"Bet he has a hot piece of ass in Boston." Tony nodded Mack's way.

Before Mack could confirm or deny that—not that he planned to—the doorbell chimed. Saved by the bell. He wasn't up for the ribbing his buddies would give him if they learned he hadn't been out with a woman in eight months.

Leaving his friends to finish their pizza, he made his way around the maze of unopened boxes to the door.

The minute he opened it, Grace rushed in, grabbing him around the waist. "Daddy, look what Grammy bought me for my new room!" Grace pointed at the lamp his mother held in one hand while she clutched a large shopping bag from the mall in the other. "And she got me a new comforter that matches the lamp. Can we go put it on right now?"

Mack took the items from his mother. "You didn't need to do this," he said, even though he realized his words were falling on deaf ears. His parents spoiled their two grandchildren, and nothing he could say would change that fact.

"I know that." His mom closed the door then hugged him with her typical kiss on the cheek. "But I wanted to and Grace wants her new room to match Brianna's."

Brianna, Grace's cousin and best friend, seemed to be the defining entity on anything and everything in Grace's world these days.

"So can we go put it on my bed?"

Mack placed the items on the couch. "I haven't put your bed together yet. As soon as I do, we'll make it with all the things Grammy bought you."

"Let's put it together now!" Grace grabbed his hand and pulled.

His daughter might have gotten her looks from her mother, but she'd gotten her impatience from him.

"In a few minutes. I'm almost done eating."

Just as he expected, Grace pouted but didn't argue.

"Did you get everything moved in?" His mother ruffled his hair, something she'd done for as long as he could remember. "If not, I can bring Grace back later."

"We got everything off the truck. Now it's just a matter of unpacking." Grace had spent last night and all day with his parents, so he could move everything into their new house. "She's fine here."

"If you're sure. I don't mind if she stays with me a little longer. Or I can stay and help you unpack."

"We're all set, Mom. The guys will be leaving soon, and then Grace and I will tackle the unpacking. The two of us can handle it. Right, buddy?" Reaching out, he ruffled his daughter's hair and instantly a smile replaced her pout.

"Right," Grace answered with the kind of determination and enthusiasm only a five-and-a-half-year-old could muster.

"Okay, but if you change your mind, call me." His mom gave Grace a hug and kiss. "Will we see you tonight at the block party?"

"I don't—"

"I want to go. Please," Grace said before he could finish his sentence.

"It would be a great way for Grace to meet more children her age before school starts."

Mack looked from his mother to his daughter's expectant face. The very face she knew he couldn't say no to.

With an audible sigh, he nodded. "Okay, but only for a little while. I want you in bed on time tonight." He looked back at his mother. She always claimed Grace went to bed around her normal time, but he knew better—not that he would ever fault her for it. As a kid, when he'd stayed over at his grandparents' house, he'd never made it to bed on time either.

"Great. Then your father and I will see you there. Don't forget to call if you need anything." After giving them both a kiss, Rose left.

Reaching down, Mack scooped Grace up so that their eyes met. "Did you eat already? We have some pizza in the kitchen."

Grace hooked an arm around his neck. "Grammy took me to lunch. We met Auntie Erin and Brianna."

"Okay then, let me finish my pizza, and then we can start on your room." He carried Grace into the kitchen where his friends were hanging out.

"Hi, Sean. Tony." Grace sat in the seat next to Striker when Mack put her down. "Hi, Striker."

"You remember them?" Although he kept in regular contact with his friends, he could only recall a handful of times when Grace had been around them.

"Your parents take her all over town when she visits," Sean explained before Grace answered. "She probably knows more than half the people in North Salem already."

When he'd first decided to move back, he'd worried how Grace would handle it. She'd lived in Watertown in the same condo complex her entire life. Evidently, he'd had nothing to worry about.

***

Music from the Town Common greeted Mack as soon as he pulled open the front door. The town always arranged for live music at each block party. Most of the time they hired local bands, but occasionally they'd pull in someone from Providence or Hartford. At the moment, he was still too far away to see who was in the bandstand tonight.

"Don't forget. Only one special treat tonight," Mack

said as he and Grace crossed the street. In addition to food from the many grills, there was always an abundant supply of sugary snacks on hand at this gig. As a kid, he'd once managed to consume cotton candy, ice cream, and a bag of mini homemade donuts all in one night. He'd then proceeded to spend the remainder of the night sick in bed with a stomachache.

Next to him, Grace nodded, but although she hadn't argued with him, it didn't mean she wouldn't try to get more than one treat later on.

Cutting through Saint Mark's parking lot, Mack led his daughter toward Main Street. As they got closer, the air around them changed as the smell of burgers on the grill mixed with the scent of popcorn in the old-time popping machine the senior center brought over for every town event.

At the edge of the Common, Mack paused, his daughter's hand still clasped in his, and he took in the view. The scene before him looked like every block party he remembered. Everywhere he looked, people he'd known all his life interacted. Some danced to music performed by Gage Larson's band, while others sat at the tables enjoying food and conversation. A sense of coming home washed over him, and he realized how much he'd missed this place and these people.

"Can I try the games?" Grace asked, shaking him from his thoughts. "I won the ringtoss with Grammy."

"Lead the way." No sooner did he speak the words, then Grace started off as fast as her legs would carry her toward the carnival games the elementary school's PTA had set up.

"Which one first?" Each one already had a short line of children waiting their turn.

Going by the look on Grace's face as she considered the booths, one would've thought he'd just asked her how she'd solve the government's national debt.

"The ringtoss," she answered after several moments.

As they joined the line, Mack pulled out his wallet. He knew the PTA used the games as a fundraiser, so dishing out a few dollars didn't bother him.

"Mack Ellsbury."

At his name, Mack looked up at Kenny Adams. They'd graduated high school together. Back then, they'd hung out a lot, but had lost contact since.

"I heard you were moving back. You bought the Kerry place, right?"

Mack nodded. "Moved in today."

"Welcome back. Is this your daughter?"

"This is Grace." Mack and Grace stepped forward as the line moved.

"She looks about the same age as my son, Gabe. He's starting kindergarten this year." Kenny put a hand on his son's shoulder.

"Me, too." Grace pointed toward herself.

"Then I guess we'll be seeing you around." Kenny clapped him on the back and then led his son toward the food tables.

The next hour or so went much the same way as people came up and welcomed him back. Over the years, he'd kept in contact with some of his childhood friends, like Sean and Striker, but others he hadn't seen in years despite his regular visits back to see his family. Most looked like they did in high school, but there were others he barely recognized.

"So are you ready for a snack?" Mack asked as Grace climbed down from the bounce house the Parks and Recs department had set up. She'd already gone in the thing three times since they'd been there, each time coming out with the name of a new friend she'd made while inside.

"And something to drink," she answered with a pink face.

Pleased that she'd agreed without any fuss, he took her hand. "Sounds like a good idea. What do you feel like tonight?" Together they crossed the makeshift dance floor, which was empty at the moment while the band took a break. "The ice cream truck is still here." During the summer, the ice cream truck still made daily runs through town. He didn't think there were many that still did that. At least, he'd never heard one in Watertown.

"Nope. I want a donut."

He liked the way his daughter thought. The homemade donuts the church sold were better than the ones from the store or popular coffee shops. "A donut it is. Let's go."

Weaving through the crowd, they headed for the table where Mrs. Mitchell and Mrs. Quinn manned the electric pan fryers cooking up homemade doughnuts and fried dough on the spot.

"You did make it tonight," a female voice called out as he passed a table.

Mack turned, ready to reply, but his daughter let go of his hand and rushed forward before he could speak.

"Jessie!" Grace called out with glee as she rushed toward Jessie, then proceeded to hug the woman.

With no hesitation, Jessie's smile widened and she hugged Grace. That afternoon, she'd mentioned she knew Grace, but he hadn't realized they were so friendly.

"Jessie, I live here now." Grace released her and bounced up and down as she shared her news.

"I know. Your father told me today."

Jessie smiled at him briefly, but then turned her attention back to Grace, giving him a chance to give her a once-over. Now, like earlier, he was surprised by how much he liked what he saw.

"How do you like your new house?" Jessie asked.

Grace shrugged her little shoulders. "It's okay. I don't like the color of my room. It's light green." She pouted before she continued. "Daddy promised we'd paint it."

"Let me guess. You want it pink?"

"Or purple. Daddy said we'd see."

Grace sighed and Jessie looked back up at him as she tried to hold back a laugh.

"I promised we'd stop in the store and decide on a color we both like." Mack put a hand on Grace's shoulder.

Jessie turned back to Grace again. "We have a lot of nice colors at the store. You'll find something you both like."

"Will you help us look?" Grace asked. "Daddy's not a girl, and girls are better at picking out colors."

"You got it." Jessie gave one of Grace's pigtails a playful tug. "What do you think about the rest of the house?"

"It has a big backyard." Grace's voice went up an octave. "Daddy promised to get me a swing set and a dog."

Grace had been asking for a dog since her fourth birthday, and he kept telling her a dog needed a yard, something they didn't have in Watertown. When she'd seen the backyard of their new house, it had been one of the first things out of her mouth. "I said I'd think about the dog." He didn't want Grace getting her hopes up.

"But, Da—" Grace started.

"We'll talk later, Grace. Besides, I thought we were getting donuts." Perhaps a minor distraction would get her mind off a dog, if only for the night.

Grace's pout disappeared as if just remembering their initial destination. "Oh, yeah. Can I wait here with Jessie while you get them? My feet are tired."

He didn't believe her feet were tired for a second. She just didn't want to wait in line. "As long as Jessie doesn't mind." They would have to sit down and eat somewhere anyway.

Jessie pulled out the seat next to her. "She can stay. I don't mind."

"Can I get you anything?" Mack asked as Grace zipped into the chair.

"Just finished some popcorn, but thanks."

"Okay, I'll be right back." Alone, Mack joined the line for donuts. Every once in a while, he glanced behind him to check on Grace—not that she noticed. His daughter was too busy talking Jessie's ear off. The little girl loved to tell stories, and she'd talk to just about anyone, even complete strangers in supermarket checkout lines.

"Decided to join everyone tonight?" Striker asked as he got in the line.

"Yeah, Grace wanted to come." The person in front of him at the concession table moved and Mack stepped forward. He glanced over the freshly-made donuts. "I'll take two of the apple cider and two of the powdered, please, Mrs. Mitchell."

"I was so glad when I heard you were moving in next door, Matthew," Mrs. Mitchell said.

Although everyone else in his life called him Mack, Mrs. Mitchell insisted on calling everyone by his or her true name.

"Where's your daughter?" she asked, looking around.

"With Jessie." He pointed in their direction.

"Grace does love my granddaughter," Mrs. Quinn chimed in. "If your mom brings Grace to quilting club, she doesn't leave Jessie alone."

Mack accepted the donuts, surprised he was hearing about all of this now. To the best of his knowledge, Grace had never mentioned Jessie. Mack moved down the line to pick out drinks and pay.

Before he left, Mrs. Mitchell called out to him. "If you ever need anything, please just stop in, Matthew. That's what neighbors are for."

Mack nodded.

"And what can I get you, Alfred?" He heard Mrs. Mitchell ask his friend, and for half a second, he wondered who she was talking to. He, like just about everyone else in town, had called his friend Striker so long, he'd forgotten his real name.

Next to him, Striker grumbled a response but didn't correct the old widow. No one in town ever did. Man, it's good to be back.

"Anything else, Mack?" Mrs. O'Brien, who sat with the other two women, asked.

Mack held out a ten. "Two bottles of water, please."

With a nod, Mrs. O'Brien grabbed two waters from the cooler. "The same goes for me, Mack. If you need anything, please don't hesitate to call or come over." She handed him his change.

"Thanks."

Mack waited for Striker to pay for his food and then they walked back toward Jessie and Grace.

"I don't know why she does that. Not even my mother calls me Alfred." Striker opened his water bottle.

Mack couldn't blame his friend. He wouldn't want to be called Alfred either. "You could always correct her."

Striker threw him a 'get-real' look.

"Do you want to join us, Alfred?" Mack asked when they stopped at the table.

Striker elbowed him in the ribs. "Another time. Nicole's waiting for me." He gestured toward a woman seated at another table.

Mack tried to place Nicole as he put down the food.

"Who's Alfred?" Grace asked from the other side of Jessie.

"What?"

"Who's Alfred?" Grace asked again as she reached for a donut.

"Just giving Striker a hard time. His real name is Alfred." To make the conversation with both his daughter and Jessie easier, he took a seat on the other side of the table.

Grace considered his answer as she started on an apple cider donut. "Why do you call him Striker?"

"It's a nickname. Like you calling Jessie 'Jessie,' when her real name is Jessica."

"But Striker doesn't sound like Alfred. I thought a nickname sounded like your real name."

He could understand how she'd reached that

conclusion. "Sometimes, but not always."

"Striker is his last name," Jessie added.

Happy with the answers, Grace fell silent as she munched on her snack.

Before Mack could continue his conversation with Jessie, she raised a hand and waved at someone.

"Maryanne and Kelsey just got here. I'm going to say hello." She pushed back her chair, prepared to leave. "I know you have your mom and sister to help out, but if you need anything, let me know. I'm always around."

"Thanks." Mack watched Jessie walk toward Maryanne and Kelsey, both life-long North Salem residents, and was again surprised by the physical changes in her. Maybe everything in North Salem didn't always remain the same. Jessie Quinn certainly hadn't, and he wasn't the only one who noticed how great she looked tonight. He saw several other guys watching her as she walked away, and he understood why.

CHAPTER 2

Jessie turned the corner just in time to stop the blue painters' tape with her foot before it could roll any farther down the aisle. Then she turned the cardboard display, which held the tape, upright again.

"I'm really sorry about that," Tina Adams said as she bent to help Jessie pick up the rolls now covering the floor. "Gabe, help Miss Jessie pick up this mess."

"Don't worry about it, Tina. It was an accident." An accident most likely caused by Gabe, who still stood with both hands on the handle of his baby brother's stroller.

Tina haphazardly stacked a few rolls of tape on the shelf. "Gabe likes to help me push his brother," she said, confirming Jessie's suspicions that he'd knocked into the display.

"This thing gets knocked over at least once a week." Jessie exaggerated a little. Actually, in the two months it'd been up, only one other person had knocked it over. "It'll only take me a few minutes to fix it. You can finish your shopping." *And head home before your son causes any more damage.* Jessie watched as Gabe took off down the aisle, pushing the stroller as fast as he could, his baby brother laughing the whole time.

"Thanks, Jessie." Leaving the mess behind, Tina hurried after her sons.

With a little shake of her head, Jessie finished putting the display back together and then continued on toward aisle six, her original destination. Earlier that morning, Phil Larson had called looking for ten more cases of slate tiles. She'd promised to check and get back to him. Although a simple task, this was the first time all day she'd had the opportunity to check.

Once in aisle six, Jessie scanned the shelves, looking for the right item code. After finding it, she counted the number of cases left. Perfect; they had three here and nine in the backroom, enough to give Phil what he needed and not wipe out their inventory. With one more thing crossed off her morning to-do list, Jessie made her way back to her small office. As a child, she'd spent countless days in this same office with her grandfather as he managed the store. Now it was hers.

In a way, she knew her grandfather would've loved to turn everything over to his only son. Unfortunately, her dad had never been interested in the store. All her life, he'd driven tractor-trailers cross-country, sometimes spending a week or more away from North Salem. As a result, she'd been raised more or less by her grandparents, with her father stopping home between runs. These days, he was around more, but he still had no interest in the family business. Instead, he spent his days driving trailers for a New England-based grocery store, which at least allowed him to return home each night. That didn't mean they saw each other all that much more. Not long after her father had given up cross-country driving and moved back into Blackthorne Farm, her grandparents' home, she'd moved into her own apartment.

For the most part, she tried not to resent her father's decision to keep driving those long hauls after her birth. After all, he had only been twenty when she was born and his wife had died during childbirth. Then the woman he'd married two years later divorced him. Finding oneself as a single parent at that age would be rough on anyone. And her grandparents had given her the love of four parents, but still, it would've been nice if her father had been around more.

As if thoughts of her grandfather had conjured him up, he appeared in the doorway. He still came in a few days a week, but it was more of a way for him to get out of the house than because the store needed him. As someone who had worked hard all his life, he found retirement difficult.

"Sean's out front looking for you, honey. If you're busy, I can help him."

"I got it, Gramps. Thanks. But I saw Rex come in a little while ago." Jessie came around from behind her desk. Rex often stopped in to enjoy the free coffee and talk with her grandfather. "I just made a fresh pot fifteen minutes ago and grabbed some of those crawlers you like from Peggy Sue's. There were still some left when I checked." After dropping a kiss on her grandfather's cheek, she went to the front of the store where Sean stood talking to Brian, a high school student who worked there.

"Sorry I never got here yesterday," he said, after ending his other conversation. "I had dinner with Taylor and my father," he explained, referring to his much younger half-sister.

She noticed that when he mentioned his dad, Sean no longer sounded bitter, a huge change from a few months ago. "Don't worry about it. How's Taylor?" She'd only met Taylor once since the girl had entered Sean and Charlie's lives, but she seemed like a nice kid.

"Good. She's looking forward to skiing this winter." Sean followed Jessie toward the backroom where special orders were stored.

"This one is yours." She pointed to the huge box as she hit the button that raised the garage-style door. Sean had picked up enough orders over the years to know he should park his truck near the door.

"Do you want me to get Brian to help you?" She stepped outside for a moment of fresh air.

"I'll help you with it," Mack said from the parking spot next to Sean's truck as he helped Grace out.

"You promised we'd pick out paint," Grace said, stepping between the two vehicles, a slight whine coming out in her voice.

"We will. This won't take long. Promise."

Jessie heard the note of irritation in Mack's voice and wondered if the father and daughter had a rough morning. "If you want, I can bring Grace inside to start looking. Just close the door when you're done."

"Please, Daddy."

"Go ahead. I'll be right in."

Jessie took Grace by the hand and led her through the back room. "Did you have fun last night?"

"I got to stay up past my bedtime."

As a little girl, staying up past her bedtime had always seemed like a major event to Jessie, and evidently it was universal for all children. "I'll tell you a secret. So did I." Jessie kept her voice low as if she didn't want anyone else to hear.

Grace giggled. "Adults don't have a bedtime."

"Says who?" Jessie led her toward the display of paint cards.

"Adults go to bed when they want," Grace answered with authority. "Nobody tells Daddy when to go to bed."

A vision of Mrs. Ellsbury telling an adult Mack to brush his teeth and go to bed passed through Jessie's head and she laughed. "I guess you're right." Together they stopped, a rainbow of color before them. "Let's start over here. That's where all the pinks are." Jessie pointed to an area filled with everything from pastel to neon.

When Mack joined them a few minutes later, Grace already had several color samples in her hand.

"I see you've already found some, buddy."

Jessie hadn't noticed last night, but now, seeing Mack next to his daughter, she realized they looked nothing alike except for their eyes. They were the same shape and the same shade of light hazel. But while Mack's hair was almost black, Grace sported two lopsided strawberry-blonde pigtails. Her skin was fair with a dusting of freckles across her nose, and Jessie suspected she burned easily if she spent too much time in the sun. Mack's skin was a few shades darker.

"These are just the pink ones." Grace handed her father the cards and moved down toward the purples, her hand immediately going for the brightest, most vibrant shade available.

Mack shuffled through the cards, then looked up at Jessie. "People buy these colors?"

"You'd be surprised." *You're in big trouble, Mack.*

"Here, Daddy." Grace held up another set of cards.

Without a word, he added them to his stack and began sorting them, discarding some on a shelf as he went.

"That's my favorite," Grace said when one particular card joined the stack forming on the shelf.

A pink almost as bright as a highlighter, Jessie cringed at the thought of an entire room that shade.

"Way too bright." Mack continued to add cards to his rejection pile. "How about this one?" He held up a card and pointed to the third square on the bottom; a shade of pink so light it appeared almost white.

Grace shook her head, her pigtails swinging back and forth. "I like this one." She grabbed the bright pink card from the rejection pile.

"Sorry, Grace, but we're not painting your room that color," Mack said.

Understanding Grace's displeasure in Mack's choices, Jessie pointed to the card in Mack's hand. "I think we have something similar to that, but with a touch more color." A quick glance over at the display revealed what she wanted. "What about this?" She handed Mack the card, her hand brushing against his. The brief contact sent a spark of excitement up her arm.

"This would be okay."

"It's too light." Grace crossed her arms and frowned.

"I think it is really pretty, and maybe your dad will let you get some decals to decorate the wall. They come off easily so you can move them around when you're ready for a change."

Grace studied the color again. "Can I get some?"

Mack nodded just as his cell phone went off. "Grace, it's work. I have to take this," he said as he pulled the phone from his pocket.

"I can show Grace the decals if you want." Jessie figured it would keep the little girl occupied while he took the call.

"Thanks. I'll be as quick as I can, Grace."

Mack stepped away and Jessie took Grace farther down the aisle. "We just got in a bunch of new princess decals and I know we have some animal ones, too."

Grace looked through various decals, picking out her favorites and handing them to Jessie. Soon, she held several packages containing various princesses and one with puppies. "Do you think Daddy will let me get them all?" She handed Jessie yet another package.

Unsure of just how many Mack would get, Jessie was careful with her answer. "Maybe you should pick the ones you like the most for now."

"Hell." Mack's muttered oath had her looking up in his direction. As he came toward them with a scowl on his face, he raised his phone to his ear again. "We need to go, buddy. I'm sorry." He looked down at Grace, the phone still next to his ear as if waiting for someone to answer.

"But, Daddy, we didn't—"

Mack pulled the phone away from his ear. "We'll come back this week." He looked away from Grace and at Jessie.

"Have you seen my mother or father today, Jessie?"

"No. Is everything okay?"

"Emergency at work. I need to go in. Erin's on her way to New York to see her in-laws and neither my mother nor father are answering. I need to find someone to watch Grace."

Mack worked as a task force officer with the FBI now, and if he was getting called in on his day off, it must be serious. "She can stay with me. I'm leaving here at one when Ty comes in," she said, referring to her assistant manager.

Mack considered her offer. "I don't know when I'll be home."

"I can keep trying your mom and bring Grace over if I get her."

"Are you sure?"

"Positive. Don't worry about it."

Relief replaced the concern on Mack's face and he knelt down in front of Grace. "As much as I'd rather stay with you, I need to go into work. You be a good girl for Jessie. We'll get decals and paint tomorrow."

"I'll be good. Promise," Grace answered, all the excitement from earlier exiting her body.

"My cell number is on here." Mack handed Jessie a business card he pulled from his wallet. "Text me if you bring her to my mom's house. If I don't hear from you, I'll pick her up at your house. Are you still at your grandparent's place?"

Without looking at the card, she slipped it into her jeans pocket. "No, I live in the apartment building next to the Jade Orient on the second floor."

"Okay. Thanks again. I owe you one, Jessie." Then, after giving Grace a kiss and hug, he hurried out the door.

Oh, man, she'd love to collect on that promise.

***

The phone call that morning from his ex-wife should have given him an idea of how the rest of his day would play out. For the most part, Bethany called every Thursday to talk to Grace and then arranged to see her once or twice a month. Since today was Sunday, he'd known something was up as soon as he saw the call was from her. Sure enough, she'd called to let him know she couldn't see Grace this upcoming weekend as planned. This was the second time in a row she'd canceled. The last time Grace had seen her mother had been almost five weeks ago. Much to his gratitude, Grace had taken the news well this morning, perhaps because Bethany's behavior wasn't anything new. Since their initial separation, she often canceled planned visits. Even before the divorce, she'd not been what he'd call a hands-on mother. While during the week they had both worked and Grace had gone to daycare, on the weekend Bethany had often gone shopping or spent time with friends rather than with him and Grace. When Grace had taken swim lessons at the local gym, he'd been the one to take her most Saturday mornings. Yeah, Grace had spent her entire life coming in second place in her mother's life, which explained why she'd handled Bethany's absence so well.

Nope, the change in plans hadn't been the thing to set Grace off into a thirty-minute-long temper tantrum, a fit that might not have been so bad if she had not gone to bed so late two nights in a row. He should've anticipated the meltdown the moment she asked about the dog again. Instead of flat-out saying no, he should have said he'd think about it. Those simple words would have allowed him to bypass the resulting fit. He hated to lie to his daughter though, and while he was open to getting a dog at some point, it was not happening this month.

The icing on the cake had been the phone call from his supervisor. The lieutenant governor's sixteen-year-old daughter hadn't been seen since going to a friend's house the night before and all hands were being called in to look for her. So rather than spend a relaxing Sunday afternoon with his daughter, he spent much of the day talking to a sixteen-year-old's friends and canvassing the area where she'd last been seen. At least they'd found her safe, not abducted like her parents feared, but with her college-age boyfriend.

Leaving the highway behind, Mack headed toward North Salem. He didn't want to entertain the idea of Grace pulling a stunt like the lieutenant governor's daughter had. When he hit a red light, Mack checked his cell phone again. Several times already he'd checked, expecting a message from Jessie telling him she'd dropped Grace off with his parents, but despite the late hour, he still hadn't gotten one.

Thank God she'd been around today. If she hadn't offered to watch Grace, he didn't know who he would have called with his parents MIA and his sister away. Sure, he had several good friends in town, but they were all single guys who wouldn't know what to do with a five-and-half-year-old girl. In the past, before they'd moved back, he'd relied on Tonya, the analyst who lived in the condo next to theirs and worked in his office. She and her husband had children of their own, but those kids were in high school. As much as he liked Tonya and her family, he always felt guilty when he had to drop Grace off with them. Not having to rely on his neighbor like that had been just one of the many benefits of moving home.

He could see lights in several windows on the second floor when he pulled up in front of Jessie's apartment. As soon as he opened his car door, he got a whiff of Chinese food from the restaurant next door and his stomach rumbled. He'd grabbed a fast food burger around one, but that had been nine hours ago. Food would have to wait until he got home. Jessie had been babysitting Grace since late that morning.

The stairs creaked as he took them two at a time. On the second floor landing, he found two apartment doors. Jessie hadn't said which was hers and he glanced between them before he picked one. The door on the right was a solid green with no decoration of any kind except for the gold A in the center. The other, however, had a border of tiny white flowers stenciled all the way around it and a wooden doorplate, which read *Welcome* just below the peephole. The Jessie he remembered from high school would've taken the time to stencil in flowers.

After knocking on the door, he waited. He heard a deadbolt turn and then the door opened.

"Hey, Mack. Come on in," Jessie said, stepping to the side. "Grace is asleep on the couch."

He entered a rather large kitchen, considering it was an apartment, and the faint smell of popcorn lingered in the air. "Sorry it's so late." Mack closed the door behind him. "You never got in touch with my parents?"

"I got your mom about ten minutes ago, but they were still in Portland."

His mom loved to go shopping there. Most of the time, she took his sister with her, but if Erin was not available and his dad couldn't come up with a good excuse, she'd drag him along. "I owe you big time."

"Honestly, Mack, it was no big deal. We had fun. After we left the store, we stopped at the playground. Grace met another girl who's starting kindergarten this year. Then we came here and had some pizza. Afterward, we made popcorn and put some movies on. Grace fell asleep about halfway through the second one."

His stomach gave a little rumble again. "You still saved me big time. If I can help you out in any way, just let me know."

Jessie waved a dismissive hand in his direction, letting him know she didn't expect anything in return. "Grace is in here." She walked into the next room.

As often happened after a long day like today, the sight of his little girl filled him with so much love it helped him remember why he did the job he did. Bending down, he scooped her up, careful not to wake her. With some luck, he'd get her into the car and buckled without disturbing her too much. Cradling her against him, he noticed the pigtails he'd fashioned that morning had been replaced by some fancy braids.

"She's always begging me to do something different with her hair. Ponytails and pigtails are all I can manage. She must have loved when you did this."

Jessie shrugged. "She wanted her hair to look like Heather's, the little girl she met at the park."

Mack carried Grace back to the kitchen door, Jessie following close behind. "By the way, how much do I owe you for the pizza?"

"You don't. I planned on ordering pizza tonight anyway."

He wanted to press the issue, but didn't want to get in an argument either. "If you say so, but you'll have to let me buy you dinner sometime. Thanks again."

Before he could reach for the doorknob, Jessie pulled it open for him. Her arm brushed against his and his body picked that moment to remind him how long it had been since he'd had sex.

"Anytime, really. We had fun." Jessie's voice pulled his thoughts away from the discomfort he suddenly felt. "Oh, and before I forget, she picked out the decals she liked the best. I put them aside for you to see. She was worried someone would buy them."

"I'll stop in later this week and get them."

Mack managed to get Grace into the car without waking her, but the second he stretched the seatbelt across her lap, her eyes popped open.

"I love you, Daddy," she said, her unfocused eyes a clear sign she wasn't awake.

Leaning forward, he kissed her forehead. "I love you too, buddy." No sooner did he say the words than Grace's eyes drifted closed again.

He didn't hear another peep as he drove home. She did open her eyes once when he lifted her from her car seat, but otherwise, he got her tucked into bed with no trouble.

After locking his gun in the safe and dropping his

wallet and handcuffs on his nightstand, he went in search of food. He'd polished off the leftover pizza last night. He'd intended to hit the grocery store after their trip to Quinn's that morning, but the call from work had killed that, which meant he had few options. Grabbing a box of cereal, he poured himself a bowl and slapped together two peanut butter and jelly sandwiches. Tomorrow he'd try to leave work early and shop. Back in Watertown, there had been a large chain grocery store that would deliver groceries right to his door; a service that came in handy after Bethany had left. His ex-wife hadn't been big into helping around the house, but she had always kept the kitchen well stocked.

Unfortunately, the grocery store in North Salem provided no such services, so he'd have to fit food shopping into his weekend routine.

***

Dressed in her favorite T-shirt and shorts, Grace sat across the table from Mack bright and early the next morning.

"What do you feel like?" With such limited options at home, he'd decided to stop for breakfast at Masterson's Restaurant before heading into Boston.

"A waffle and chocolate milk." She didn't look up from the picture she colored on the place mat.

After giving their waitress his own order, he turned his full attention on his daughter again. "Jessie said you picked out the decals you liked. We can pick them up on the way home tonight."

At the mention of her decals, Grace looked up, the end of one long braid brushing the table. That morning she'd insisted he leave her braids alone, and since they looked neat despite a night in bed, he hadn't touched them. "Can we go now?"

"You know I have to work today."

"I wish you could stay home. Then we could stay home

together and I wouldn't have to see Noah," she said, referring to a boy at her daycare center. Ever since Noah had started there this winter, Grace complained about him.

Reaching for his coffee, Mack took a long gulp. "Next week you start school and won't have to see him anymore." As much as he wanted her to start school, it would be odd not having her just floors below him. Ever since he'd gone to work with the FBI, she had attended the daycare and preschool located on the second floor of the building.

She considered his words. "Why can't I stay with Grammy or Auntie Erin?"

They'd already gone over this. "Auntie isn't back yet and Grammy is getting ready for the start of school. Next week you'll see Auntie Erin and Brianna everyday after school." Earlier that year, his sister had decided to leave her part-time position and be a full-time stay-at-home mom. When Mack told her his plan to move back, she'd offered to watch Grace after school.

"I still don't want to see Noah." Grace dropped her elbows onto the table and propped her chin in her hands. "He makes fun of everyone."

Mack, as well as a few other parents, had spoken to the teachers, and while Noah's behavior had improved, he still sometimes bothered the other children. "Just a few more days, buddy."

"Here we go," Nicole, their waitress, said, appearing at their table. "One waffle for you, Grace." Nicole placed a Belgian waffle down. "And a Mediterranean omelet for you." One of the biggest omelets he'd seen appeared in front of him, along with toast, sausage, and corn beef hash.

"Is there anything else I can get you?" Nicole asked, her hand coming down onto his and he felt paper slip under his palm.

He stared at the hand covering his, unable to respond at first. Hadn't Nicole been at the block party with Striker? "Just some more coffee, Nicole. Thanks." He gave her a tight smile. The last thing he wanted was to encourage her or make her think he was interested. Even if he were on the look-out for a girlfriend, Nicole wouldn't be on his radar. At least four or five years younger than him, she reminded him too much of Bethany.

Nicole gave him a bright smile. "Coming right up."

"Can I stay with Jessie today?" Grace asked between bites of her waffle, her mind still fixated on the day ahead.

Without being obvious, Mack glanced at the note under his hand. Sure enough, it contained Nicole's phone number and a message for him to call her. Moving his plate so it covered the note, he got ready to dig into his own breakfast. "She's probably working today, too."

"You could call and check."

"I take it you liked staying with Jessie?" He covered his toast with strawberry jam as he waited for an answer.

With her straw in her mouth, Grace could only nod until she finished. "I want to stay with her again."

"Is that my Grace I hear?" Rose Ellsbury appeared at their booth, interrupting their conversation.

Breakfast forgotten, Grace jumped out of her seat. "Grammy!"

Rose smiled and hugged her granddaughter. "Now this is the perfect way to start a Monday morning." She kissed Grace and then gave Mack a hug. "If I knew you two were going to be here, I would've come sooner." She sat next to Grace as Nicole appeared with coffee in hand.

"Can I stay with you today?" Grace used her best please-give-me-what-I-want-because-I'm-cute look.

"I wish you could, but I need to get ready for the big kids to come back next week."

"I can help you."

"You'd be bored watching me get my office ready. How about you and your dad come for dinner this week? Then, on Friday, if you're not seeing your mom, you can sleep over."

Although not the answer she wanted, Grace didn't

offer any further protests.

"Bethany canceled for the weekend, so if Grace wants, she can stay."

Grace bounced in her seat and smiled. "Can we invite Brianna, too?"

Slipping an arm over Grace's shoulders, his mom gave her granddaughter a little squeeze. "Sounds like a good plan. I'll call Auntie tonight and ask."

Pleased with the unexpected plans, Grace turned her full attention back to her breakfast, thoughts of Noah and daycare gone.

"I'm sorry about yesterday. I left my cell in the car while your father and I shopped."

With his toast gone, Mack started on the sausage. "Jessie came to my rescue."

"That doesn't surprise me. She helps out everyone."

"She did my hair," Grace said, taking a break from eating.

"It looks very nice. Did you have fun?" Rose added sugar to her coffee as she waited for an answer.

Grace nodded. "We went to the playground and later watched two fairy movies. I want to stay with her again."

"I owe her one. I didn't pick Grace up until about ten o'clock."

His mother's head tilted to the side and an expression he couldn't identify formed on her face as she looked from him to Grace and then back again. "I've always liked Jessie. So what movies did you watch, Grace?" The expression on his mom's face disappeared and Grace launched into a full description of the two movies. Right now, fairies were her obsession and she couldn't get enough of them.

"How does your new room look?" Rose asked once Grace finished.

Grace reached for the fork she hadn't touched in several minutes and shrugged. "Okay."

"Just okay?"

"Daddy promised he'd paint it soon, and I picked out

some decals to decorate with. We're going to buy them tonight."

"We'll stop at Quinn's tonight after the grocery store. We can get paint while we're there, too. This weekend, while you're with Gram, I'll paint. Does that sound like a plan?" He couldn't deny his daughter's bedroom was a rather ugly color.

Across from him, his mother signaled to Nicole that she wanted more coffee. "I have an even better idea. I'll stop at Quinn's and pick them up. Text or call me when you get home and I'll bring them over. That should save you some time tonight."

He appreciated his mother's offer, but he didn't want to make more work for her. As a high school guidance counselor, the start of school was already a busy time for her. "I got it, Mom."

"Please," she said with a wave of her hand. "It won't take me long and it'll give me a chance to see this cutie again." She squeezed Grace's shoulders.

***

Hanging up the phone, Jessie rubbed her forehead over her left eye. Of all the distributors she worked with, Jansen was the worst. They often didn't get her orders when promised and their sales staff had no clue. Unfortunately, they were the only distributor in New England that carried the line of light fixtures Mrs. Osborne wanted. If the company still didn't get the order in by the end of the week, maybe she'd just call other stores in the area and buy them. For now though, she'd leave things as they were.

After grabbing two aspirins from her desk and washing them down, she left her office. So far, she'd spent most of the morning and early afternoon cooped up at her desk. Although she had employees who stocked shelves and helped customers, she liked to spend time in the store itself. She found the time not only let her make sure things got done the right way, but also allowed her to connect with her employees and customers. One of the reasons people came in was because they liked Quinn's welcoming atmosphere as opposed to the impersonal environment found at the box stores.

"Can I help you find something, Mrs. Rizzo?" Jessie asked the high school principal's wife when she came around the corner.

"I need two things. Some mousetraps, but not the ones that kill the mice. Do you have any of those?"

"We have both the catch-and-release kind and the more traditional type in aisle three."

"And something Donald can use to mount my new mirror in the bathroom."

"You'll find mirror-mounting hardware in aisle five."

"Great. Thanks." Mrs. Rizzo headed toward aisle three.

Jessie stopped once more to chat with a customer before making it to the registers. Prepared to start a conversation with Patti, a long time employee, she paused next to the battery display she restocked. Before she could utter a single word, Mrs. Ellsbury entered the store.

"Jessie! Just the person I wanted to see."

She couldn't guess what Mack's mother needed. "What can I help you with?"

"Grace mentioned you were holding some things aside for her. I want to pick them up along with the paint."

Before they'd left the store, she'd placed the packages on her desk. It had been the only way to reassure Grace they'd still be available when she came back. "They're in my office." Jessie gestured for Mrs. Ellsbury to follow. "Did Mack and Grace decide on a color?"

Judging by Mrs. Ellsbury expression, that tiny detail had slipped her mind. "Come to think of it, no, but I think I can manage. Do you know what they were thinking?"

Jessie grabbed the items Grace picked out as well as the color samples she'd left behind. "This is what she liked. Mack was trying to convince her to go lighter."

Mrs. Ellsbury looked through the various shades.

"Maybe I better let Mack get the paint." She looked back up. "I will take these now."

Together, they headed for the front registers again. "I had breakfast with Grace this morning. She couldn't stop talking about you. She wanted Mack to let her stay with you again." Mrs. Ellsbury placed the items she held on the counter.

"She's a sweet little girl. I told Mack anytime he needs help to just ask."

The smile on the other woman's face broadened. "I'll remind him." Mrs. Ellsbury leaned forward a bit and dropped her voice. "He'd never admit it, but sometimes I think he finds being a single parent difficult. I'm so glad he has good friends like you to help him out." She patted Jessie's hand as she spoke.

Heat burned the back of her neck at the compliment and she wanted to contradict the woman. They were more like friendly acquaintances than friends. "That's the great thing about this town," she said. "Everyone helps everyone else."

Mrs. Ellsbury stood upright. "Perhaps, but Mack wouldn't trust his Grace with just anyone in town."

Without a good response, Jessie handed Mrs. Ellsbury her change.

"Mack will be in later this week for paint. He told Grace he'd paint this weekend while she sleeps over at my house."

Once again, Mrs. Ellsbury's comments left her at a loss for words.

"When you see your grandmother, tell her I said hello. I'm going to try to make it for quilting club on Sunday. Will you be stopping in?"

Jessie had learned to make quilts because her grandmother wanted to teach her, not because she enjoyed it. In all honesty, she found it a tedious endeavor, and over the past year, she'd joined her grandmother and grandmother's friends less and less on Sundays. "I'm not sure yet. Maybe."

"Well, maybe I'll see you then. Thanks again."

CHAPTER 3

"Plans for the weekend?" Dakota Smith asked as he walked alongside Mack Friday night.

Mack pushed open the door to the stairwell. "Painting. I promised Grace I'd get her room done while she stays with my mom." He also needed to get more unpacking done. Other than the boxes he'd emptied last weekend, he'd yet to tackle anymore. Time just hadn't been on his side that week, despite his best efforts.

On his way out as well, Dakota followed him down the stairs. "Stop by on Sunday. Josh and Bruce are coming to watch the game," he said, referring to two other agents in the building.

He doubted he'd have the time, but he appreciated the invite. When he'd first made the transition from his position as a detective with the Boston police department to task force agent with the FBI, he'd worried whether or not it'd be a good fit. Other guys on the police force who'd worked with the FBI complained about the bureau. They claimed the agents considered local law enforcement good for nothing but handling crimes beneath them. In his three years working with the agents in Boston, he'd found none of that true. Sure, as with every job, there were the jerks, but overall, the agents considered the task force officers part of the family.

"I promised Grace I'd take her someplace special Sunday night to celebrate starting school on Monday." Mack stopped at the second floor where the daycare center was located.

"What happened to starting school after Labor Day? We have almost three more weeks left in August." Dakota moved toward the next flight of stairs. "Wish her luck, and have a good weekend."

Most nights, Mack could get in and out of the daycare center in a matter of minutes. After being there all day, Grace wanted to go home. Tonight, though, was a different story. Despite her complaints about going, she insisted on giving everyone a hug before leaving. He could understand her sentiment. She had spent more time with the daycare employees and other children than she had with him in the last few years. Still, Friday night traffic out of the city always proved heavy and tonight's rain would only add to it.

"Can we stop and get the paint before Grammy's?" Grace asked from the backseat as Mack took the exit off Route 1 an hour later. As he'd expected, traffic had been slow going since he'd pulled out of the parking garage. Thankfully, he'd grabbed Grace's overnight bag before leaving the house that morning.

"Up to you. It'll mean you get to Gram's later." Other than grabbing some takeout and watching a movie, he had no plans for the night ahead.

Silence came from the backseat, a sure indication that Grace was considering his answer. "Let's get the paint first."

Two nights earlier, they'd decided on a color. Still, Mack wondered if his daughter was going to use this opportunity to get a different color. She'd wanted a much darker shade of pink called Fabulous Fuchsia, but it was so bright he feared it would keep her awake at night. He'd wanted the Baby Girl Pink, a shade that would merely give the walls a hint of color. However, he'd conceded and promised she could get the Cherry Blossom Pink, the color Jessie had suggested the previous weekend. He'd also promised to paint the room so it looked like her cousin Brianna's. He'd asked Erin to send him a picture of Brianna's room to use as a sample.

By the time Mack and Grace pulled into the parking lot, the rain had stopped. Or at least it had stopped for the moment. The weather forecast called for rain off and on all night and much of tomorrow. In true child-like fashion, Grace skipped through all the puddles in the parking lot, soaking both her sneakers as well as her legs, though it didn't bother her.

Once inside, he expected Grace to head straight for the paint area, but instead, she made a beeline for the back of the store. Mack followed behind, always keeping Grace in sight. While North Salem was one of the safest places he knew, that didn't mean Grace couldn't get herself into trouble.

When Grace paused at the open office door, he figured he should've known she'd look to see if Jessie was around. Several times over the week, she'd mentioned Jessie and how she wanted to see her again. And each time she did, an image of Jessie formed, reminding him just how much she'd changed.

"Jessie," Grace said from the doorway.

Through the glass windows, he saw Jessie glance up and smile.

"We're getting the paint for my room," Grace explained as he stopped behind her.

"That's exciting. What color did you pick?"

Grace tilted her head back and looked up at him. "What's it called again?"

"Cherry Blossom Pink." He placed his hands on her shoulders.

"Nice choice."

"I wanted a different one, but Daddy said no." She sounded disappointed but resigned. "He promised to make the walls look like Brianna's before we put up the princesses and puppies."

The corners of Jessie's mouth twitched, but she didn't go into a full-blown smile. "I love Cherry Blossom Pink, Grace. I used it in my bedroom."

"Really?" Grace's voice perked up at the news. "I guess it will be okay."

This time, Jessie grinned. "Come on." She stood. "Let's have Brian get that mixed for you." She came around the desk and headed out with Grace joining her.

Forgotten for the moment, Mack followed behind, his eyes drawn to the petite woman in front of him. She wore a pair of jean shorts and a fitted t-shirt. The outfit once again drove home the physical changes in her, and he found it hard to look away from her cute backside.

Back in high school, when she'd played soccer with his sister, she'd been a skinny little thing. The type who could blow away if it got too windy. Then in college, she'd gone the opposite direction and gained more than the traditional freshman fifteen. Now though, she'd reached a happy medium and he could see why Tony was interested. Not that he thought Tony should take her out. Sean was right when he'd said Jessie wasn't Tony's type. Nicole from the restaurant was better suited to Tony.

"How many cans do you want?" Jessie asked when they stopped next to the paint station where the same teenager he'd seen on his last visit stood.

"How many does it usually take?" He'd never painted inside before. In fact, he'd only painted once before and that had been a clubhouse his dad built him.

"Depends on the size of the room," Jessie answered as she handed a color card to Brian. "I'd start with three or four cans and go from there. If the walls are a dark color, you should use a primer first. If you don't mind spending a little more per gallon, you can have this made using a base that has a primer in it."

If it meant saving some time, he'd spend the extra money. "Give me four cans with the primer to be on the safe side. I'd like to finish this up this weekend."

Jessie passed the instructions on to Brian. "Anything else you need?"

"Can you tell me how to make the walls look like this?" Mack pulled up the photo his sister had sent him and handed the phone over. Each wall in the room had been divided into two parts with the top half painted a solid pink. The lower half had a design to it.

"You can divide the wall in half by using painters' tape. The rest they did using a combination of brushes and sponges." She handed him the phone and pulled a discarded shopping cart closer to them. "Everything you need is down aisle seven. If I were you, I would also grab a paint edger for between the wall and ceiling. I always use one and put painters' tape around the trim."

He considered Jessie's answers. He'd assumed paint went on with a simple roller. He'd never heard of using a sponge for anything other than cleaning dishes or his car. "Tell me what I need and I'll get it."

"You've never done this before, have you?" Jessie asked as the swirl of the paint-mixing machine filled the background.

Mack shook his head while Grace skipped from one tile to the next beside him. "Never where it had to look nice."

"If you want, I'll put together everything you'll need." She reached for the shopping cart. "It'll take me a minute."

Jessie disappeared down an aisle in search of supplies. "How's this?" Brian asked from behind the counter.

The color in the can appeared darker than it had on paper but it was still better than Grace's original choice. "Fine, thanks."

"I'll get the others ready then." Brian pounded the cover onto the can and then started on the next one.

"Can we go?" Grace asked, her excitement over getting the paint now replaced with excitement to get to her grandmother's house.

"Soon." He should have taken her straight to his mother's and then came here regardless of what she had said. There was no place she liked better than her grandparents' house, especially if her cousin was going to be there.

"Here you go." Jessie reappeared with various objects in the cart. "I added some plastic floor covering too just in case. But if you don't want it, leave it here and I'll put it back later."

Mack eyed the items. "You've done this a lot I take it? Don't suppose you want to come over and help me tomorrow?"

He was joking, though, with Jessie around, Grace's room might actually come out looking like Brianna's. But while he knew he wasn't serious, Jessie didn't. At least her expression suggested she didn't.

"I can come by tomorrow around ten."

Although he hadn't expected that response, he wasn't about to turn down the offer either. "If you're serious, that would be great."

"I'll be by right after the gym."

After the hardware store, Mack drove to his parents' house where he found his younger sister and mother deep in conversation. Judging by the way they both clammed up the moment he walked in, they'd been talking about him. Although why he'd be the topic of their conversation escaped him.

"Grace forgot I existed the minute she saw Brianna." Mack stopped at the kitchen table.

"Get used to it. It only gets worse as they get older," his mother replied. "By the time she's a teenager, she'll only want you when she needs a ride somewhere."

The idea of his little girl being a teenager downright scared him.

"Did you remember to set everything up with the school?" Erin asked.

"All taken care of. The bus will drop Grace off with you every day."

Erin sighed and frowned. "I still can't believe they're both starting kindergarten on Monday."

Mack shared his sister's sentiment but kept the thought to himself. "Soon you'll have another baby in the house, Erin. How are you feeling?"

Erin's frown disappeared, and she ran a hand over her belly. "Good. I go back to the doctor next week."

For several minutes, he hung around catching up with his sister, but eventually she stood. "Marcus and I are going to the movies and dinner with friends. I'll see you on Sunday, Mom." She picked up her purse before addressing him. "Mack, I'll see you on Monday."

"I'm going to head out, too. Big plans myself with the couch and television tonight." He expected a comment from either his mom or sister. Over the past six months, they'd been encouraging him to date more. Tonight, no such comment came from either of them.

"Good luck with painting tomorrow. I know you want to get that done and the house in order, but don't work all day," his mother said.

Mack dropped a kiss on her cheek. "Trust me, I won't. After Jessie and I finish painting, I'll call it a day."

He didn't miss the glance between his mom and sister.

"I wasn't serious when I asked her, but I guess she didn't know that. Besides, I could use the help."

"And Jessie can never say no when someone asks her for a favor," his mother said.

"If you say so. Anyway, if you need me, just call."

"We'll be fine. I'll bring Grace back home on Sunday." His mom patted his arm. "Have a nice quiet night."

***

Jessie dragged a brush through her wet hair, her upper

arms protesting at the movement. Her personal trainer, Mary, had put her through a vigorous upper body workout that morning. She'd started seeing Mary once a week about nine months ago. The first month or so, Mary had taken it easy on her, but then she'd started to push her more and more. To be fair, Jessie had told Mary she needed someone to push her, to keep her on target. Thanks to Mary's workout routines and her own dietary changes, she now liked who she saw in the mirror. In fact, she'd shed twenty-five pounds and now fit into the same size clothes she'd worn her sophomore year of college.

Yup, Mary's butt-kicking workouts were worth a few sore muscles. Using the elastic band from her wrist, she tied up her hair in a short ponytail with several of the shorter pieces coming free. That was the only downside to her hairstyle. Still, it would do for a day of painting. Jessie shook her head as she zipped up her bag. Why the heck had she even agreed to help him? Talking with him at the store wasn't a big deal. Neither was a conversation at the block party where other people and his daughter had surrounded them. But being stuck in a room with just him was another story. Already anxiety zigzagged through her body. Evidently, even though she was now an adult, Jessie was still affected by Mack as much as she'd been in high school.

"How long can it take?" Jessie asked her reflection in the mirror. Grace's bedroom couldn't be that big.

When she stepped from her car, she spotted Mrs. Mitchell outside, pruning the rose bush near her front door. As anxious as she felt about the task ahead, Jessie didn't want to put it off by getting into a long conversation.

With just a friendly wave in her former piano teacher's direction, she crossed the lawn. Before she managed to place a finger on the doorbell, Mack appeared in the living room, gesturing for her to come in through the screen door. Much like the day he'd moved in, he wore faded jeans with a small hole above the knee and a t-shirt so old she could no longer read the logo on the front. He also wore a baseball hat, this one sporting an emblem for a team she didn't recognize.

"Make yourself comfortable. I just need to finish up this call." Mack pointed to the phone near his ear and headed out of the room.

She'd never stepped inside the old house before, but she'd passed by it her whole life. She'd even gone trick-or-treating there. From the outside, the house looked small, but the living room was much larger than she'd expected. A couch took up the longest wall while two armchairs and a coffee table sat in front of the windows. A large flat screen television hung over a stone fireplace and, in front of the fireplace, a dollhouse, which almost reached Jessie's waist, sat open with each room set up and the dolls positioned.

"Sorry about that." At Mack's voice, Jessie looked away from the dollhouse. "Work stuff."

She gripped her hands behind her back. "No problem. I'm ready to start if you are."

Mack gestured she should follow him. "I managed to get the furniture covered and taped most of the trim."

She followed him up the stairs. A few unopened boxes, some with the word *Toys* written on them, had been left in the hallway.

"Ignore the mess. I made Grace wait to unpack her stuff until I painted." He pointed to the boxes as he pushed open a door. "As long as she has the dollhouse downstairs and Mr. Whiskers, she's happy."

She assumed Mr. Whiskers was some kind of stuffed toy since she saw no evidence of a live pet anywhere.

"Everything I got at the store last night is in here."

Jessie's gaze swept around the room. Like the living room, it was much larger than she'd expected. "This is almost as big as the room I had growing up."

Blackthorne Farm had been in her family since the late

1800s when one of her ancestors had purchased the land and turned it into a dairy farm. A man with a large family, he'd constructed a four-thousand-square-foot house, and while the house might lack several bathrooms or an attached garage, it made up for those things in the size of its bedrooms. In fact, several of her friends growing up had been jealous of how large her bedroom had been.

"It's hard to tell by the street, but this house is bigger than it looks."

Comments about the size of the room out of the way, Jessie latched onto the only other topic she had. "If you want to hand me a roll of tape, I'll finish taping around the electrical outlets."

Mack grabbed a roll and tossed it to her. "While you do that, I'll get these cans open."

In no time, they fell into a comfortable silence as they worked with Mack handling the top part of the divided wall and Jessie using the various sponges on the bottom half.

"I don't blame Grace for not liking this color," Jessie said. "It looks like pea soup." So far, she'd forced herself to stay focused on her work. With him so close, though, she couldn't help but look over at him now.

He took a step back and eyed the wall. "It reminds me of the green slime along the marsh behind the elementary school."

Jessie looked at the color again. "That, too." She set the sponge into the paint tray and watched as Mack got within a few inches of the ceiling. "Don't worry about getting close to the ceiling. I'll go around with the edger once we finish everything else."

"I appreciate your help today. If Grace had wanted something plain, this wouldn't have been bad, but if I did the part you're working on, it wouldn't have come out well."

"I used to paint my room almost twice a year. My grandparents didn't mind and I don't think my dad ever noticed." Jessie went back to work. The longer she stared at Mack, the harder her heart beat. "One time, I even painted each wall a different color with different patterns. My dad noticed that, but he let me leave it." At the time, she'd assumed her dad knew she'd get sick of the multiple colors and paint over it.

"How is your dad? Does he still drive trucks?"

"He's still driving, just not long-distance anymore. Last year, he took a job with Heartland, so he only does deliveries in New England," she said, referring to the New England-based grocery chain.

Once again out of conversation material, Jessie became silent and focused on her work. Painting the walls with a roller or sponge was the easy part. It was all the trim work that would take time.

"It must be nice having him around more."

She glanced over her shoulder. Although they'd started at the same time, he'd covered more ground than her. Then again, he did have the easier task. "It is. We usually get together once a week or so for dinner. Sometimes we meet at Masterson's or the Jade Orient. Other times, he comes to my place. Honestly, I think he misses the long-distance drives."

She watched Mack pour more paint into his tray. "Change can be difficult. Why'd he give it up?"

Rather than return to her own work, she watched the way the muscles in Mack's arm flexed as he moved the roller on the wall. By the looks of it, Mack kept himself in top shape, despite a full-time job and daughter.

"I think he wanted to be around for his parents. My grandfather is almost eighty-three."

Turn around and work. She allowed herself one more moment of watching Mack and turned. "When I'm done here, I'll swap sides with you and get that part near the ceiling."

"Consider it done."

***

One of the worst parts about being short and painting was the constant up and down the ladder. Considering all the climbing she'd done that day, it was okay that she'd skipped the leg part of her workout.

"I think that's it." Jessie took a step into the middle of the room. In just a few hours, the room had undergone a complete transformation.

Mack dropped his own paint roller and joined her. "You're right. I thought it might need a second coat, but it looks good to me. Grace will love it, especially after she puts up those decorations you helped her pick out."

"And when she gets sick of the puppies and princesses, you can peel them off the wall." Whether because Mack stood so close or because of the paint smell, Jessie suddenly felt light-headed. Taking a step away from him, she said, "Do you need help cleaning up before I leave?" She picked up a discarded paint roller.

"Forget about it. I'll clean up later. I'm starving; what about you?" He took the roller from her and his fingers brushed against hers.

She'd arrived before lunchtime and neither had stopped for anything but a drink since. "Now that you mention it, I'm hungry. On my way home, I think I'll grab something."

Mack covered the leftover paint. "How about we grab something together? My treat. It's the least I can do for all your help today and last weekend with Grace."

At one time, she'd dreamed about Mack Ellsbury asking her out. None of those invitations had been because he wanted to repay her. "I appreciate the offer, but I don't think either of us is dressed for going out."

Rather than respond, he focused his gaze on her, starting at the top of her head and traveling down. Under his intense inspection, the self-consciousness she'd just begun to control returned full force, and she fought to not fidget.

"You look great to me," he said, his voice taking on a new degree of warmth. "There's not a speck of paint on you." Mack stepped closer.

Unable to maintain eye contact, Jessie glanced away. "You might want to look in the mirror before you decide to go out." Although he'd stayed clean for the most part, he did have some paint on his baseball hat as well as on his left bicep and t-shirt.

Mack glanced down at his clothes then back up. "I don't see anything."

"Check your left arm, right about here." Jessie showed him the spot on her own arm since touching him was out of the question. "And on your back there's a spot, too."

"That's nothing. Come on. People have shown up at Masterson's looking much worse. I'll change my shirt and we can go."

She had no good excuse. She'd already said she only planned to go home, and she was hungry. At the same time, though, showing up at the restaurant together might just send the rumor mill into action.

"After all your help, Jessie, dinner is the least I can do."

Whenever someone did her a favor, she liked to repay them, so she understood Mack's sentiments. "Okay."

Ellen, Mr. Masterson's granddaughter and the hostess at Masterson's Restaurant, greeted them and whisked them to a table on the patio. The usual Saturday night dinner rush hadn't started, but still, several of the tables inside the restaurant and on the patio were occupied. Originally a small diner opened in the 1950s by Lou Masterson, the restaurant had grown over the years. Now, the once-tiny diner could seat about two hundred people and had an additional banquet hall attached.

"I'm so hungry, everything on the menu sounds good. What are you ordering?" Mack asked.

Jessie lowered the menu and looked at him. "I should go with the grilled chicken salad, but I'm leaning toward the Portsmouth pie."

Salads made great additions to meals, but they weren't a meal, at least not to him. "What's that?" He'd only glanced at the menu, assuming it hadn't changed since the last time he'd eaten dinner there. He didn't recall anything called a Portsmouth pie.

"Look under seafood. It's one of the new dishes they added last winter. It contains shrimp, scallops, and lobster."

Mack raised the menu again. Perhaps it warranted a closer look. Sure enough, several new dishes filled each section of the dinner menu.

"Mack Ellsbury, I heard you moved back."

Mack glanced up and saw Brendan Michaels at their table. A fellow classmate, they'd played on a lot of the same sports teams as kids. Even back then, Brendan had been a pain in the ass, always picking on the kids he didn't like. Once in high school, he'd given up sports and taken up partying. Mack hadn't seen the guy since their last high school reunion and had no desire to catch up now.

"Hey, Brendan. Moved back last week."

Brendan slapped him on the back and Mack caught a whiff of beer. "Well, welcome back. We should catch up sometime." Without another word, he headed off to a corner table where his older brother and sister-in-law sat.

"He hasn't changed, has he?" Mack put his menu off to the side.

Jessie placed hers on top. "No. I think a lot of people wish he'd move somewhere else. Earlier this summer, he even got into a fight with Sean."

Sean had never been one to get into fights, so Mack was curious what could have provoked him. Before he could ask about it though, their waitress appeared.

While they waited for their appetizer, they discussed the recent happenings in town. Then when the buffalo tenders, one of Mack's favorite appetizers, arrived, he pushed the plate toward Jessie so she could take one.

"So, if you weren't here tonight, what would you be doing?" Mack grabbed the last buffalo tender from the plate between them. While Jessie had eaten one or two, he'd more or less polished off the entire appetizer himself.

"Depends." Jessie stirred her ice tea with her straw. "A few months ago, I would've been up to my eyeballs with everyone's taxes. When it's not tax season, I sometimes visit my grandparents and dad. Occasionally, I do a girls' night out with Kelsey and Maryann. But most Saturday nights, I stay home and watch a movie."

It didn't escape him that she hadn't mentioned a boyfriend or dating. Had Sean threatened every guy in town against asking Jessie out? The guy had always treated Jessie as a second sister. Rather than ask her about her romantic life, which really wasn't any of his business, he latched onto something else she'd mentioned. "You're an accountant?" From behind him, the waitress came back to remove the empty appetizer plates.

"I double-majored in management and accounting. Besides running the store, I take care of the accounting for Peggy Sue's and The Hair Cottage. Then, during tax season, I do taxes for a bunch of people."

Sounded like a busy but boring life to him. "Don't be surprised if you find me knocking on your door next April. My old accountant quit and I don't have the patience for doing my own."

"I'd prefer if you didn't wait until April. It's much better when I get all the materials early, but I'd be happy to do them for you."

When their dinners arrived a few minutes later, they both started on their meals. While he'd dated a good deal before his marriage, he hadn't done much since the separation and divorce. And while this wasn't a date, but rather two acquaintances sharing a meal, he found himself enjoying her company. In fact, he'd enjoyed her company all day.

"What would you be doing if you weren't here?" Jessie

asked.

"Saturday night is movie night. Grace and I get takeout, usually pizza, make popcorn, and watch a movie together." Other single guys might find that a horrible way to spend a Saturday night, but he wouldn't trade it for anything. "If she's at my mom's or it's a weekend she's with Bethany, I might go out with friends or sometimes I just chill at home and try to unwind from work."

"Grace must love doing that with you. She talked a lot about you when she stayed with me." Jessie reached for her iced tea as she spoke. "She really is a great kid."

"That's funny because she hasn't stopped talking about you. She keeps asking when she can stay with you again. Grace said you were the best babysitter she ever had."

At the compliment, Jessie shifted in her seat. "Whenever you need a babysitter, she's more than welcome at my place."

As they finished up their meals, they talked about general things, never again touching on anything personal. After he paid the bill, they headed back to his house where Jessie had left her car.

"Thanks again for the help today. Grace is going to love it."

Jessie gave him a warm smile that transformed her whole face. For a moment, it was like he was seeing Jessie Quinn for the first time, and he wondered why Tony or another guy in town didn't just ask her out regardless of Sean's objections.

"Glad to do it. And if you need help with anything else, just call or stop by the store."

Mack remained outside until Jessie pulled out and then went inside. With the painting done and a whole empty house to himself, he grabbed a beer from the kitchen and switched on the baseball game. Tomorrow, he'd put Grace's room back in order before she came home. Tonight, he planned to just relax.

***

"Mrs. Mitchell told your grandmother you spent the day at Mack Ellsbury's house yesterday."

Her father's words stopped Jessie in her tracks as she carried the dirty dinner plates to the sink. Her dad had stopped by for their weekly father-daughter meal, and so far they'd talked about general things going on in town. Not once had either of them brought up her personal life. In fact, they didn't discuss her personal life much ever, not that it bothered her. In many ways, she'd always felt a closer connection to her grandparents than her dad, and who could blame her? Her grandparents had been like parents to her. Her grandfather had taken her to all but one father-daughter dance in school. Her grandmother had attended every one of her soccer games and taught her to cook and sew. Her grandfather even taught her to drive. Her dad had been on the road too much to do any of those things. Since his change in jobs, he'd been trying to strengthen their relationship, and while they were much closer now, she doubted they'd ever have the same tight father-daughter bond as Mack and Grace. From the little she'd seen, it appeared as if he put Grace first all the time. He seemed to go out of his way to make sure the little girl was happy.

"He needed some help with a painting project." Jessie wished the image of him working alongside her on Saturday would disappear. "I wasn't there all day, just for a few hours." She grabbed the Boston cream pie she'd made. It had always been one of her dad's favorites and something she enjoyed as well.

"She said she saw the two of you leave together." Her father didn't wait for her; instead, he cut the pie while she went for clean plates.

With her back to her father, she rolled her eyes. Mrs. Mitchell was a sweet lady, but she loved to gossip. "We went out to eat. We were both hungry after painting."

Her father took the plates she held out. "Just telling

you what I heard, Jessie." He dropped a huge slice of pie on one plate. "If you want to see Mack, that's fine with me. He always seemed like a good guy." He cut another slice, this one much smaller. "He's a Boston cop, right?"

"Sorta." She didn't feel like explaining at the moment. "But I'm not seeing him, Dad."

"Maybe you should consider it. I heard he got divorced."

She didn't want to discuss her romantic life with her father of all people. "I'm not interested in Mack like that, but even if I was, I'm not his type." So she'd lied a little. She'd love to get to know Mack in a more amorous way. But she wasn't lying about not being his type. She'd seen his ex-wife on television plenty of times. The woman was gorgeous. It was no wonder she'd landed an anchor position on a national news network.

Her father paused in his endeavor to polish off his pie. "You're beautiful and smart. That's every guy's type."

"You're my father, you have to say that." Jessie cut another slice of pie and added it to her dad's plate before he could ask. "Do you want some coffee?"

"I can take a hint. Yeah, I'll have a coffee, thanks."

CHAPTER 4

Mack never considered himself the type to get teary-eyed and emotional. Even still, that morning when he'd watched his little girl climb onto the school bus, he'd gotten choked up. Time was flying by and she was growing up so much faster than he'd thought possible. His own parents had warned him that would happen, but he'd blown off their comments. He'd assumed it was just another line older people told you. As he watched the bus drive away that morning, he'd realized just how true the statement was.

Now, as he headed for his sister's house, he couldn't wait to hear how Grace's first day had gone. He hoped it had gone well because, even now, he remembered his first day of kindergarten and how embarrassing it had been. First, he'd missed the bus because he couldn't find his sneakers and arrived at school late. Then, when he'd walked into class, all the other students stared at him when Mrs. Truman stopped circle time to get him settled. Later, during lunchtime, he'd spilled his entire thermos of milk on himself and Striker. Perhaps all that wouldn't have been bad if he hadn't fallen asleep on the bus ride home and the bus driver had to wake him up. Mack couldn't imagine a worse first day.

His niece's and daughter's voices reached him when he opened his car door. Rather than head into the house, he went around to the backyard where he found the girls in the sandbox while his sister sat on the patio.

Engrossed in whatever they were working on, neither girl said hello, so he took the opportunity to watch them work together. When they'd managed to get the bucket tipped over, Grace glanced up. Without any hesitation, she jumped up and sprinted across the yard toward him, her lopsided pigtails swinging as she ran.

"Daddy!" she shouted, throwing her arms around him. "Come see what Brianna and I built." Letting go of his waist, she grabbed his hand and tugged.

With a wave in his sister's direction, he allowed Grace to lead him over.

"Do you like it, Uncle Mack?" Brianna asked, looking up from where she was making a path in the sand.

Although parts were crumbling and other areas did not connect, it still resembled a castle. Crouching down so he could get a better look, he said, "Let me guess. Cinderella's castle?" Cinderella was one of Grace's favorite princesses.

"No. This castle is for my horse, Stormy." Brianna pulled a gray plastic horse from the sand.

"And her sister, Cloud." Grace held up a white plastic horse.

"It looks great, ladies. Are you all set to go, Grace?"

"Can we finish? We are almost done."

"Please, Uncle Mack?"

"You have to be careful when those two gang up on you," Erin called from the patio.

Mack looked from one expectant face to the other. "Tell me about it," he answered. "Ten more minutes, then it is time to go."

Happy to have won some more time, the girls went back to work, dismissing the adults while Mack joined his sister.

"They got off the bus talking nonstop about their day. It sounded like they loved school."

"Good. I'm glad she didn't have a first day like mine."

"The school sent home all the emergency paperwork. It's in Grace's folder. They want it back by next week."

At least he didn't need to do it all tonight. He'd spent enough of his day on paperwork already.

"They ask for three emergency contacts besides myself. I added you as one. Hope you don't mind." Erin reached for her glass of juice.

"Why am I not surprised you already filled yours out?" His sister never put things off. "Yeah, of course, that's fine."

"Before I forget, I can't watch Grace on Friday. I'm having another ultrasound that afternoon."

Mack ignored the first part of her comment. "Is everything okay?"

Erin waved a dismissive hand. "It's more a precautionary thing. The doctor says I'm measuring a little smaller than normal and he wants to play it safe."

Erin's response didn't cancel out all of his worry, but since she didn't seem concerned, he accepted her answer. "Don't worry about Grace. I'll figure something out. Who's watching Brianna? Mom?"

"Mom has an administrators' meeting after school and Dad is doing interviews at the station. Brianna will go home with her friend, Melanie. They went to pre-school together."

Okay, that crossed his parents off his list. "Like I said, I'll figure something out." Mack checked his watch. "Time to go, buddy. Say goodbye and grab your stuff."

In the sandbox, Grace stopped but didn't make a move. "But we're not done."

"You can finish tomorrow." Mack used a sterner tone, one that Grace didn't argue with.

With a sigh he heard from across the yard, she gave her cousin a hug and stood. "Bye, Auntie," she said as she walked toward the door.

"Just a little bit of a drama queen." Erin laughed as Grace disappeared inside the house.

"Tell me about it. See you tomorrow. Bye, Brianna."

Too busy with her castle, Brianna only waved in his direction.

Mack started his car and backed out of his sister's driveway once Grace buckled herself in the backseat. "I thought we could go out for dinner to celebrate your first day of school." For better or worse, his daughter loved to eat out. "Does that sound good?"

"Yes," Grace answered with no hesitation. "Can we go for Chinese?"

He'd had his heart set on something Italian, but since this was her celebration, he'd do Chinese instead. Besides, The Jade Orient was closer to their house than Tuscany. "If that's what you want." Mack turned onto Highland Street, which would eventually bring him to Pleasant Street where the restaurant was located. "Tell me about your first day. What was the best part?"

From the backseat, Grace started to fill Mack in on all the details starting with the bus ride, which in her opinion had been the absolute best thing ever. By the time they pulled into the restaurant's lot, she'd made it up to their morning snack.

"You got to play at the sand table and do an art project, but the bus was the best part of the day?" he asked while Grace got out of the car.

She slipped her hand into his and nodded.

"What was so great about the bus?" His own memories of the school bus were less than exciting. He remembered them as noisy and hot in the summer and cold as hell in the winter.

"We didn't have to wear any seatbelts or sit in car seats."

Rather than say anything, he pulled open the door for Grace. After all, how could he argue with logic like that?

Besides, he assumed that, in time, the novelty of riding the bus would wear off and she'd find another aspect of school to fall in love with.

"Someone will be with you in a moment," a waitress carrying a full tray said as she passed Mack and Grace.

He nodded, his attention more on Grace. "How was lunch? Did you like eating in the cafeteria?"

"I got to sit with Brianna and her friend Melanie. Melanie is in our class, too. Her sister has Mrs. Hockner," she explained. "Brianna said they're twins, but they don't look alike."

Before Mack could explain that not all twins looked alike, an older woman approached them with menus. "This way, please."

Still holding hands, they followed the woman around the half wall that separated the waiting area from the main dinning room. Being a Monday night, much of the restaurant remained empty.

"Daddy, look. Jessie's here." Grace tugged his arm and pointed to a booth along the wall. "Can we say hi?"

The hostess stopped at an empty table feet from where Jessie sat. "She probably already heard you." In fact, he assumed everyone in the restaurant had heard her.

Taking that as a yes, Grace bypassed her own seat and went to Jessie's booth. And much like she had every other time she'd seen Grace, Jessie gave his daughter a warm smile. "Hi, there. What are you doing here?"

"Daddy said we could celebrate my first day of school with dinner."

Jessie looked at him, giving him a smile as well. "Sounds like fun. And how was your first day? Who do you have this year?"

He assumed Jessie was waiting for someone since there were two glasses of water and two menus on the table, yet she didn't give any hint that she wanted Grace to buzz off. He'd discovered since becoming a parent that sometimes people without children wanted to be left alone when they were out. Even people with children got that way if they didn't have their own around. Jessie, though, didn't give him that impression, at least not during any of the times they'd met since his return.

"It was great. Brianna and I have Mrs. Wilks, and you know what the best part was?" Before Jessie could guess, Grace continued. "The bus. I can't wait to go on it again tomorrow."

Looking up, Jessie caught his eye and smiled.

"You know what else, Jessie?"

Jessie's lip twitched as if she wanted to laugh, but didn't when she glanced back at Grace.

"I love my room. Daddy painted it when I was at Grammy's and I put up the princesses and puppies. Can you come over and see it?"

"I'd love to, but not tonight. I'm meeting a friend for dinner."

He'd only been half-listening to the conversation, but her admission caught his full attention. He'd guessed she was waiting for her dad. She'd mentioned they met for dinner once a week. For some bizarre reason, when she stated otherwise, he couldn't help but wonder who she was meeting. While it was none of his business, he wanted to know who the friend was. Had Tony ignored Sean's warning and asked her out? He couldn't wrap his head around the idea of Tony and Jessie together.

The friend could be female. Why had he immediately assumed she referred to a guy? And why did he care anyway? She had the right to see whoever she wanted. Until last weekend, he hadn't seen Jessie in months. Despite knowing it was none of his business, he wanted to ask.

"Can you come after dinner?" Grace asked.

"Afterward, Maryann and I are going shopping, but I promise I'll stop by soon and see your room."

The unease in his chest evaporated when she mentioned Maryann. "Let's sit, Grace, and leave Jessie alone." Mack dropped his hand onto Grace's shoulders. About to turn her to head toward their table, he stopped as an idea came to him. Maybe Jessie could watch Grace after school on Friday. He did need to find a solution for the afternoon and Grace liked her a lot. Not to mention, Jessie had told him to just ask if he needed help.

Don't do it. Just because she offered didn't mean she meant it. Then again, the Jessie Quinn he'd grown up with and tutored in high school always meant what she said and was known to go out of her way to help others.

Even knowing all that, something bothered him, but he couldn't put his finger on what. Still, he needed a babysitter and he didn't have many options.

"Jessie, I understand if you can't, but is there anyway you could watch Grace after school on Friday?" Mack ignored whatever bothered him. "Erin has a doctor's appointment and my parents have meetings."

"Please, Jessie." Grace clasped her hands together.

Jessie bit down on her lip as she considered his request. "Sure. Do I need to pick her up at school?"

He hadn't considered that part. "No, I can have the bus drop her off at my house if you want to meet her there." Since she was doing him this favor, he didn't want to make it difficult for her. "I'll put a key in the front pocket of Grace's backpack so you can just let yourself in." As he spoke, Maryann arrived and settled in at the table.

"Sounds like a plan. What time does the bus get there?"

Another thing he hadn't considered. "No idea. School gets out at three o'clock, that's all I know."

"The bus drops my neighbor's kids off at quarter past three." Maryann lived on the same street as Mack and Grace. "Grace must ride the same bus and she'd get dropped off before my neighbors."

"Then I'll plan to get to your house at three and just wait." Jessie looked back at him.

Although she'd agreed with little hesitation, his conscience bothered him for once again asking for her help. "Are you sure you don't mind?"

"Don't worry about it. We'll have fun."

His mother's words from the week before popped up. He didn't want to take advantage of her generous nature. "If you change your mind, let me know. I'll understand."

"I'll see you on Friday, Grace," Jessie said, ignoring his comment as the waitress appeared.

"Come on, Grace. Let's sit and let them enjoy their dinner." With a final goodbye to both Jessie and Maryann, Grace let him lead her away.

From his table, he kept looking back over at Jessie as they waited for their dinner and Grace told him all about her first day of school. Every time he did look, Jessie had a smile on her face as she and Maryann talked. Even before tonight, he noticed what an attractive woman she'd become, but when she smiled, her face transformed from pretty to beautiful. Perhaps not Hollywood beautiful, but she had a girl-next-door beauty, which he found himself attracted to more so now than ever before.

"My cubby at school is purple and it's next to Brianna's, but I have to share it," Grace rattled on. "I share with Sydney. She has a princess backpack just like mine."

"And do you like her?" Mack's gaze wandered over to Jessie again, and this time their eyes met for a moment. As soon as they did, Jessie looked back at her dinner.

"She's okay. I like Maggie more. She shares a cubby with Brianna."

Mack nodded since his daughter's statement didn't require a response. In return, Grace launched into a description of morning circle time while the waitress set their food out. Then, without pausing to breathe, she continued telling him about class centers, which happened right before lunch.

As she spoke, Mack spooned food onto her plate, careful to make sure none of her food touched. Heaven help him if her fried rice mixed in with the chicken chow mien.

"You can tell me everything else later. Right now, eat." It wasn't uncommon for his daughter to talk her way through dinner.

She hadn't meant to look in their direction again. She'd already reminded herself how rude it was to stare. Even still, she glanced over at Mack and his daughter. She'd often done the same thing when he'd tutored her in high school. Then, he'd been none the wiser—much like tonight. Rather, all his attention stayed focused on Grace. Or, at least, it had seemed that way. When she'd shot that last look at him and met his eyes, she'd wanted to crawl under the table. While he'd most likely assume she'd just been looking around the room, she hated that he caught her.

"Can you pass me the soy sauce?" Maryann asked.

Without looking up from her plate, Jessie grabbed the bottle and handed it over.

"You and Mack seemed friendly earlier."

Jessie ignored the curiosity in her friend's voice. "You know this town. Everyone is friendly with each other."

"I guess." Maryann's tone let Jessie know there was a *but* in there. "My mom said she saw you two together at Masterson's."

Maryann's mom worked at Masterson's in the kitchen, but Jessie didn't remember seeing her that night. For the first time in a long while, Jessie wished she'd moved away from North Salem after college like her friend, Charlie Sherbrooke.

"I helped him paint Saturday afternoon, and afterward, we grabbed an early dinner. No big deal."

Maryann shot a quick glance over at Mack and his daughter, then at Jessie. "Didn't you have a thing for him in high school?"

Jessie adored her friends, but they never forgot a thing. "Me and half the girls in our class. Even you had a crush

72

on him for a while freshman year."

"It lasted maybe a month for me and then Colin moved into town," Maryann said, referring to her first boyfriend. "You liked Mack until he left for college."

She'd liked him long after that, but Jessie kept her mouth shut. "I helped him out and we grabbed some dinner. People can do that." She was an adult now with no time for old high school fantasies.

"Then why do you keep looking over at him?" Maryann asked, raising an eyebrow.

The back of Jessie's neck grew hot. She tried not to be obvious. "I looked over once."

The corner of Maryann's mouth twitched upward. "If you say so." She glanced in Mack's direction. "You know what I think?" Before Jessie could ask, Maryann continued. "You should ask him out. We're all adults now."

Ask Mack out? She'd rather have her hand cut off. "I'm not interested in him."

"You're a coward, Jessie. If you asked him, I bet he'd say yes. I noticed the way he was looking at you when I walked in."

Jessie didn't want to continue this conversation or encourage her friend, but she couldn't contain her curiosity either. "And how was that?"

Maryann leaned forward. "Like he wanted to pull you in a corner and kiss you senseless."

Why had she asked? "Oh please. Now I know you're nuts. Come on. Let's finish dinner so we can go shopping." By this point, they'd both stopped eating.

"Just think about it. You haven't been out with anyone in a long time."

Maryann's words stayed with Jessie long after they left the restaurant. In fact, they still buzzed around as she got ready for bed. Regardless of how she'd felt about Mack as a teenager or even now, she couldn't ask him out. She doubted she could ever ask anyone out, let alone him. And despite her friend's insistence, she knew Mack hadn't been looking at her with anything more than gratitude. She didn't grab men's attention. Although her grandparents and dad called her beautiful, it was only because they were related to her and they were supposed to say things like that.

Patting her face dry, Jessie glanced at her reflection. No, she wasn't ugly, but she wasn't beautiful either. She considered herself average. The kind of person who could just blend into a crowd, not the type men fantasized about dragging into a corner to kiss. She was okay with that. Not everyone could be gorgeous enough to stop traffic.

Jessie switched off the bathroom light and went into her room. As for not going out in a long time, well, Maryann didn't know the whole story. Jessie pulled her shirt off and tossed it into the hamper. As if pulled by an outside force, her eyes zeroed in on the scar on her side, a visible reminder of Jeremy. If Maryann or any of her friends knew the truth about her last relationship, they'd understand her reluctance to date now. None of them knew, and she liked it that way.

The oversized nightshirt she pulled on covered the scar; however, it remained crystal clear in her mind, as did the cold smile Jeremy had given her that day in the coffee shop. She'd called Sharon the day after the block party. When voicemail picked up, she'd hung up rather than leave a message. Perhaps she should try again. After all, if not for her friend, Morgan, who knew where she'd be now? But if she did that, though, one more person would know her secret.

If it helps Sharon get away from Jeremy without being hurt, it's worth it. Tomorrow, she'd try again. If she got Sharon's voicemail again, she'd leave a message this time.

CHAPTER 5

In less time than Mack expected, he and Grace fell into a regular routine. He'd wake her up after he ran on the treadmill in the basement and showered. As she got dressed, he prepared them breakfast, and then once they finished, he helped her brush her teeth and hair. In fact, after five consecutive days, they finished everything fifteen minutes early on Friday morning, allowing them time to read more of the book he'd started with her. Despite the easy routine they'd adopted since moving home and starting school, he was looking forward to the weekend. With nothing planned, he and Grace could do whatever they wanted Saturday and Sunday.

"Let's go over this arrest plan one more time," Bruce Conklin said late Friday afternoon to the other members of the squad gathered around.

Mack looked at Dakota seated across from him and shook his head. They'd already reviewed the plan for Monday's early-morning arrest. Everyone knew what was expected of him. They'd done enough arrests together that they worked like a well-oiled machine. However, no one argued with Bruce. They all realized this was Bruce's first time as lead agent on an arrest and they'd all been in his shoes. Not to mention, this case involved a high-profile suspect as well as several dangerous individuals who all had long criminal records. If all went according to plan, the suspects would be apprehended with no issues. To make the situation a little more challenging, however, other agencies were involved, including the DEA and the Massachusetts state police.

Settling back in his chair, Mack pushed aside all thoughts of his daughter and the weekend ahead as Bruce started at the beginning and worked his way through the detailed plan. Halfway through, another agent asked for clarification on a matter, but otherwise, Bruce got through the entire plan without any other questions or interruptions.

"I'll see everyone at the staging point Monday at five-thirty," Bruce said when he wrapped up the meeting.

With the group conference done, Mack turned back to his computer. Five-thirty. Christ, that was early. While he enjoyed the excitement and sense of the fulfillment that went along with an arrest like this, he hated the early hours planned arrests were scheduled for. While he understood the reasoning behind it, the older he got, the earlier five-thirty seemed. Of course, it didn't help that most times he got little sleep before a big operation like this. He didn't know how it was for others involved, but for him, the night before a take-down like this, anticipation combined with adrenaline overwhelmed his body and kept him on high alert until the suspects were apprehended. Then, once at home, it'd drain out of him faster than a balloon losing helium. The energy up-and-downs he experienced before and after an arrest had driven Bethany crazy and had been something they'd argued about a lot before their separation.

"Jesus, I hope I wasn't that bad my first time as agent in charge," Dakota said when Bruce left the area.

"You were worse, Smith," Oliver called out from his desk.

"At least I remember my first time, old man," Dakota came back with. At forty-eight, Oliver was the oldest agent on the squad, though to look at him, you'd never know it, which partially explained how he'd landed himself a wife thirteen years younger than him.

Mack listened as Oliver and Dakota tossed insults at each other, something that occurred all the time among the squad members. While outsiders might see it and assume no one got along, the opposite was true. Especially between Oliver and Dakota, who often worked as partners.

"You guys can bullshit all you want, but I'm out of here." Mack turned off his computer and locked his desk drawer. "See you both on Monday."

The calendar said summer didn't end for several more weeks, but Mack noticed a few orange and red leaves on his way home that night. He'd already noticed there was a little less daylight each day when he left work, but the colorful leaves drove home the fact that fall was just around the corner. Not that he minded. Fall was one of his favorite times of year. In a few weeks, he and Grace would go apple picking, something they had been doing since she could walk. Before the divorce, Bethany would sometimes come with them. This year, it would be him and Grace and maybe his niece. Grace had already asked if they could bring Brianna with them, but he kept forgetting to ask his sister. They would also need to buy a Halloween costume soon. He'd already seen some at the mall when he stopped for lunch earlier that week. He knew from past experience, though, it was best to wait as long as possible. Grace had a tendency to change her mind five or six times before Halloween ever arrived.

While he'd rather get off the highway and take the back roads home, he'd promised Jessie he'd get home as early as possible when they spoke Thursday night. If traffic remained light, the highway was a shorter route.

As expected, she told him not to worry, but still, he was

eager to get home. Thanks to his long hours, he already didn't get to spend as much time with his daughter as he'd like. Then there were the weekends when she went with her mother—like next week—and he saw her even less.

The eagerness inside him now, though, stemmed from more than just spending time with Grace. The thought of seeing Jessie again contributed to it. Ever since they'd painted and had dinner together, she had been popping up in his thoughts.

He'd enjoyed their conversations. They'd been easy-going and open. They both contributed, unlike the conversations he and his ex-wife had. Maybe that should have been a clue that their relationship wasn't going to work, but he'd never noticed back then. Only after the separation had he noticed how Bethany needed to dominate their conversations. How she need conversations focused on *her* thoughts and desires. If he'd paid closer attention, perhaps he would've saved himself a lot of headaches. Then again, if not for his marriage, he wouldn't have Grace.

Thanks to the light traffic—an unusual occurrence for a Friday night—Mack pulled into his garage forty minutes after leaving the office. Opening the door into the kitchen, the smell of peanut butter greeted him, but all the lights remained off.

"Grace?" he called out as he stopped by the counter where two trays of cookies sat, and he grabbed a few.

"We're outside, Mack," Jessie answered.

Mack bit into a cookie and turned toward the French doors that led onto the deck.

"Daddy." Grace smiled at him when he came outside but remained seated.

Dropping a kiss on his daughter's head, he surveyed the project before him. Newspaper covered the table and several paper cups sat in a line, each filled with a different color of paint. Off to one side sat a painted birdhouse, and judging by how neat it looked, he guessed Jessie had done it. In front of Grace sat another wooden birdhouse, but this one still needed its roof painted.

"I love the bird houses," he said as he watched Grace finish one side.

Grace stopped and looked at him. "They're fairy houses, Daddy." Then, before he answered, she went back to work.

Mack looked over at Jessie who tried not to laugh. "Right. Fairy houses. I should have known that." He pulled out an empty chair near his daughter. "Did you make these delicious cookies, Grace?"

His daughter looked up long enough to answer. "Jessie helped me."

"I hope you don't mind. I brought the ingredients with me from home."

Mack finished the cookie in his hand and shook his head. "No, they're delicious." He watched as Grace spread paint on the fairy house roof. "How much do I owe for the bird—I mean, fairy houses?"

"Don't worry about it. They were on sale at the craft store." As she spoke, Jessie came to her feet. "Now that you're here, I'm going to go."

Immediately, Grace stopped painting and looked at Jessie. "No, not yet."

Although he didn't say it, Mack shared his daughter's opinion. After thinking of Jessie often during the week, now she stood here in the flesh. "I plan to throw some burgers on the grill. Why don't you stay and eat with us."

"Daddy promised we'd roast marshmallows tonight. He bought huge ones at the store. You can roast some, too."

Indecision filled Jessie's face and Mack wondered what enticement might push her into staying.

"Please, Jessie," Grace pleaded, her head tilted to one side and her large eyes fixed on Jessie.

He noticed a slight change in Jessie's expression the moment she made up her mind.

"Okay. If you really want me to." Jessie sat back down.

Mack almost shook his head. His daughter had a way of getting people to do whatever she wanted without pitching a fit or even raising her voice. "Great. You two stay here and I'll get the burgers going." Mack switched on the gas grill before he headed inside.

Big turkey dinners and casseroles he'd never mastered, but cooking outside he excelled at, if he did say so himself. Over the years, he'd prepared everything, from burgers and hot dogs to venison and salmon. More nights than not, he cooked dinner on the grill, even in the winter. Tonight, after placing enough patties on the grill, he went back inside and prepared a salad while Grace and Jessie cleaned up their painting project. Unlike most children he knew, his niece included, Grace liked salad. In fact, she preferred it to most cooked vegetables. As a result, they had one almost every night with dinner, regardless of what he cooked.

While he worked chopping up the celery, he could hear Grace chatting away outside. Every once in a while, he'd hear Jessie's voice when she answered whatever question about fairies and fairy houses Grace threw at her. For the past month or so, they were all she talked about. He'd long ago run out of ideas for answers to her questions. From the sound of it, Jessie was holding her own, though.

"Brianna says fairies can live anywhere," Grace said as they ate. "I told her she's wrong. Fairies only live in the woods like in the movie I watched at your house. Do you think fairies can live anywhere?"

"How about we give fairies a rest and finish eating?" While he'd started on his second burger and Jessie was almost done with her first one, Grace's remained almost whole.

"It's my last question, promise."

"Last one. Then you eat, right?" He tried to maintain his stern tone. "Otherwise, no marshmallows after."

"Promise."

Mack looked over at Jessie who was smiling at the two

of them. Behind her, the setting sun bathed her in light, and he noticed for the first time the blonde highlights her hair. "I never win with this one." He pointed his thumb in Grace's direction.

Jessie's smile grew wider at his comment and a tiny dimple appeared in her left cheek. "Gran says the same thing about me all the time."

The flames in the fire pit danced, making shadows on the side of the house as the smoke curled into the sky. Next to him, Grace sat licking the remnants of her last marshmallow from her fingers while he roasted one for himself.

"Can I have another?"

Mack thought for a moment, trying to remember how many she'd already eaten. He wasn't positive, but he guessed four. While she had decided to just eat the marshmallows and not the s'mores like him and Jessie, she'd still consumed a fair amount of sugar. "Just one, and then it's inside to bed."

Grace didn't wait for him to help her. Instead, she reached into the bag. After sticking what she'd described as "perfect pillows for her dolls" on the end of her stick, she inched a little closer to the flames.

"There is something extra tasty about a marshmallow toasted over a fire," Jessie said from the other side of the fire pit. "I make s'mores in my microwave at home and they never taste this good." She added her marshmallow to the chocolate and graham crackers she'd prepared.

"I'm still shocked Grace refused to try one." Mack turned the stick in his daughter's hand before the marshmallow caught on fire.

Grace, unwilling to wait for the sugary treat to get any more color, pulled it away from the flame, and without pulling it off the stick first, she stuffed half of it into her mouth.

"I like them this way," she said with a mouthful. "Can I

have one more?"

Taking the stick away, Mack shook his head. "It's time for bed." Her expression alone said she was about to protest, so Mack beat her to it. "This isn't open for negotiation. You should've been in bed an hour ago." Since he had promised her roasted marshmallows and they did have a guest, he'd let her stay up late, but if she stayed up much later, she'd be a bear in the morning.

"Can we do this again tomorrow night?" Grace stood, her movements slow and drawn out.

Giving her a slight push, he stood behind her. "We'll see. Say good night to Jessie."

Finding a new way to stall, Grace ran around to the other side of the fire pit and threw her arms around Jessie. "Good night, Jessie. I had fun with you."

He watched as Jessie hugged Grace. "Any time. I had fun, too."

Before Grace realized it, Mack scooped her up and tossed her over his shoulder. "I'll be back as soon as I put this monkey to bed." He tickled Grace's side as he spoke.

In the past year, bedtime had gone from being a chore to just another routine part of the day, so it didn't take him long to get Grace tucked into bed. "No story tonight, buddy. It's too late." Mack kissed her on the forehead. "We'll do something fun tomorrow."

"Can Jessie come over tomorrow? I liked having her here tonight."

Funny, so had he. "We'll see. No promises."

Grace gripped her stuffed dog, Mr. Whiskers, tighter, her eyes already starting to droop. "Love you, Daddy."

"I love you, too."

When Mack went back outside, he found Jessie still sitting near the fire. "She's already asleep." Rather than take his seat from before, he sat in the one to Jessie's right.

"I guess she had to run out of energy at some point. I ran out of it an hour ago."

In the fire pit, a log crackled, sending tiny sparks up.

"Tell me about it. I wouldn't know what to do with all her energy." Mack watched the flames dancing for a moment, the sight a bit hypnotizing. "She liked having you here tonight." He realized that now, with Grace in bed, Jessie would be leaving. Although he'd never once considered spending an evening with Jessie before, he didn't want her to leave now. "She wants you to come back tomorrow." He leaned a little closer, his forearm brushing hers.

Jessie moistened her bottom lip and swallowed. "Don't you—?"

Before she could finish her sentence, he leaned even closer. "*I* want you to come back tomorrow." Mack closed the distance between them and touched his lips to hers.

Jessie remained rigid, reminding him of a stone pillar with her hands gripping the chair, but she kissed him back as if not 100 percent sure she should. When he slipped an arm around her waist and pulled her closer, she relaxed, but her kisses stayed tentative.

Slipping his other hand under her hair, he cupped her head as he traced her lips with his tongue, hoping she'd get the hint and open her mouth to him. He didn't have to wait long. The moment her lips parted, he surged forward. She tasted like marshmallow, chocolate, and something unique and appealing, something that was a part of Jessie and Jessie alone. Applying more pressure with his lips, he let his tongue meet hers, allowing them each a chance to get to know each other better.

A feather-light touch brushed his arm then moved higher until it left his bare skin and continued up his shirtsleeve. A similar touch slid across his other arm, and soon both of Jessie's hands rested on his shoulders, sending warmth through the cotton material and into his body.

After a week of Jessie popping up in his thoughts, the feel and taste of her was taking over his brain and bringing other parts of his body online. It had been months since he'd last had sex and his body was taking this opportunity to remind him of that fact. As if sensing where his thoughts had headed, Jessie pulled away. In the firelight, he saw her eyes grow wide as her brain registered what they'd been doing. She opened her mouth as if to speak, but snapped it shut just as fast. Then she dropped her hands back into her lap. Even without her hands on his shoulders, *want* coursed through his body.

With his arm still around her waist, he kept her close while his other hand rubbed the soft skin on the back of her neck. "So will you?"

Jessie swallowed and licked her lips. "Will I what?" Her usually soft voice was almost inaudible now.

His gaze dropped to her lips, surprised by just how much he wanted to kiss her again. Rather than remain there, though, he looked back up. For as long as he'd known her, she'd worn glasses. With those gone now, he noticed how beautiful her eyes were. Framed by long, dark lashes, her eyes were not just a simple shade of brown—rather flecks of chestnut and mahogany mixed with a hint of gold to create a shade unique to the woman in his arms. Unable to look away for a moment, he lost himself in the depths of her eyes, catching a glimpse of the questions and apprehension reflected there.

No, there was more than just apprehension. He saw some fear as well, or at least, he thought it was fear. Then she blinked and whatever emotion he thought he saw disappeared, leaving only the questions behind.

Mack gave himself a mental shake. "Come back tomorrow?"

"I'm opening the store tomorrow. I'll be there most of the day."

If he hadn't been so close to her, he never would've heard her response.

At the moment, her coming back meant a great deal to him, but he'd ask himself why later. "How about afterward? On Saturdays, Grace and I usually get takeout and watch a movie. Come and join us."

Jessie bit down on her lip as she considered his invite. "That sounds like a special tradition between the two of you. I shouldn't intrude."

Mack moved the hand that rested on her neck forward, tracing her jaw with his index finger. "You wouldn't be intruding. We both want you here, remember?"

The crackling logs remained the only sound while Jessie considered his comment. Then, when Mack assumed she needed more convincing, her chin dipped down and she nodded.

"Okay," she whispered. "If you're sure." This time her voice increased a bit in volume.

An invisible string attached to both of them pulled him toward her again. "Positive," he answered, his lips mere inches from hers. "It'll be fun." The words left his mouth and he kissed her again.

Oh, dear God! His lips moved against hers and the same words repeated over again. Mack was kissing her. She'd been kissed before, but it had never felt like this. Okay, true, she'd only been kissed by a handful of men, but none had kissed her like this. Like Mack. And although his mouth touched only her lips, her entire body prickled with awareness as if he was touching and kissing her everywhere.

It's a dream. It had to be. Why else would Mack Ellsbury have his arms around her as he kissed her senseless? She didn't usually have dreams this lifelike, but so what? Maybe the teenage daydreams she had of Mack had grown up, too, and this was the end result. Either way, she planned on enjoying it.

The cotton on her back slipped upward and warm flesh replaced it. Like a bungee cord, the contact yanked Jessie back to reality as confusion and some fear jabbed her. Wrenching her mouth away, she stared at Mack, her heartbeat racing out of control. "It's late. I should go." To her own ears, she sounded out of breath.

"It's not even nine-thirty, Jessie." He leaned forward.

Afraid he intended another kiss, she leaned all the way back in her chair. Perhaps noticing her retreat, he reversed direction himself.

"Hey, what's the matter?" He moved his hand on her skin up and down.

This is Mack. He'd never hurt anyone. He's not Jeremy. Jessie reminded herself of all the things she'd learned in therapy as she forced her sudden fear back into its little box.

"Nothing," Jessie lied, not wanting to discuss what she felt or the fact that this was the first time she'd been kissed in years. "It was a long day and I have to be at the store early." She also wasn't going to tell him about the confusion still running rampant in her head.

Mack studied her; there was no other way to describe the way he looked at her. "Are you sure? You look..." He paused. "Worried." He finished his sentence, but his voice suggested he wasn't confident of his word selection.

Jessie forced a smile. "Just tired. The store's been busy and I expect it to be another busy day tomorrow. Our anniversary sale kicks off this weekend and we're opening an hour earlier than usual."

The warm fingers on her back disappeared and, instead, Mack took her hand. "I'll walk you to your car then." He pulled her up as he stood.

Neither spoke as they passed the drying fairy houses on the patio and exited through the side gate that led to a stone path.

"Watch your step. Some stones are loose. I need to fix them and replace some of the solar lights." Mack held her hand as they walked.

Happy that their conversation had returned to non-personal topics, Jessie nodded. "Sounds like a good weekend project." They stopped next to her car, but rather than release her hand as she'd expected, he took another step toward her, then pulled her closer so they stood less than an arm's length apart.

"Come on over whenever tomorrow, okay?"

Before her mouth could say no, her brain made her head nod in agreement. Not seeing any way of getting out of it and not really sure she wanted to anyway, she said, "Can I bring anything?"

Mack tugged her closer. "Just yourself. Like I said, we get takeout and just watch a movie."

He planned to kiss her again. Anticipation grew, even as questions popped up in her mind. *Examine the questions later!* her body yelled, drowning out her mind as his chest pressed against her breasts. Then, in slow motion, his mouth came down on hers again. The kiss remained light and over all too soon.

"Okay."

Mack remained in the driveway as she backed into the street. Even as she headed down Union Street, she caught a glimpse in her rearview mirror of him still in his driveway.

She'd driven every street in town so many times she could do it on autopilot, and as she made the short trip from Mack's house to her apartment, her mind focused on the events of the night not the drive. When Mack had invited her for dinner, she'd assumed it was a way to say thank you. Although not expected, she understood why he might feel a need to show his appreciation. Then, of course, there was Grace. She'd more or less invited her before her father could stop her. Once the little girl made the invite, Mack may have felt unable to avoid a guest for dinner. All that made perfect sense to her and it had been her way of explaining Mack's invite. The kiss, though… How did she explain that?

He kissed me. Jessie shut her car door with the statement repeating in her head. Mack had kissed her not once but *twice*. While friends sometimes shared a peck on the cheek, they didn't kiss the way he kissed her.

Jessie climbed the stairs to her apartment, the scene in Mack's backyard replaying in her head. When he'd come back outside, the last thing she'd expected was a kiss. She'd thought maybe they'd talk for a few more minutes, and then she'd leave with no idea of when or where she might see him again. Instead, he'd sat down beside her, sending a dizzying current of attraction racing through her. If that hadn't been enough, he'd asked her to come back the next night before kissing her.

Jessie paused in the kitchen and replayed the glorious kiss in her head. Not even Hollywood could have scripted a more perfect first kiss. The one by her car had also been nice, but not as intense. With a sigh, she headed into her bedroom. What did it mean? Did it mean anything? Maybe he'd just been caught up in the moment. The atmosphere around them had bordered on romantic. Right now, he might be sitting outside, thinking how their kiss had been a mistake. Tomorrow, he might keep his distance. Perhaps even call her and say he changed his mind about her joining them. If that happened, she'd understand. People made mistakes when they got caught up in a moment. But what if he *didn't* cancel? What if the kiss tonight meant something? What if he did it again?

Since her recent weight loss, she'd noticed the occasional once-over she got from men, though no one ever made any advances. Well, except for Tony, but she didn't count him because he came on to all women. She assumed it was because she'd known everyone for so long that they never asked her out, and for the most part, she rarely left North Salem.

Thanks to her limited experience with men, she didn't know how to interpret tonight's events. Did she even *want* Mack's actions to mean something? Sure, she'd had a crush on him in high school; a lot of girls had. But they weren't in high school anymore. Hadn't been in a long time. What did she really know about Mack anymore? He'd moved from North Salem a long time ago, and she had only seen him occasionally during his years away. People changed. Sure, he'd been a nice enough person when he tutored her, but who knew about now?

Jeremy had been kind and considerate in the beginning, too. It had taken him a while to show his true colors.

Jessie slammed her bureau drawer shut. *But Mack is one of the good guys.*

Angry with herself, she tossed her pajamas onto the bed, then stripped off her jeans and shirt. She'd come a long way in getting her life back on a track. After her six-year relationship with Jeremy, she'd let her life coast. She'd shut out most of the outside world and lived a sheltered existence, afraid to let anyone or anything new in. Over the past year and a half, she'd succeeded at breaking out of that bubble. She'd finally moved out on her own. She'd changed the way she looked and had started doing things she enjoyed rather than the things her grandparents enjoyed.

Whatever this thing with Mack might be, it needed to be treated in the same way. She couldn't run from it. No, she needed and, honestly, wanted to see where it might go. It might go nowhere.

Pulling on her pajamas, she glanced in the floor-length mirror. After she'd gained weight in college, she'd avoided mirrors. When she'd decided enough was enough, that she had to take control of her life and change the things she didn't like, she'd bought a freestanding, full-length mirror. It was a symbol, a reminder that she would no longer hide away.

"Just go with the flow," Jessie said to her reflection. "Act like nothing has changed and see where things go tomorrow." Her resolve set, she switched off the light and headed for the couch and an hour or two of her favorite television shows.

CHAPTER 6

Jessie spent much of the morning assisting customers. Annette, who worked Saturday mornings, called in sick, and Jessie couldn't get anyone to cover Annette's shift until eleven o'clock. With Brian there now, Jessie could retreat to her office and finish the schedule for the rest of the month. With the kids back in school and high school sports in full swing, her summer schedule no longer worked. The same thing happened every year. While the store did have regular full-time employees with set schedules, it also had a number of part-timers, some of whom were students or parents who worked there for additional income. It was these part-timers who messed with her well-ordered schedule.

Jessie opened up the spreadsheet program she used for the schedule. Much of the month was done. If she didn't have any more interruptions, she could get it wrapped up in another hour or so. Distractions from the store she could block out without a problem. All she had to do was close the office door. It was the mental distractions she couldn't shut out.

Thoughts of Mack and the night ahead plagued her. Would he kiss her again? Grace would be there for some of the time and she doubted he'd kiss her then. But what about afterward?

At some point, Grace would go to bed. She hoped he kissed her then. Or should she make the first move this time? This was the twenty-first century. Women could let a man know how they felt.

Jessie's mind wandered away from the schedule and she pictured them outside again. This time, however, she wrapped her arms around his neck and pulled his mouth to hers. In her vision, they kissed, his fingers sinking into her hair.

"You'll never do it," she muttered under her breath and wished she was a little more like Charlie or Mia. Both women were very sure of themselves. If they wanted something, they went after it.

The vision evaporated and Jessie looked back at the computer screen. She'd scheduled herself until three o'clock. That gave her three more hours. If she remained on task, she could get everything done by then.

Once Jessie finalized the schedule, she moved down her to-do list. She was still reviewing the materials she'd received from a new manufacturer of eco-friendly cabinetry when Charlie appeared on the other side of the window. Before she could even knock, Jessie gestured for her to enter. She'd last seen Charlie over the Fourth of July weekend.

Jessie had known Charlie O'Brien—now Sherbrooke— all her life. They'd become friends in preschool and had remained best friends all through school. They'd slept over at each other's houses and played soccer together. After high school, though, they'd gone their separate ways. Jessie had stayed in North Salem while Charlie became a doctor and joined the Navy. Two years earlier, they'd reconnected and their friendship was like it'd been back in the day.

"I figured I'd find you here when you didn't answer your cell." Charlie entered the office.

Jessie had left the cell behind when she'd gone into the

store to help customers and hadn't bothered checking it since. "Annette called in this morning, so I was on the floor." She put aside the brochures she was holding. "I'm glad you stopped in. You didn't say you were coming up this weekend." Distance might keep them from regular visits, but they exchanged text messages all the time and spoke on the phone.

"Jake and I decided at the last minute." Charlie took a seat on the other side of the desk. "I left him at Sean's. They're gutting one of the upstairs bathrooms."

Sometimes Jessie still found it unbelievable that Charlie had married Jake Sherbrooke, a man once known in the media as Prince Charming. Almost as unbelievable as that was what a nice guy he was. From the very first moment she'd met him when her grandfather fell and needed help, Jake had been kind and compassionate. Nothing at all what she'd expected from someone from such a wealthy and powerful family.

"I think he loves tearing things up more then he does putting them together." Not only did Jake run a disaster relief foundation, he often worked alongside his employees when his team went in.

Jessie could picture Jake and Sean tearing apart one of the outdated bathrooms in Sean's old house. "How is Jake?"

"Busy. He spent last week in Kansas after that tornado hit," Charlie said. "What about you? Anything new and interesting?"

"Same old things. You know me."

"You should come visit us more often. Get away from here." Charlie grew serious. "You're always welcome."

Jessie appreciated Charlie's concern. She'd never discussed with anyone her intentions to take control of her life and move it in a direction she wanted. However, Charlie had noticed and once commented on the changes she saw in Jessie. "I'll visit soon," Jessie answered, and not just because it was the answer Charlie wanted. She'd never traveled much. In fact, she'd never been any farther south than Virginia and no farther west than New York City. Her grandparents had been too busy running the store when she was younger and her father spent so much time on the road for work, he considered staying home a vacation. While she couldn't imagine living anywhere but North Salem, she did want to see more of the world.

Charlie didn't push for an exact date; instead, she moved to the edge of her seat. "I'm heading over to pick up Taylor and bring her to Sean's," she said, referring to her younger half-sister. "He's having a cookout tonight and told me to invite you. Tony and Striker will be there, too."

Any other time, she'd say yes. She thought of Sean as the brother she never had. While Tony had been driving her a little crazy the past few months, he was an okay guy. She didn't know Striker as well, but when he and Tony got together, things got entertaining. "I'm going to Mack's after work."

Charlie leaned forward, her brow wrinkled with confusion. "Mack as in Mack Ellsbury?"

Jessie nodded.

"Wow. I haven't seen him in ages, although Sean stays in contact with him. Didn't he move to Worcester or Boston?"

"He lived closer to Boston for several years. A few weeks ago, he and his daughter moved back here. He bought the house next to Mrs. Mitchell."

Charlie sat back in her chair again. "Daughter? I didn't know he ever married."

Sometimes, Jessie forgot how out of touch with the town her friend had become after graduation. "He was married to Bethany Lewis. They got divorced a couple years ago. She used to be on channel 7 news. Now she's on *USA This Morning*."

"I didn't know any of that." Charlie paused and Jessie could see her friend's brain processing their conversation.

"How long have you two been together?"

The question made sense, considering what she'd shared so far. "We're not together."

"Then he's having a party? I'm surprised he didn't invite Sean and the guys."

Was Charlie searching for information? That wasn't her typical way. Charlie tended to be straightforward. If she had a question, she asked it. Then again, they didn't usually discuss Jessie's love life or, better put, *lack* of a love life.

"No, it'll just be the three of us."

The corner of Charlie's mouth inched up. "But you're not together. Come on, Quinn. Out with it."

"I've helped him with his daughter a few times when he needed it and stuff." She thought about her interactions with Mack since his return. "Yesterday, he needed a sitter after school, so I watched Grace until he came home. Then I stayed for dinner." The memory of their kiss rose up and her body temperature spiked.

"And I'm guessing you did more than eat dinner," Charlie said, sounding almost happy about the fact.

"We kissed, nothing else." Jessie's lips tingled with the memory. "Then he invited me—well actually, he said his daughter and he wanted me to come over again tonight." Jessie reviewed his exact words in her head. Yes, he'd said Grace wanted her to come back when he returned from tucking her in. Then he'd continued by saying he wanted her there, too.

"You look confused or worried. I'm not sure which." Charlie broke into her thoughts.

Even though they'd reconnected and their friendship was much like it had been, Jessie had never told Charlie about her last relationship. Rather than share anything now, she shook her head. "Neither. I'm just not going to assume anything. One or two kisses don't always mean something." It was true. During her first semester at college, she'd met a guy at a freshman get-together. They'd kissed a few times that night and then gone on two dates.

After that, she never spoke with him again.

"But sometimes it does."

Charlie hadn't dated a lot in high school, either. Jessie had a feeling that had been because most guys hadn't wanted to get on Sean's bad side. Even before Charlie's dad walked out on them, Sean had been protective of her. Once their dad left, though, he'd taken over the roles of both protective brother *and* father. She assumed Charlie had dated a lot in college as well as in the Navy, which meant she had a lot more experience with men.

"I guess."

Once again, Charlie moved to the edge of her seat. "I have to go, but are you around tomorrow or Monday? Jake and I are here until Tuesday morning."

"I'm off Monday, but I have to work tomorrow morning."

Charlie stood. "Perfect. Do you want to plan on meeting Monday around noon? I can come to your place if you want."

"Sounds good."

"Have fun tonight." Charlie picked up the keys she'd placed on Jessie's desk. "See you on Monday."

Jessie watched her friend walk back into the store, again wishing she were a little more like Charlie. People had often wondered about their friendship. On so many levels they were complete opposites. Charlie was tall and one of the prettiest girls in their class—confident, driven, and she never backed down. All the things Jessie wasn't. Somehow, though, their similarities had over-shadowed their differences. Right now, however, Jessie wished for just a touch of her friend's confidence. Heck, she'd like to have a bit of Charlie's height as well.

With Charlie gone, Jessie picked up the brochure she'd been reading and checked the wall clock. Another hour until she called it a day. Mack had said to come over after work, but she planned to stop home first. When she'd left this morning, she'd dressed for a day at work, nothing else.

Regardless of whether Mack kissed her or not tonight, she wanted to look nice. She didn't want to show up in the Quinn's hardware golf shirt she'd thrown on or the jeans she managed to get paint on while mixing a can for Ray Larson.

At the last minute, Jessie made a small detour on her way to Mack's. While he told her not to bring anything, her upbringing told her something else. Since she didn't have time to make anything, cupcakes from Peggy Sue's would have to do.

"I'll take three chocolate and three vanilla cupcakes," Jess said and watched the high school student behind the counter fill a box.

"Anything else?"

Jessie accepted the box and handed over a ten-dollar bill. "That's it."

"Jessica?" an unfamiliar voice said from behind her.

Accepting her change, she turned and found Sharon Pelletier behind her. She'd tried calling the other woman twice now and had even left a voice mail, but Sharon had never called back. Now here she stood and the words she'd prepared vanished from her head. "Hi Sharon." *I can do this.* "How are you?"

"Busy. The wedding is in a week and there are a million things left to do."

Jessie leaned against the counter for support. "You're getting married?"

Sharon shook her head. "No, Keira," she said, referring to her older sister. "Edward and I only got engaged last month."

Edward. She'd said Edward. Not Jeremy. Then she wasn't dating the monster.

"Sorry I didn't call you back. I meant to. When you said you needed to talk, you made me curious."

Now that Jessie no longer had to share her secret, she struggled for an answer. "I saw you with someone I thought I knew the other day at The Coffee Press. I wasn't sure if it was him or not." As far as on-the-spot excuses went, it wasn't bad.

"You must have seen me with Jeremy. We stopped in on our way back to the office."

She almost hugged Sharon. "You work with him?"

"For a little longer anyway. He's transferring to the Worcester office. Would you like me to tell him you said hi?"

"No!" Jessie shouted and a few customers looked in her direction. "I was just curious. I thought he moved after we graduated." She couldn't recall the last time she'd improvised like this. "We weren't close friends or anything."

"I'm not surprised. He's a bit of a jerk."

You don't know the half of it. "I'll take your word for it. It was nice seeing you." Jessie took a step backward. "Congratulations on the engagement."

"Bye."

Back outside, Jessie got in her car, feeling a thousand pounds lighter. The weight she'd carried since seeing Sharon and Jeremy no longer existed, and best of all, she didn't have to tell Sharon her secret.

***

Through his upstairs bedroom window, Mack heard a car stop in his driveway. Pulling his t-shirt on, he opened his bedroom door as Grace's voice floated up the stairs.

"Daddy, someone's here."

"It's probably Jessie." Mack reached the bottom of the stairs, anticipation like he hadn't experienced in a long time running through him. "I'll get the door. Why don't you find the takeout menus in the kitchen?"

Grace nodded, causing her wet hair to fall forward before she skipped off to the kitchen, her dollhouse forgotten.

They'd spent the day in the yard cleaning an area for Grace's new swing set. Or perhaps *he'd* cleared an area while Grace played. Either way, they'd both needed showers when they'd come inside.

Opening the front door, he saw Jessie still seated in her car, her eyes locked on the garage door. Then her gaze swung toward him. For half a heartbeat, she watched him and then her lips formed a tentative smile, and the memory of their kiss washed over him. When he'd come home the night before, kissing Jessie hadn't been on his mind. Sure, he'd thought of her often during the week and had looked forward to seeing her, but kissing hadn't occurred to him. Once he'd put Grace to bed and seen Jessie seated in the dancing firelight, the idea took root and there had been no stopping it.

After she'd left, he'd lain in bed thinking about her and the kiss. He'd even woken up thinking about it. Now, as he stood there looking at her, all he wanted was to kiss her again and see if it would affect him the same way it had the night before. Like he was a thirteen-year-old experiencing his first kiss again, only better.

Breaking eye contact, Jessie pushed open her car door and stood. He'd told her to come over right after work, so he'd expected her to be in either jeans and a Quinn's hardware golf shirt or perhaps one of those loose flowing dresses she sometimes wore. Today, though, she wore neither, and he had to keep his mouth from dropping open.

Unable to help himself, he let his eyes rake across her body, starting at her face and working his way down. She'd left her hair down and it skimmed across her shoulders. Her dark red short-sleeve top clung to her body, its V-neck drawing his eyes to her cleavage where they remained for several seconds before traveling lower. While she wore jeans, they were nothing like the loose-fitting ones she wore in the store. Instead, these molded to her trim thighs. She even wore footwear he never would've guess she owned. Unlike the comfortable sneakers or sandals she wore most of the time, tonight she wore black boots that ended just below the knee.

"I hope this time is okay." Jessie stopped on the top step. "If not, I can come back later."

Mack forced his eyes to met hers and hoped surprise didn't reflect on his face. "It's perfect. I just finished my shower."

Jessie held out the box in her hand. "I know you said not to bring anything, but I stopped at Peggy's for some cupcakes."

"Thanks. Come on in." He accepted the box, his fingers brushing hers, and a jolt of awareness shot through him. And just from that simple touch, he knew that when—not if, because there was no doubt in his mind it would happen—he kissed her again, it would be just as incredible as last night.

The door closed behind Jessie, but neither of them moved. Not wanting Grace to walk in and see them kissing, he raised a hand and trailed a finger down Jessie's cheek. "I'm glad you're here."

Jessie swallowed and gave him a small smile, this one not as tentative as before. "Me, too."

He didn't miss the hint of unease he heard. "Come on. Grace is in the kitchen digging out the menus. She wants Chinese again, but I'm more in the mood for pizza." He took her by the hand. "There is also that Indian restaurant in Salem that delivers now."

Without any hesitation, Jessie entwined her fingers with his, and it dawned on him that Jessie had come back into his life for a reason. Okay, maybe he couldn't count tutoring her in high school and playing soccer with his sister as *in his life* before, but that day she'd helped with Grace had crossed their paths and he wanted to see where things went.

In the end, they ordered pizza since they'd all eaten Chinese earlier in the week. Considering she hadn't gotten her way, Grace didn't complain at all even though Chinese was one of her favorites.

"You have to see the fairy village I made." Grace removed a mushroom that had accidentally gotten on her pizza before lifting it from her plate. "I used the houses we painted, but it needs more. Come on. I'll show you." Grace began to slip from her chair, but Mack stopped her with a hand on her arm.

"After dinner."

"I'll be quick."

Part of him wanted to say *okay*, but he knew from past experiences that if Grace went out now, she'd never finish dinner. "Eat first. Then you can show Jessie anything you want."

Grace scowled, a look that made him laugh. Rather than make her look angry, the expression only made her look cuter.

"I'm hungry anyway, Grace. I want to finish my pizza." From across the table, Jessie threw him a glance as she spoke. "As soon as we're both done, we'll go outside."

Her plans foiled by two adults, Grace reached for her pizza again. "Daddy promised he'd get more houses for me to paint after work this week."

Why, he'd never know. He'd rather arrest members of a drug ring than walk into a craft store. The smell alone was overwhelming, not to mention, the crowded aisles and little old ladies with blue hair moving slower than snails. Maybe he could just build her some instead. How hard could it be? He'd once built a doghouse with his father. A fairy house just needed to be smaller.

"I can stop by the craft store and pick more up," Jessie said.

Wondering if he'd somehow given away his feelings, Mack looked at Jessie.

"But if you'd rather have your dad pick them out, I understand." She smiled at him. Not a tentative smile like before, but one filled with humor that let him know she'd guessed his thoughts about the craft store.

"You know, Grace, it might be better if Jessie does it. She knows what a fairy house should look like."

Grace finished her mouthful, unaware of the unspoken conversation going on. "Okay." She reached for her milk. "But can you get some different kinds?"

"I'll see what they have," Jessie answered.

Saved from the dreaded trip into the craft store, Mack went back to eating his pizza as Grace filled Jessie in on all the items she'd added to her village. Every once in a while, Jessie would ask a question or make a suggestion, but for the most part, she listened while Grace rattled on. Once again, Mack noted how good she was with his daughter. He knew for a fact that if Bethany sat in Jessie's seat, their dinner conversation would be much different.

Regardless of who else was in the room, Bethany liked to take center stage. He hadn't noticed it that much when it had been only them, but once Grace began talking, he'd noticed it. Sure, Bethany spoke to Grace, but she always tried to monopolize his attention.

Jessie, on the other hand, let Grace dominate the conversation. Not once last night or tonight had she tried to change the subject, even though he couldn't imagine she found fairies interesting.

She'd also painted and baked with his daughter, two rather messy projects. He'd once baked a box mix of brownies with Grace, so he knew what a fun, but hazardous, endeavor it could be. To the best of his knowledge, Bethany had never done either activity with Grace.

"I'm done. Are you, Jessie?" Grace held up her empty plate. Tonight, she'd finished everything, including the pizza crust.

Jessie's soft laugh made him smile. "I think so. I want to save room for a cupcake. But maybe we should help your dad clean up first."

"All set. You two can go out, and then we can decide on a movie." He still had a slice of pizza to finish.

Grace leapt from her chair. "Come on, Jessie. Let's go."

Through the French doors, he watched Grace take Jessie by the hand and lead her over to what he guessed had once been a garden and listened as she described how the various sticks around the houses were a fence and the rocks she'd placed inside them were benches. She'd used a bunch of leaves to create a pond and pinecones acted as trees. When she'd showed him, he'd been impressed with her imagination. Judging by the comments he heard Jessie making now, she was impressed as well.

"Maybe you can use one of the new houses I buy as the village school," Jessie said once Grace finished pointing everything out. "Fairies need a school."

"Or maybe a library," Grace said with enthusiasm.

"They need that, too." Jessie stood. "Ready to go back inside?"

Grace stood, too. "Just one more thing." She took Jessie's hand and walked her toward the area he'd cleared for her new swing set.

He could no longer hear every word she said, but once Grace had given Jessie the whole scoop, they returned to the house, where he still sat with half a slice of pizza. He'd been so enthralled watching the two of them that he'd stopped eating.

"Grace created quite the village out there." Jessie stood behind his daughter, her hands on her shoulders. "I'm impressed. She's got a great imagination."

Like it would for any father, pride filled him at Jessie's words. "That she does." Done with his food, Mack stacked the dirty plates. "I'll take care of this. Why don't you two go pick out a movie?"

After putting the dishes in the dishwasher, Mack switched off the kitchen lights and joined Grace and Jessie in the living room. They had already picked a movie, and the opening scene was frozen on the television screen.

"Good. You found a movie." Mack sat and put his arm

around his daughter and pulled her close. They were both in their normal spots on the couch, Mack at the end, near the table, and Grace right up against his side.

"Jessie needs to sit over here." Grace looked at him when she spoke. "You can't see the TV from over there."

Jessie sat in the chair near the windows.

"If you want her to move, ask her, Grace." The chair was fine for watching television. He'd sat there several times and watched the news.

"You'll miss all the good scenes if you don't sit on the couch, Jessie."

Jessie smiled at him. "I don't want that to happen, so I guess I better move." She stood and crossed the room.

Now, the three of them sat together in what would be a perfect pose for a family photo. And while that might make another man uncomfortable, it filled him with a sense of contentment he hadn't experienced in a long time. Not only did he have his daughter, whom he loved more than life itself, but he had someone he enjoyed spending time with and who accepted Grace.

Since his divorce, he'd done some dating, but none had led to anything more than dinner and occasional sex. While some of the women he'd gone out with might have been interested in more, the moment he mentioned Grace, they backed off. As a result, he'd decided not to look for anything serious until Grace was older. That was why the last few times he'd gone out, he'd done so because he just wanted a night out with someone other than his daughter or his buddies, not because he hoped they'd be the right one.

Now, though, he reconsidered his decision. Being with Jessie felt right. No, the word *right* didn't describe it, but it was the only word he could find. Not only did he enjoy her company, but he found himself physically attracted to her in a way he'd not experienced before. While he didn't know how to explain it, he knew it was true.

Even now, as they sat there, he thought about their

previous kiss and the ones he intended to share with her later. He couldn't remember any other time as an adult he'd been so consumed by thoughts of kissing. If all those reasons weren't enough to make him reconsider his earlier decision, her treatment of Grace added even more. In the short time since his return, she'd shown Grace nothing but affection. Judging by how Grace had reacted the night of the block party, Jessie had also shown her attention in the past.

"So what do you think? Will she marry the awful prince?" Jessie asked and Mack once again looked in her direction, something he'd done a lot that night.

"Nope. She's gonna marry Wesley." Grace reached for another handful of popcorn.

"I still don't believe you've never seen this movie," Mack said. While he'd seen *The Princess Bride* years ago and knew how it ended, neither his daughter nor Jessie ever had.

"I don't even remember it being in the theaters." She turned her attention back to Grace. "How's she going to marry Wesley? He's locked up in that dungeon."

"The prince is a bad guy. They always lose. You'll see."

Mack wished his daughter's statement was true, but he didn't correct her. She'd learn the truth soon enough.

Jessie looked at him over Grace's head. "She sounds rather confident. Do you think she's right?"

"You're just going to have to watch and find out."

***

Jessie stayed on the couch while Mack tucked Grace into bed. Unlike the last time she'd visited, Grace had given her dad a bit of a hard time. Although past her bedtime, she'd insisted she wasn't tired and wanted another movie. Jessie had all but laughed when Grace told her father that. As it was, the girl had almost not made it all the way through the movie. More than once, she caught Grace's eyes starting to droop.

In the end, Mack carried Grace upstairs, and as Jessie waited for his return, her thoughts turned to the night ahead. Although he hadn't said anything, she'd caught the once-over he'd given her when she'd arrived. And while some women found it rude or insulting, it had boosted her confidence. Men in town—at least to the best of her knowledge—didn't view her as a potential girlfriend. Rather, they saw her as plan old reliable Jessica Quinn, the manager of the hardware store, the person they looked to when they couldn't find the saw they wanted or when they needed to special-order a new bathroom sink.

The way Mack had looked at her, though, let her know he saw something else—and better yet, liked what he saw. At least she thought he did. Not having a lot of experience with men, it was possible she'd misread him. She hoped not.

She heard footsteps upstairs and then a door close. A thrill of anticipation mixed with nerves settled in her stomach. When he'd kissed her the night before, he'd sent excitement coursing through her body, awakening parts that had been dormant for so long. Then tonight, when he'd touched her face, he'd sent shock to those same parts, awakening them even more. What would the rest of the night bring? Would he kiss her again? Or, instead, say goodnight now and walk her to her car with a "see you around"?

"She almost fell asleep brushing her teeth. I think she gave me a hard time because you're here. She really likes you."

Jessie watched him as he came back into the room and her self-confidence slipped. For a moment, she wondered if she'd imagined the kiss they'd shared. This was Mack Ellsbury. The guy so many girls in town had wanted to date. The man who looked even more gorgeous now than he had back in school. Why would he kiss her?

You didn't imagine the kiss or the way he looked at you.

Her thoughts bolstered her confidence.

"I like her, too. She's a sweet girl."

Mack sat next to her, his thigh rubbing against hers. "Can I get you anything?"

Yes, you. The thought popped into her head, but, thankfully, not out of her mouth.

"I know I was thinking about another cupcake," he said.

The cupcakes from Peggy's weren't the normal sized ones people baked at home. They were huge. Earlier in the night, she'd split one with Grace. "No, thanks."

Mack's arm slipped over her shoulders, his fingertips brushing her arm. "I'll get the cupcake later, then. Can you stay for a little longer?" His fingers caressed her skin, leaving goose bumps behind.

She nodded and enjoyed the simple physical contact. Nothing short of an all-out emergency could get her to leave now.

"Good," he said, his voice taking on a huskiness that hadn't been there before. "I'm glad you came tonight." He touched her cheek, sending a ripple of awareness through her.

Kiss me. Jessie clenched her fist to keep from reaching for him.

"I missed you after you left last night." He leaned forward, his gaze dropping to her lips for a moment before going back to her eyes. "All day I've been thinking about one thing."

Before she could ask him what, his mouth came down on hers. The kiss started slow and gentle as if he wanted to see how she would respond.

After spending a good portion of the day thinking about their last kiss, she wanted to bask in this one. Leaning in, she put her arms around his neck and kissed him back.

Following her actions, Mack's kiss changed. His lips became more demanding as he caressed and coaxed hers apart. Caught up in the moment, she opened to him and his tongue surged forward. A wave of desire shot through her body.

Jessie had no idea how long the kiss lasted, but she knew she didn't want it to end.

Unaware of her desires, Mack pulled away and switched his attention to the erratic pulse in her neck. "I missed you last night, too." Since he'd shared his feelings, it seemed only fair she do the same. "I'm glad you invited me over tonight."

His hand moved from her waist and traveled up her side as his lips once again took possession of hers. Immediately, blood surged from her fingertips to her toes and she lost herself in the kiss. Only when his hand brushed the outside of her breast did sudden panic reel her back to the present. Even through her t-shirt and bra, heat from his hand burned her skin.

This is Mack. He'd never force you. The reminder set her mind at ease, leaving Mack none the wiser. *Just enjoy this.*

With a mental shove, she pushed her negative thoughts away and threw all she had into their kiss. Slowly, one kiss flowed into another.

"Do you have plans tomorrow?" Mack pulled back from another incredible kiss.

"Work until two."

He pushed some hair away from her face. "Come over after."

"Are you sure?" She'd already intruded on his time with Grace.

He kissed her cheek. "Positive."

Jessie fought to form an answer as he kissed a path toward her mouth. "Okay." She got the single word out before his lips covered hers again.

"Grace is spending next weekend with her mom." Mack ended their kiss. They'd more or less been making out like a couple of teenagers for the past two hours and Jessie didn't want it to end. "I thought we could go out, just the two of us. Do you have to work?"

"I'm off Friday night and free all day Saturday and Sunday."

Mack raised her hand to his lips and kissed it. "Not anymore you're not."

The independent woman in her said she should object to his bossiness, but the truth was, she wanted to spend time with him, wanted to explore this thing between them.

"I'll pencil you in."

CHAPTER 7

With Charlie due over at any minute, Jessie hid the basket of unfolded laundry in her bedroom. It had been one of the many things on her to-do list that weekend, but like everything else, she hadn't gotten around to it. Between work, then babysitting on Friday night, and spending time at Mack's Saturday and Sunday nights, she'd been away from her apartment most of the weekend. Despite the untouched list, it had been the best weekend she'd had in a long time.

She let her mind wander back to their first kiss on Friday night. Soon her thoughts turned to the rest of the weekend. They hadn't done anything but talk and kiss. She didn't know if that was because Grace had been upstairs or because he didn't want to rush things, but either way, she was grateful. She enjoyed kissing him and being in his arms, but she wasn't quite ready for anything else. Or at least, her brain wasn't ready. Her body, on the other hand, had wanted so much more when he'd been kissing her last night. Just how much her body ached for his touch scared her. Never had she experienced an actual yearning to have someone's skin against hers, to have a man love her with his whole body. With Jeremy, the only man she'd ever slept with, it had been all about his needs and desires. If he wanted sex, they had sex. End of story.

Anger flared at the mere thought of Jeremy. She'd let him control her life for way too long. Even after she'd left him, he'd controlled her life. Now, complete control rested in her hands.

The doorbell brought Jessie back from the past. Closing the bedroom door to hide the unfolded laundry, she headed out, prepared for a nice afternoon with an old friend.

"So what did you do all weekend?" Jessie asked as she prepared a pot of coffee for Charlie, the biggest coffee fanatic she'd ever met.

"We hung at Sean's place on Saturday. He said to say hello, by the way. On Sunday, I drove Taylor back to my dad's and visited with him."

Charlie's father had come back into her life that summer after eighteen years. "How are things going?" She watched her friend for a reaction. Charlie, much like her brother, kept certain emotions under lock and key. Sometimes, the only way to know her true feelings was by her expressions.

"Okay. Strange. Jake insists it'll get better, but I'm not convinced. What about you? I noticed your car at Mack's again last night when I drove by."

Jessie ran through the adjectives in her vocabulary. "It was nice."

Charlie made a noise in the back of her throat and accepted her coffee. "That's all? I hoped you'd say incredible or fantastic. For some reason, I imagined he'd be capable of more than just a nice night."

Oh, it had been so much more than just nice. Jessie didn't know why she'd settled on such an inappropriate word. "Both days I spent time with him and his daughter. They made me feel like part of their family." She knew that sounded ridiculous. She'd only just reconnected with Mack. She wasn't part of his family, but she could see herself that way.

"And when we were alone…" Jessie's voice trailed off, and she shifted in her seat. "We only kissed, but it… I don't know how to explain it. It felt like more than a kiss. Does that make any sense? I've been kissed before, not a lot, but it never made me feel like this."

Charlie nodded. "I know what you mean. So what's the problem?"

"I didn't say there was a problem." Jessie glanced at the table.

"You didn't have to. If you're attracted to him and like spending time with him, what's the problem? Is it because he has a daughter?"

When she'd dated Jeremy, Charlie had been away from town and they hadn't seen much of each other. In fact, Jessie hadn't seen much of anyone. Those she had seen never knew how Jeremy treated her when they were alone.

"That doesn't bother me. I just haven't dated a lot." No way was she going to admit she hadn't been on a date since college. "The last relationship I was in, well, it didn't go well."

If Charlie found her statement odd, she kept the thought to herself. "So that happens. I dated a few losers before I met Jake. Everyone does."

Only a handful of people knew the truth about Jeremy. Charlie never would have stood for Jeremy's crap. She would've left him in a heartbeat.

"I never should have stayed with my ex-boyfriend as long as I did. It took me a long time to find myself again after I left him."

A light bulb went on over Charlie's head. "You don't have to worry about that with Mack. We've both known him and his family for a long time. He's a good guy. I say see where things go if you're interested in him. The worst that'll happen is you go back to being friendly acquaintances."

Lifting the coffee she'd poured herself, she sighed. "I

know you're right. I'm still nervous."

"I didn't say you couldn't be a little nervous, just don't let it stop you. Take things one day at a time and see where they go." Charlie gave her a mischievous smile. "Who knows? Maybe I'll be here next year getting ready for *your* wedding."

The comment was so uncharacteristic of Charlie, Jessie burst out laughing.

"I knew I could get you to loosen up." Charlie picked up her coffee again, a pleased expression on her face.

With a roll of her eyes, Jessie shifted the conversation from her love life. "Enough about me. Let's talk about you. Your life's a lot more interesting."

"Not much new going on. Jake and I started looking for a new place."

Jessie thought the townhouse they lived in now was beautiful. She didn't see why they'd want to move. "What is Jake up to today? Did Sean leave him a list of jobs?"

"You know Sean better than that. He'd never trust Jake to work on the house without him." Charlie took a sip of her coffee. "He went to visit his cousin, Trent, in Providence."

"I saw a picture of his cousin on the cover of *The Star Report* last week. He looks just like Jake. They could be brothers."

She and Charlie continued their conversation as they enjoyed the soup Jessie had prepared them. Again, Jessie marveled at how easily they'd fallen back into a close friendship despite the years they'd gone without seeing each other.

When Charlie left a few hours later, Jessie returned to the basket of laundry waiting for her. As she went through the mundane task, her thoughts revisited Charlie's advice. Her friend's words reinforced what she already knew about Mack. While she knew Charlie had been joking about the wedding, it didn't take any effort for her to envision spending her life with Mack and his daughter.

That weekend, spending time with the two, had felt natural, as if they'd done it a thousand times before. Had it been that way for him, too? She hoped so. Only time would tell.

Her doorbell rang. She wasn't expecting anyone. Had Charlie forgotten something?

"Who is it?" While North Salem remained a safe town, it never hurt to stay cautious.

"It's Mack, Jessie."

Mack? Jessie checked her watch. It was only three in the afternoon. Curiosity mingled with her excitement as she opened the door. Prepared to embrace him, she took a step forward, but then stopped. She knew he worked in law enforcement, but she'd never seen him with a gun. The last time she'd seen him after a day of work, he'd had his golf shirt untucked, concealing his weapon. Today though, the handle protruded from the waistband of his black cargo pants, and an extra magazine sat on the other side. She'd seen guns before. Her grandfather, a retired Marine, had been an avid hunter when she'd been young. But the sight of the weapon on Mack drove home what a dangerous job he had.

When she didn't move, Mack stepped toward her and hugged her. The contact brought her voice back online. "Mack, what are you doing here? Shouldn't you be at work?"

"I left the house at four o'clock this morning. I'm done for the day." He kissed her and pushed the door closed behind him at the same time. "I decided I'd stop in and see you before I pick up Grace. I hope that's okay."

His kiss and words sent a flutter of excitement through her chest. "Of course." She wanted another kiss; the first one had been too short. So far, she hadn't initiated anything. She'd followed his lead. How would he react if she turned the tables? Some men wanted everything on their terms. Only one way to find out if Mack fit into that category.

Before she lost her nerve, Jessie captured his mouth for a light kiss. When he didn't pull back with anger, she let the kiss become more demanding. As the kiss sent shivers of desire racing through her, Jessie parted her lips, an open invitation for Mack to enter.

He didn't disappoint.

In a heartbeat, Mack's tongue met hers and, right away, her senses reeled from the delicious sensations his kiss sent through her.

When he did pull away, she noticed how the pulse in his neck beat faster, just as her own heart did. In a flash, embarrassment washed over her and she kept her eyes focused on his chest rather than his face when she spoke. "Four? Why so early?" Right now, she needed a mundane conversation.

With his index finger, he tilted her face toward his while his other hand remained locked on her waist. "We did a big arrest along with the state police and the DEA." His hand moved from under her chin and he brushed a few stray hairs from her face.

Jessie's mind latched onto his comment. "Do you like working with the FBI?"

His fingers outlined her ear before moving down her face and neck. He stopped for a moment when he reached her shoulder, before continuing down her arm. Then he wrapped his arms around her waist and clasped his hands behind her back. "Love it. I've been doing it for three years now."

Locked in his embrace with his body pressed against hers, her mind struggled to keep focused on their conversation. The longer they stayed together, the faster her heart beat. "Are there others like you with the FBI?"

Mack's head lowered again. "Task force officers?" He brushed a feather-light kiss across her mouth and then pulled back just enough to speak. "Not a lot, but there are others from various police departments." He dropped another kiss onto her mouth, this one firmer. More demanding.

Driven by passion and the way he'd responded to her earlier, she returned his kiss with reckless abandon.

All too soon, he pulled back, his breathing heavy, leaving her mouth on fire. "I'd like nothing more than to stay and do this for a few hours, but I need to get Grace."

Still in a kiss-induced fog, Jessie nodded.

"I haven't seen her since yesterday. She spent last night with Erin, so she could get her off to school this morning." Mack took a step back, his arms still locked behind her. "We're still on for the weekend though, right? Bethany's picking Grace up at five on Friday."

"As of Friday afternoon, I'm free all weekend." A dose of apprehension bolted through her. They'd be alone, and she didn't know how far things might go or how far she even wanted them to go.

Mack's arms fell back to his sides. "Good." He dropped a quick kiss on her lips. "Are you free to come by for dinner this week?"

"I can come on Wednesday." Jessie's apprehension disappeared and was replaced with something that she suspected could easily turn into love.

"Good. I'll see you then." He took a step toward the door. "Does six-thirty work?"

Mack glanced back up at Jessie's apartment before he pulled away from the curb. Again, today, much like yesterday, his attraction toward her had him shaking his head. Never in a million years would he have expected the type of relationship that was developing between them. Before his return, he'd considered her that nice girl in town who got along with everyone, but the one who spent her Saturday nights with her grandmother.

Since he'd seen her running the day he'd moved in, however, he'd viewed her in a whole new light. Sure, she was still the Jessie Quinn everyone liked. The one who wouldn't think twice about doing anyone a favor. At the same time, however, she wasn't the girl everyone overlooked anymore. She'd changed into a sexy woman men noticed, though she did appear oblivious to the attention. He'd sure as hell noticed her.

When he'd stopped at her place, he'd only intended a quick hello and a brief kiss. He might have managed that if she hadn't given him that soul-searching kiss. At first, it'd surprised him. So far, he'd always been the aggressor. He assumed the nervousness he sometimes glimpsed in her was what held her back. Whatever the case, it didn't bother him. He knew eventually she'd be comfortable enough to make the first move. He just hadn't expected it today.

However, when she'd taken possession of his lips and then opened her sweet mouth to him, it had nearly brought him to his knees. Even now, his blood pooled below his belt, urging him to turn around and go back. Thankfully, while his body might not know it, his head did realize now wasn't the time to take things further. Maybe this weekend, but definitely not now.

The physical reaction he had wasn't the only thing that had him shaking his head. After all, Jessie was, as Tony said, hot, and he was a single guy who hadn't had sex in months. The emotional attraction between them surprised him the most. He'd known Jessie all her life and had never considered how much he might enjoy her company. Now, he looked forward to their time together. In fact, even though they'd spent much of the weekend together, he'd missed her yesterday afternoon when she left. Then, the thought of not seeing her today had caused him to make a detour on the way to his sister's house.

As he drove, the memory of Jessie and Grace painting the previous Friday night popped up. Many women he'd considered dating hadn't been interested once they learned he had a child. Jessie hadn't blinked an eye at the fact. Rather, she treated his daughter much the same way a mother or aunt would. While she'd never said it, he knew she cared about Grace, and there was no question that

Grace adored Jessie.

Mack passed by the river and the new Stonefield Dam before turning onto Church Street. The apartments that had once lined the street were all gone. Hurricane Andrea had destroyed them a few years earlier. Now, single-family homes and young trees lined the street, another reminder of all the changes around him. When he reached the stop sign, he turned right and pulled into his sister's driveway.

Yeah, a lot of things were changing, but while that might bother some people, he embraced it. He didn't know what more would change between him and Jessie, but he was eager to find out.

The door flew open before he pressed the doorbell. "Hi, Uncle Mack," Brianna said.

Prepared to scold her for opening the door, Mack opened his mouth, but his sister beat him to it.

"Brianna Stone, what have I told you about opening that door?" Erin stood in the hallway, her arms crossed.

Brianna's grin disappeared. "Not to unless you or daddy tells me it's okay." His niece glanced at him as if she hoped he'd save her.

When he remained silent, she looked back at her mom. "But I saw it was Uncle Mack through the window."

Erin shook her head. "It doesn't matter. Now go upstairs and tell Grace her dad's here."

His niece darted up the stairs, the fairy wings on her back bouncing.

"Last I checked, they were playing dress-up. This might take awhile." Erin headed back down the hall and indicated Mack should follow. "Help yourself to anything." She stopped at the crockpot and stirred its contents, the scent of the meal inside making his stomach rumble.

Passing his sister, he opened the refrigerator and grabbed a can of soda. "Thanks for all your help."

"Anytime. Those two play well together." Replacing the cover, Erin turned from the counter. "Grace filled me in on how Jessie spent much of the weekend with the two of you. Care to share or should I wait and hear it all from Mom, who will no doubt hear about it from one of her friends?"

He heard a loud shriek upstairs, followed by running feet. For a moment, he considered checking it out, but when Erin remained unconcerned, he pulled out a kitchen chair. "Since you got everything from Grace, what do you need me to tell you?" His sister had always been a bit of a busybody.

Erin's eyes narrowed. "I assumed there was more to tell, smart-ass. I didn't even know you two were seeing each other."

What he and Jessie did wasn't anyone's business, but then again, this was North Salem and people noticed everything. "I'm just seeing where things go, Sis. Okay?"

"Fine by me. It just surprised me when Grace told me. I like Jessie, but she doesn't seem like your type. I thought you liked women more like Bethany." Erin's voice took on a sour note when she mentioned his ex-wife. From the day he'd first introduced Erin to his ex-wife, they had disliked each other.

While he had no desire to have a relationship with a woman like Bethany, his sister was correct. Jessie wasn't his usual type. Since his days in college, he'd gone for the more worldly women, for lack of a better word, rather than those who preferred small town life. His ex-wife had grown up in Philadelphia and done some modeling in high school and college before moving to Massachusetts. Jessie, on the other hand, was the living, breathing definition of small town. Unlike in the past, though, he no longer found that a turn-off. He found it the exact opposite.

"People's preferences change, and the last thing I want is another Bethany."

"You and me both. You know how I feel about her." Erin grabbed his soda and took a sip. "I've been craving cola all day. I have to get some caffeine-free soda next time I'm out." She passed the can back to him; then her face turned serious. "I don't think Jessie has dated much. I can't recall ever seeing her with anyone."

Jessie's relationship history didn't matter to him, although he found his sister's revelation odd. "So?"

"So I think you should take things extra slow with her. I don't want you to hurt her feelings. We're not best friends, but I like Jessie a lot."

Big surprise there; everyone in town liked her.

"Daddy!" Grace flew into the room and hugged him before he said anything else. "Look at the dress Brianna said I could have." She pulled back and did a little twirl for him. "She already has one just like it."

Mack looked at his sister for confirmation.

"Brianna does have two. I bought one and then my mother-in-law gave her one. If Grace wants it, that's fine."

"In that case, why don't you get your regular clothes on and put that one in your bag? Then we'll head home."

"Can she stay for dinner?" Brianna asked, popping into the room. She'd ditched the fairy outfit and now wore the same princess gown as Grace.

"You're more than welcome to stay." Erin passed a hand over her stomach and he realized he'd never asked how her ultrasound went the week before.

Grace and Brianna stared up at him as if they could control his mind. "I guess so." Grace loved being with her cousin and liked visiting with her aunt and uncle, not to mention he was exhausted and not up for cooking tonight himself.

"Come on. Let's get the stuff for the tea party." Brianna grabbed Grace's hand and yanked her from the room.

"Those two are like sisters."

Erin's words echoed his thoughts. Not having another baby with Bethany had been the right decision, but he regretted that Grace was an only child. While he realized he could rectify that situation since his divorce, he'd never pictured it happening.

"I'm glad they're so close," he said before he drained his soda, reconsidering his thoughts from a moment ago. He'd never pictured it happening with the women he'd dated since his ex-wife; however, he had no trouble picturing it when he thought of Jessie. He didn't doubt for a moment she'd make an excellent mother.

With that thought, Mack headed to get another soda. It was too soon to be thinking of Jessie in those terms. Even still, now that the thought had materialized, he couldn't shake it. In fact, the thought stayed with him all through dinner and all the way home.

CHAPTER 8

Although he would've preferred his ex-wife pick Grace up on Saturday morning rather than Friday night, Mack had agreed Grace would be ready at five o'clock. In order to make sure that happened, he'd helped Grace pack her overnight bag the night before and arranged to leave work early that night.

Now, as they waited for Bethany, he wished he'd pushed for Grace to leave in the morning instead. He'd seen his daughter before the bus came and for about fifteen minutes tonight. Then he wouldn't see her again until late Sunday afternoon. While it wasn't that much time calendar-wise, it always felt like a lifetime when Grace spent weekends with her mom. Oddly, it didn't feel as long when she spent weekends with his parents. He was no shrink, but he suspected his feelings toward Bethany these days influenced his emotions in that regard. Despite how he felt about his ex now, she was Grace's mother and she had the right to see her. Thankfully, she didn't do that on a regular basis.

"Can I take Mr. Whiskers and Brown Bear?" Grace asked while they waited for Bethany.

As long as she had Mr. Whiskers, she'd be fine. The

stuffed dog had been her favorite toy since her first birthday, but he saw no harm in letting her take along more than one friend.

"Fine with me. You better hurry upstairs and get him. Your mom will be here any minute." He may have issues with many of Bethany's traits, but she was punctual. And if she was running late, she called.

Grace jumped up. "Be right back." Like a bullet train, she flew up the stairs. Before she made it back down, the doorbell rang.

Right on time.

Bethany never wanted anyone to see her as anything less than perfect. Today wasn't any different. Her blonde hair hung loose, each curl arranged just so. Her makeup appeared perfect, not too much but just enough. Although she wore jeans, they looked brand new and he'd bet a whole paycheck they had a designer label on them.

"Bethany, come in." He stepped back. Yeah, his ex-wife looked just as beautiful today as the day he'd met her eight years ago, but unlike that day, not an ounce of attraction filled him. "Grace ran upstairs for Brown Bear." While he didn't intend to be rude, he didn't ask her to sit either. He'd told Jessie to stop by whenever tonight and he wanted Bethany gone before that so they could enjoy their time together.

"I'm not in a rush. We're only staying in Boston this weekend, so it won't take long to get there."

Since she'd accepted her new position with a major television network, she'd moved to New York City. To help cut out the long commute when she visited Grace, she sometimes got a room in Boston and they stayed there all weekend.

"Grace will love that. She thinks sleeping in a hotel is cool." Perhaps he had at her age, too. He couldn't remember. Now, though, he found it more of an annoyance.

Bethany moved toward the stairs. "Tomorrow, I'm

going to take her to the children's museum. It has a special exhibit I think she'll like." She started up the stairs as if she lived there. "I'll check and see if she needs any help."

More than likely, either Grace couldn't find Brown Bear or she'd gotten distracted with something else. Either way, he didn't stop Bethany. Grace would want her mom to see her new room before they left.

As his ex disappeared from view, the doorbell rang again. *Damn.* He'd hoped to avoid Jessie meeting his ex-wife tonight. Why, he didn't know, but the idea of Bethany and Jessie in the same room made him uncomfortable. Even with the unease, Mack opened the door and placed a quick kiss on Jessie's lips when she walked in. He'd seen her on Wednesday and they'd talked for a few minutes the night before, but he'd missed her. For a good portion of the day, he'd tossed around ideas for the weekend. So far, nothing had jumped out at him.

"I would've been here sooner, but I left work late and had to stop home." She gave him another kiss, this one on his cheek.

"Jessie!" Grace called out from the stairs. "I'm going to Boston and staying in a hotel. Mommy said we can get room service." She headed in their direction, Brown Bear in one hand and Bethany right behind her.

Next to him, Jessie stiffened, but her mouth curved up in a smile. "That sounds like a lot of fun. I've never had room service."

While Grace added Brown Bear to her overnight bag, Bethany joined them. "I don't think we've met." Bethany gave Jessie a quick but definite once-over before she shot him a look that he couldn't decipher.

Uncertain on how to label Jessie, he decided to make introductions as short and sweet as possible. While he might think of Jessie as his girlfriend, they hadn't discussed their relationship in those terms.

"Bethany, this is Jessie Quinn. She's a good friend of mine." He nodded toward Jessie. "Jessie, this is Grace's mom."

"It's nice to meet you. Grace is a great little girl." Jessie smiled.

"She is." Bethany looked over at Grace as the little girl rushed to them. "Did you go to high school with Mack?"

Mack had an answer prepared, but Grace didn't give him a chance to share it.

"Jessie is Daddy's girlfriend," she informed them, sounding rather pleased with the situation.

Bethany glanced at Jessie again and then sent him a strange look while Jessie turned as red as a tomato.

"I saw him kiss her on Wednesday."

He'd never thought it possible, but Jessie's face grew a darker shade of red.

"Well, it's nice to meet you." Bethany broke the uncomfortable silence. "Come on, Grace. Let's go." She grabbed the overnight bag from the floor. "I'll bring her back around three on Sunday."

She'd never wanted magical powers more than when Grace had announced she was Mack's girlfriend. If she could have snapped her fingers and disappeared, she would have. While she assumed their relationship was headed that way, to have Grace blurt it out like that had been too much. If she'd said it in front of just Mack, it would've been one thing, but with his gorgeous ex-wife standing there, she'd thought she'd die. To make matters even more uncomfortable, something she'd believed impossible, Grace had said she'd seen them kissing. Even now, with Mack outside saying goodbye, her face burned with mortification.

Please don't mention it. Perhaps if she launched a conversation the moment he walked in, Grace's comments would slip from his mind.

"I think Grace is more excited about room service than the exhibit Bethany told her about," Mack said when he came back inside.

"Room service does sound rather nice." Jessie forced herself to look at him, and once again, she was struck by just how out of her league he was. A guy as handsome as Mack belonged alongside an equally beautiful woman… one who looked like his ex-wife.

Whether he sensed her discomfort or not, he didn't say. Instead, he came over and put his arms around her waist. "You've never had room service?"

His show of affection and physical proximity made her senses spin, and any embarrassment from before disappeared. "I've only stayed in hotels a few times and I've never splurged on room service."

He pulled her closer. "We'll have to remedy that someday."

Heat once again surged through her, although this time, it wasn't caused by embarrassment. Clearing her throat, she searched for a safe topic. Right away, her thoughts turned to Grace. "Grace looks just like her mom. No wonder she's such a beautiful little girl." Standing in the same room with Bethany, she'd felt a little like one of the ugly stepsisters.

"Grace does have her mom's physical characteristics. Thankfully, that's all she got." He gave her a short quick kiss then pulled away. "Let's go figure out what we want to do tonight."

In the end, they decided on dinner from the grill, followed by relaxing around the fire pit outside. Unfortunately, the rain forecasted for much later in the evening arrived early, extinguishing the fire before they could enjoy it. Rather than complain about their ruined plans, they moved inside where Mack built a fire in the fireplace.

Despite the change of plans, Jessie remained on cloud nine. Part of it came from the atmosphere. She'd always loved a fire, whether it was outside or in a fireplace. When she'd been growing up, her grandfather would often build a big fire in the fireplace and she and Charlie would cook hot dogs and tell ghost stories. On weekends, if her dad was home, he'd build a fire out back, and the two of them would roast marshmallows before camping out in the backyard. Some of her best memories with her dad involved those campouts.

Her companion for the night, though, contributed even more to her current state. All evening, Mack had been an attentive listener and a perfect gentleman. Although neither had touched on Grace's statement, they had discussed everything from his job to the workout regime her trainer had her on. And while Grace's new label for her never came up, she couldn't shake it as Mack went in search of a DVD.

"I couldn't find the one I wanted, but I found these. Take your pick." He handed her a heavy DVD case.

Inside, she found everything from classic black-and-white movies to recent action films. "It's weird to see a DVD with Mia's picture on it." She paused when she found her new friend's face staring back up at her.

Mack flipped the page. "Still can't get my head around Sean being with a movie star. Every time I think about it, I'm afraid I've stepped into the Twilight Zone."

Jessie attempted to hold back her laugh but failed. "She's nothing like you'd think. You'll meet her at Mrs. O'Brien's wedding. Sean told me she'll be back for that." Jessie grabbed the first movie that appealed to her before Mack turned the page again. "I still need to send in my RSVP card for the wedding. I just need to find it first."

Mack accepted the DVD Jessie held out and stood. "We can use mine. Like Grace announced tonight, you are my girlfriend. No reason for us both to send in a reply card."

His words lacked any romantic finesse, yet they answered the questions she'd agonized over all week. In fact, she hadn't realized how much she wanted clarification on their relationship until Grace's announcement that night. "Works for me. Do you want me to pick up a gift?"

Returning to the couch, he sat and then repositioned her so her legs draped over his thighs. "Sounds good." He leaned over and kissed her as the movie's soundtrack started.

After a minute or so, the music was replaced by a male voice indicating the movie had started. Even with the movie underway, neither of them made an effort to move. Instead, Jessie let herself get carried away by the maelstrom of desire building inside. Bolstered by his view that this thing between them was a real relationship with potential and not just a few make-out sessions, she changed her position, straddling his lap with a leg on either side of his.

Jessie's new position increased their intimate contact. Now, not only could she feel the hard muscles in his thighs, but she also felt his heartbeat quicken as their kiss continued, and his arousal grew against her.

Acting on pure emotion, she rubbed up against him, eliciting a groan from him. Empowered by his reaction, she did it again. This time, pleasure radiated through her. Still basking in the bliss her movements caused, she didn't realize until he'd undone her bra that his hands had disappeared under her shirt. Once he freed her from the bra, he captured her breasts, massaging them and learning all he could about them through touch alone.

Ruled by instinct, she let her hands slip under his shirt and roam up his abdomen to his chest. For a moment, he pulled away from her mouth and she feared she'd done something wrong. Before she could ask, he pulled off her shirt and then his, and then kissed her again with a hunger she felt to her toes.

Tearing his mouth away again, he seared a path of heat down her neck with his lips. Then, without any warning, he changed their position, and she found herself stretched out beneath him. He took his time letting his eyes roam across her face and down to her breasts. Under his intense gaze, her nipples hardened and she wanted nothing more than for him to touch them.

Once he finished his visual inspection, he once again met her eyes and gave her a smile that sent excitement pulsing through her. "I think this is a perfect way to spend a Friday night." He whispered the last of his sentence inches from her lips then kissed her again.

She couldn't agree more. Soon, her brain shut off as her senses took over. As he kissed her mouth, then her neck, and finally her breasts, she returned each of his caresses, loving the feel of his skin against hers. In the background, the movie played, but neither halted their current activity to watch it or turn it off. By that point, heat and desire consumed Jessie's whole body, and she barely registered the noise or anything else for that matter. Instead, only Mack existed.

The second he started with the zipper, though, her emotion-induced haze disappeared and a flashing warning sign took its place. For a moment, fear paralyzed her, but then she pushed his shoulders until he released her nipple and looked up at her.

"What's the matter?" His voice came out ragged, but she heard the concern and confusion.

Jessie sat up and used her arms to cover her breasts. Part of her knew the action was ridiculous. He'd just been sucking on her nipples. Still, the need to cover up demanded she do something.

"Jessie?" he asked again with more concern.

Tell him the truth. Don't just go with it. If he doesn't like it, better to know now. "I'm not ready for that." She moved away from him as she waited for a response. "I'm sorry if I gave you the wrong idea tonight." She looked around for her bra and shirt. Spotting both near his, she reached for them, but Mack's fingers closed gently around her wrist before she could pick them up.

He picked up her clothes and handed them to her. Did that mean he wanted her to leave? "Mack, I—"

"It's okay. Yeah, I thought you wanted more, but I understand. We both got a little carried away just now."

He pulled his own shirt on. When he spoke again, his voice remained tender and full of understanding. "Why don't we get comfortable and restart the movie?"

Jessie slumped back, not much, but enough that he noticed the motion. The movement made him consider her response minutes before, as well as the one the first night they'd kissed. As she clipped her bra back on, his sister's comment about Jessie not having much experience with men popped up. Was that why she'd gotten so unsettled tonight? Was it possible she'd never had sex? How could that be? Jessie was Erin's age. He didn't think any woman reached their age as a virgin. Then again, it would explain her unease.

Mack tossed the thought around and watched as Jessie pulled her shirt back on, his gaze drawn to the scar that started on her side and wrapped around to her back. "What happened there?" He pointed to the faded mark.

Jessie yanked down her shirt, covering up the scar. "I tripped and fell. Rather than land on the floor, I landed on a wine glass I left on a coffee table."

Her explanation sounded plausible yet his gut told him it wasn't the truth. Or, at least, not the whole truth. "That must have hurt." Despite his misgivings with her explanation, he accepted it. Maybe he spent too much time around criminals who lied all the time. After all, there was no reason for Jessie to lie now. "Do you want anything before we restart the movie?" He ignored the questions her words and actions created. Tonight, it was only the two of them, and he planned on enjoying their time together.

When Jessie shook her head, he grabbed the remote control. "Let me know if you change your mind." Restarting the movie, he put his arm around her and pulled her close.

He'd seen the classic sci-fi movie so many times he could quote it scene-by-scene, a habit that had driven his ex-wife crazy on the few occasions they'd watched the film together. Tonight, with Jessie, he made an effort not to recite a single line.

When they reached the movie's first real memorable scene, however, Jessie did the one thing he'd avoided all night and repeated the heroine's lines word-for-word. Since that particular scene was so well-known, he chalked it up to a random event. The third time she did it, repeating a much lesser-known line, he broke the comfortable silence around them.

"How many times have you seen this movie?"

"As an adult or all together? Because if we're counting when I was a kid, it would be over thirty."

"I think I have you beat. I was obsessed with this movie as a kid. Had every toy they came out with and a lunch box."

Jessie beamed back at him. "Me, too. I think my grandmother still has a few of my toys tucked away in the attic."

Pleased to learn they had something else in common, they fell into a discussion about which movie in the *Star Wars* series was best and why. Soon, the misgivings Jessie's earlier explanation evoked disappeared.

***

Since Sean had helped with his move, Mack felt obligated to return the favor. So rather than spend Sunday morning at home, he found himself at Sean's after breakfast. Even from the outside, he noticed the improvements to the old Queen Anne style house. Although it still needed a fresh coat of paint, the house had all new windows and a roof. The shrubs, which had become overgrown from years of neglect, were gone and a new mailbox stood near the street. Even with all the improvements, a lot of work remained, according to Sean. When Sean had filled him in on some of what he'd already done and what he still had planned, he'd questioned his friend's sanity.

Walking past Tony's truck, Mack started up the paved walkway and glanced over at The Victorian Rose, another Victorian era home that Sean had kept in prime condition for years. Today, like always, a No-Vacancy sign hung out in front and several cars remained in the parking lot. Even before Charlie's marriage, the bed and breakfast had done well with a steady stream of guests. Since her marriage, though, he didn't think the No-Vacancy sign ever came down. If anyone deserved that kind of success, it was Sean and his family.

"Now that you're here, we can start," Sean said when he answered the front door. "Hope you're up for some demolition."

"Always up for that." Mack followed Sean inside, impressed at the home's interior. Although a bed and chest of drawers sat in what should be a living room, there was no missing the improvements made inside. All the rooms they passed had a fresh coat of paint. Brand new light fixtures hung from the ceiling, and with the exception of the stairs, the hardwood floors gleamed.

"Off your ass, Tony. Time to get to work," Sean said when he and Mack entered a well-thought-out kitchen with brand new appliances.

Tony stuffed the last of his muffin into his mouth. "I should ask your mom to send me baked stuff. My mother's too busy traveling now since she retired."

"Good luck with that." Sean led them up a back stairway. Unlike on the first floor, old wallpaper covered the walls and the floors showed their century-plus of use.

"What's the plan for today?" Mack asked as they passed a gutted bathroom.

"Tearing down a wall to start." Sean opened a door. "I want to turn this room and the one next to it into a master suite."

Mack grabbed a sledgehammer from the floor, eager to get started. There was just something about knocking down a wall. "Easy enough."

The three men worked for over an hour in relative silence until Sean's cell phone rang. As he left the room to take the call, Tony and Mack leaned their tools against a wall and sat on the debris-covered floor.

"Seems like every time I pass your place Jessie is there." Tony used the end of his t-shirt to wipe sweat from his face.

Mack remembered Tony's comment about asking Jessie out himself. At the time, he'd guessed it was just another case of a woman temporarily catching his eye. Now, he wondered, though. While he considered Striker and Sean closer friends than Tony, he'd been friends with the guy for a long time and didn't want any hard feeling between them. "She's been over for dinner a few times." He grabbed his water and downed half the bottle.

Tony did the same before he spoke again. "Surprised O'Brien hasn't given you hell about it."

Sean walked back into the room and grabbed the last water bottle on the floor. "Given him hell about what?"

Tony took another swig. "Mack with Jessie. Every time I mentioned her, you acted like her brother and warned me away. Mack here seems to have the green light though."

"That's because I know you're a dog, Tony. Any woman deserves better than you."

"Glad you think so highly of me," Tony said, a hint of anger in his voice.

Sean and Tony were close friends. Mack suspected that was the only reason Tony didn't slug Sean for his comment. Instead, they threw a few insults back and forth. While they exchanged some choice words, Mack recalled Tony's comment about Sean acting like a brother. "Do either of you know if Jessie has dated a lot?" He wanted to ask if she was a virgin. That would explain her uneasy behavior, but he assumed neither man would have an answer to that question.

"Don't think so," Tony answered. "Then again, I don't

think I would've noticed."

"She dated someone for several years. I remember seeing them around town together. But that was a long time ago. Don't recall anyone since." Sean downed the rest of his water. "Enough rest. Let's finish this."

After leaving Sean's later that afternoon, Mack picked up some steaks before returning home. While he worked out on a regular basis, his body wasn't accustomed to swinging a sledgehammer. Already he ached from the activity, and he suspected tomorrow it would be worse. Still, taking down the wall had been enjoyable in an odd sort of way. Now, as he washed away the sweat and dust that covered him, he looked forward to having his daughter home. As wonderful as the weekend with Jessie had been, he'd noticed Grace's absence. Although he missed her, he hoped she enjoyed her weekend because it might be several weeks before Grace saw Bethany again.

Clean and dressed, he put the steaks on the grill. With Grace due home any minute, he wanted dinner ready sooner rather than later. After two nights with her mom, she'd be overtired. With school tomorrow, it would be a good idea if he got her into bed early. That was one of the reasons he hadn't invited Jessie for dinner. With her around, he'd have a difficult time getting Grace into bed. His other reason stemmed from the occasional glimpse of apprehension or whatever it was he saw in her. The last thing he wanted was to push her too far too fast. Even in the short time they'd been together, he'd become emotionally invested in their relationship. He didn't want to sabotage it before it even had a chance to develop further. If that meant taking things a little on the slow side, he'd do it.

"Daddy, I'm home." Grace walked through the front door as he checked the football score on television. "Look what Mommy bought me." She held up a boxed dollhouse family. "She got me another house, too. It's not as big as mine here. It's a vacation home."

Mack looked at Bethany. More toys were the last thing Grace needed.

"It is in the trunk. Don't worry, it's not as big as her other one, I promise."

Without a comment, he accepted her car keys. It must be big enough if Bethany hadn't carried it in herself. "Be right back."

Judging by the size of the box, the new house was almost as big as the one already in the living room. "We'll put this together later."

"When it's done, I want to invite Jessie over to show her." Grace kneeled down to examine the picture on the box, her parents forgotten.

"I heard a lot about Jessie this weekend. She sounds sweet." Bethany took back her car keys. "I need to get going. I'll see you in a few weeks, okay, Grace?"

"Okay." Grace gave her mom a quick hug and kiss and then returned to the new dollhouse.

Bethany opened the door to leave. "I'll be in touch, Mack."

With his ex-wife gone and his daughter home, all was once again right in his world. "Come on, buddy. Let's check on dinner and you can tell me about your weekend."

A little slower than usual, Grace stood and took his hand. "I loved room service." Insert chapter nine text here.

CHAPTER 9

The smell of fall hung in the air. Colorful leaves dotted every tree, the vibrant red, orange, and yellow creating a rainbow of fall colors. In another few weeks, they would fall, leaving the trees bare, but right now, they helped create a picture-perfect September day in New England. A day so perfect everyone in the area had decided to take advantage of it. The parking lot at Watch Hill Orchard overflowed with cars as Mack searched for a spot. From the passenger seat, Jessie kept an eye out as well, while in the backseat, Grace and Brianna discussed Halloween costumes.

Thanks to Jessie's observant eyes, she spotted a minivan just as it backed out of a space and Mack got to it in the nick of time. "All right, you two. No wandering away." He waited for both girls to get out before he spoke again so they'd hear him. "You need to be where either Jessie or I can see you at all times. Understand?"

Both girls nodded in agreement. "Can we get ice cream here?" Grace asked.

"Can we see the animals?" Brianna asked.

Watch Hill Orchard wasn't just a regular old apple orchard. They grew a wide variety of fruit that customers could pick, depending on the month. The orchard also had a bakery that served sandwiches as well as pie, donuts, and ice cream. A large playground had been built for the children, and not far from it, there was an animal petting area.

"We'll see. First, let's pick apples and pumpkins. If we're up for it after that, we can check out the ice cream."

Satisfied with his answer, Grace and Brianna walked together in front of them. "Those two really are like sisters," Jessie said as they walked together, Mack's arm slung over her shoulders. Even though they'd been together about a month now, a warm glow still flowed through her every time he touched her.

"They're only months apart and neither has a brother or sister. Even after Erin has the baby, I think they'll still be this close." Mack pulled her against him and kissed her forehead. "I'm glad you could come with us today."

When he'd first invited her along, she'd been conflicted. After hearing it was a tradition he'd done with Grace for years, she hadn't wanted to interfere. Neither Mack nor Grace liked her initial refusal, and both set out to change her mind, a task they'd accomplished in record time. "Me, too."

They fell silent and boarded the tractor-pulled wagon that would carry them off to the orchard. The wagon swayed and jarred them as it passed row after row of apple trees. The orchard didn't allow customers to pick just anywhere. Each day, the staff determined which grove of trees would be used.

When the wagon stopped, an employee climbed onboard. "Okay, folks. Before you get started, I have a few announcements." She waited until she had everyone's attention before she continued. "Today, we're picking Gala, Cortland, and Golden Delicious apples. Sorry, we're all out of Honey Crisp. Please remember to twist the apple from the tree; don't pull it. Finally, we realize everyone likes to eat an apple or two. Please throw your cores in one

of the white buckets at the end of each aisle."
Announcements over, the employee exited the wagon, a
trail of eager customers behind her.

"Do you make apple pie?" Mack asked as Grace and
Brianna set off in search of apples.

"Sometimes. I have a recipe for apple bread, too."
They joined the girls at a tree. At first glance, it appeared
empty, but after careful inspection, Grace spotted some
bright red apples near the top.

"Daddy can you lift me up? The apples are too high."

With ease, Mack sat Grace on his shoulders. "Just pick
a few. There are a lot more trees." While Grace chose her
favorites, Mack looked back at Jessie. "I'll make a deal with
you. If you make an apple pie tonight, I'll cook dinner."

Tonight would be only the second time since they'd
almost made love that they'd be alone. Instead, she'd
always spent time with Mack and his daughter either at his
house or someplace public. Tonight, though, after apple-
picking, the plan was to drop the girls off at his sister's
house so Erin and her husband could take them to a fair in
South Yarmouth first thing in the morning.

On the one occasion she and Mack had been alone,
they'd done plenty of kissing but nothing more. He never
commented on what had happened weeks earlier, and he
didn't push her toward anything more. Even with all that,
she didn't know how much longer he'd be willing to wait
before he told her to put out or get out. She tried to not
dwell on the possibility that he might get fed up with
waiting. Despite her best efforts, though, she did dwell at
times, and when she did, the thoughts of losing him tore
her insides to shreds. Even with the fear, she refused to
cave in and give him control. She'd been down that road.
This time, when she made love, it would be when *she*
wanted it no matter what.

Unwelcome tension stretched over her as she
considered the night ahead. *Enjoy yourself. Focus on the here
and now.*

"What do you say?" he asked as he put down Grace and hoisted up Brianna so she could grab a few apples.

"You have a deal."

Over the years, Jessie had gone apple-picking several times. Never, though, did it take as long to fill their bag as it did that day. One would've thought, with four people picking, they would have filled the bag after two or three rows, but not today. And not for lack of trying. Rather, there just were not as many apples as previous years. She'd read on the news that this year's crop was poor, but hadn't expected it to be like this.

"Time to call it a day," Mack said, about an hour after they started.

Brianna dropped an apple into the bag while she bit into another, the juice dripping down her chin. "Our bag is super full."

"Perfect for lots of pies. Now, let's grab some pumpkins, and if you girls still want, we can get ice cream."

"I hope they have Green Monster. It's the best," Brianna said.

As a group, they walked to the wagon stop for a ride back. "I thought your favorite was Chocolate Chip."

"Green Monster is my favorite now, Uncle Mack. Grace, you have to try it."

The scent of diesel fuel reached them, signaling the tractor pulling the wagon was close.

"What's your favorite, Mack?" Jessie asked. She'd learned so much about it him over the past month, but there remained many things she didn't know.

"That depends." They walked forward as the wagon rolled to a stop. "If I'm in the mood for something traditional, it's coffee. Otherwise, my favorite is Candy Dish. A place in Boston sells it." Mack followed her up the wooden steps. "What about you? I bet whatever it is, it contains peanut butter."

While Grace and Brianna sat on a bench in the center, Mack and Jessie picked a bench alongside the outer wall.

From that position, they could keep an eye on the girls and enjoy the scenery. "I do like anything containing peanut butter, but my favorite is Butter Pecan. Unless it's in a sundae; then my favorite is plain chocolate smothered with hot fudge and nuts."

"Can we get sundaes?" Grace asked, her conversation with her cousin put on hold.

Jessie hadn't considered Grace or Brianna might hear her. They'd appeared too wrapped up in each other. "Sorry."

Mack considered the request. "You two can. I'm going to pass today and hold out for apple pie."

"I think I'll do the same."

Neither girl cared what the adults did. Instead, they began to discuss what candy toppings they wanted.

***

An under-stuffed scarecrow dressed in a denim shirt and jeans sat propped against the front tree. Next to it, sat a much smaller scarecrow, this one dressed in a long-sleeved princess shirt and leggings. Jessie had helped Mack and Grace make both scarecrows the prior weekend. Since then, Mack had added black plastic bats and cobwebs to the tree and tied some corn stalks to the front light post. Perhaps because of its proximity to Salem, Halloween had always been a big deal around town and people started with their decorations the month before. Although she considered the whole thing a bit ridiculous, the decorations did add to the fall atmosphere.

"I don't know what you need for an apple pie, but if I don't have it, I can run over to the store." Mack opened the door to the house. "Feel free to check."

Jessie preceded him into the kitchen. Except for two cereal bowls in the sink, the room appeared as neat and clean as her kitchen. In fact, Mack's entire house looked tidy. Sure, Grace's toys remained around the place, but she'd never seen mountains of dirty dishes or clothes hanging around. She wondered how he managed it all. He never complained, but she imagined life as a single dad could become overwhelming, especially considering the stress of his job. Not only did he not complain, he made it look easy.

"We don't need much." Jessie opened the cupboard where she'd seen Mack grab spices the last time he'd grilled. "Thank you again for taking me today. I had a lot of fun."

Mack came around and stood alongside her as she hunted for cinnamon. "Neither of us wanted it any other way. Grace told me to invite you before I even mentioned it to her. She's crazy about you."

What about you? "She's a fantastic little girl. You do a wonderful job with her." After she located the spices she needed, she grabbed the flour and sugar, adding them to the collection on the counter. "Just need butter and water and I can get some pies started."

"I'll grab the butter from the refrigerator for you and then get dinner going." Mack pushed away from the counter.

Jessie cored and cut up apples while Mack prepared chicken kabobs for the grill. Every so often, he'd grab something else from the refrigerator and, each time he passed by, he'd kiss her.

I could get used to this. With no trouble, she pictured them preparing meals like this all the time with Grace keeping them company. "I picked up a gift for the wedding."

Next to her, Mack washed and dried his hands, eight kabobs finished. "Great. I still need to take Grace shopping for a dress."

She'd not considered that Grace might come to the wedding, but since everyone in town planned to go, that left few babysitters available. "I need to get something myself." Since she'd lost weight, she'd purchased one nice sleeveless dress. While it had been perfect for Mrs. O'Brien's engagement party, it wouldn't do for an October wedding. "I can take Grace with me if you want. Save you a trip to the mall."

"You're amazing, you know that?" His hands slid around her waist and he pulled her against him. "And that's why I love you."

The measuring cup filled with flour hit the counter and Jessie stopped breathing.

"You're as stiff as a board. Are you okay?"

Mack would never say something he didn't mean. Still, she had trouble comprehending his words. Words that she herself had wanted to say but had held back. "You love me?" She should express her own feelings. That was what people did in a situation like this. First, though, she needed to be sure she'd heard him right. That she hadn't imagined it.

"You sound surprised. I thought you would've figured that out by now." He let go of her and came around so he could see her face.

Time for some truth of my own. "No, I hadn't figured it out, but I love you and Grace, too."

He gave her a smile alive with affection and delight. "I'm glad. You had me worried for a minute there." Dipping his head, he pressed a light kiss on her mouth. "I'm going to put dinner on the grill. Be right back."

She watched him walk away and leaned into the counter. Wow. He loved her. She'd known how deep her own feelings went for a while, but she hadn't seen that coming from him.

She watched him outside by the grill. He deserved to know why she'd forced them to stop the night they'd almost made love. But could she tell him? Would he think less of her because she'd allowed someone else such control of her life? Disgust toward herself still plagued her sometimes when she thought back on that time. Would Mack decide he wanted someone stronger around his daughter? Someone who would help Grace develop self-confidence rather than someone who'd almost let a man destroy her self-esteem and self-worth?

Behind her, the oven beeped, letting her know it had reached the set temperature. The reminder took her away from her thoughts and back to the unfinished pie. If they hoped to enjoy it for dessert, she needed to roll out two piecrusts. Everything else could wait until later.

Before tonight, he'd not considered the how and when he should drop the L-word on her. He'd assumed by now she had some idea of how he felt. After all, he'd more or less made her a part of his and Grace's family. Her reaction when he told her tonight proved him dead wrong. She'd come back with an "I love you, too," but if that was the case, what kept her so quiet tonight? All through dinner she'd stayed quieter than usual. Even now, a few hours since he'd blurted out the truth without thinking, she remained quiet. Had his impromptu declaration hurt rather than helped their relationship?

"Are you feeling okay tonight?" He'd already gone through all the channels on the television while she flipped through his DVD collection, not once saying a word.

She looked up and gave him a faint smile that contained no happiness. "Fine. Why?"

In his experience, when a woman said those words the way she said them, it meant something *wasn't* fine. "You've been looking at the same DVDs for five minutes." Ready for a conversation regardless of whether or not he liked the outcome, he switched off the television. "Are you upset about what I said before?"

With a sigh, she pushed away the DVD case. "No, of course not. I love you, too, although you did surprise me."

The answer should fill him with relief. Instead, the worries jumping around inside him grew. What wasn't she telling him? "You've been quiet all night. Something is bothering you. What is it?" He took her hand, her slim delicate fingers disappearing under his. He counted as the seconds ticked by and she remained silent, her eyes downcast.

"I've been thinking about the other night." She looked up as she spoke.

Confused, he ran through the last few times they'd been together for anything unusual.

"The night I made you stop." She clarified for him.

Oh, that night. He remembered that night as well as the cold shower he'd taken when she'd left—and several times since.

"I told you I wasn't ready. That was the truth, just not all of it." Jessie bit down on her lip and looked away.

When she met his eyes again, he saw some unreadable emotion lurking there.

"Jessie, whatever the problem, you can tell me." Was she a virgin and embarrassed to tell him? While a little odd, it wasn't anything to be embarrassed about.

"I've never dated a lot. Before you, the last date I went on was in college. I met Jeremy in an accounting class. The professor paired us up with two other students for a project. When we finished it, he asked me out. We were together for six years."

"I don't care how many men you have or haven't dated." Her unease didn't mesh with the news she shared.

"My relationship wasn't normal. Or perhaps *healthy* is a better word." Jessie picked at her fingernail. "At first, it was great. He was sweet. He brought me flowers and we went out all the time. After college, we got an apartment together. Slowly, though, he changed. He got possessive. I couldn't go anywhere without checking with him first. We only did things he liked. The change was subtle. In the beginning, I didn't even notice. Soon, he controlled every aspect of my life. Who I talked to, how I dressed, when I visited my family." Jessie paused for a breath. "He had complete control over our intimate relationship, too. When he wanted sex, we had sex. The one time I said no, he hit me."

Anger flared inside him. No one should have to put up

with what Jessie described. "You left him after that?"

She pressed her lips together and shook her head. "No. He apologized and promised it would never happen again."

He'd heard that story way too many times. "What happened after that?"

"Things went back to normal—or normal for us. Slowly, he got more verbally abusive. Then, the day of our third anniversary, he hit me again. He'd been drinking and I let him use that as an excuse. I loved him and thought he loved me. I wanted to work things out. But things got worse. He started to hit me even when he wasn't drunk."

"You can never work things out with an animal like that." He squeezed her hand. "When did you end things?"

"About three years later. We got into a huge argument over what we wanted to do in Virginia Beach. He hit me so hard he knocked me out. When I fell, I landed on the wine glasses we'd left on a coffee table." She pulled up the hem of her shirt. "That's how I got this." She pointed to the scar he'd noticed before.

The fury already building inside him almost choked him now as he looked at that scar. "What happened next?" he asked, his teeth clenched.

"The nurse who treated me that night took one look at my bruises and knew what had happened even though I claimed it was an accident." Jessie let her top fall back into place, but he could still see the scar in his mind. "She convinced me to attend a support group with her. Between her help and the group, I left Jeremy soon after that and moved back in with my grandparents. By then though, I had already distanced myself from most of my friends and began suffering from depression. I started eating a lot and keeping to myself. It wasn't until Charlie and I reconnected that she convinced me to see a therapist for the depression."

"Did you ever press charges?"

"No, I didn't want anyone to know. Other than

Morgan, the nurse at the hospital, my therapist, and my support group, you're the only person I've told. I stopped us the other night because I won't let anyone force me to do anything ever again."

Mack pulled her closer and hugged her. "I'm glad you told me." He kissed her forehead. "And we can take things as slow as you want. Neither of us is going anywhere." Anger toward her former boyfriend still boiled inside him, but he fought to keep it from his voice.

"You don't…" Jessie's voice trailed off and she avoided his eyes.

With a finger, he titled her chin upward. "Don't what?"

She looked at him. "You don't mind waiting?"

"I'll never force you to do anything. And when you are ready, I'll be right here." This time, he kissed her lips, a soft gentle symbol of his promise.

Jessie wrapped her arms around his neck and leaned into him, her soft breasts pressed against his chest, and soon the anger raging inside him turned into desire. When she parted her lips and ran the tip of her tongue along the seam of his lips, he groaned then opened for her. Immediately, her tongue slipped inside and explored his mouth, leaving it burning with fire. As the kiss continued, Jessie moved her fingers up his neck and into his hair, searing a path of heat in the process.

Determined not to push her further than she wanted, he let her keep the control even though his hands ached with the need to touch her. When she pulled back, his mouth remained on fire much like the rest of him.

"I love you," she whispered before she kissed the pulse in his neck.

The contact sent another bolt of desire through his body right to his erection. Prepared to stop if she asked, he slipped a hand under her shirt and up her stomach. When he reached the edge of her bra, he paused and waited. Rather than pull away or ask him to stop, she let her own hand wander under his shirt. Assuming he had the green light, he pushed aside the cup of her bra and fondled one breast until her nipple pebbled under his fingers, then he switched to the other side.

Reclaiming his lips, she kissed with a hunger that rivaled his own, and for a moment, he considered stopping before things went any further. Moments earlier, he'd gotten the impression she wasn't ready for sex. Now, though, her action told another story. He didn't want her to do anything just because she thought she had to.

Before he could voice his thought, she straddled his lap, the intimate contact sending all rational thoughts away. When she moved against him, he groaned, grabbed her waist, and held her still. "Jessie, we don't have to do this." But, lord, how he wanted to.

She leaned back, her eyes bright with love and desire. "I know that. And while I'm not ready to sleep with you tonight, that doesn't meant I can't make you feel good." With both hands, she lifted his shirt, and then kissed his chest.

Pleasure wracked his body as her hands and mouth made a path toward his waist. Unable to do anything else, he leaned his head back and enjoyed the sweet torture.

He'd assumed she'd stop when she reached his jeans. Instead, he felt her finger work the button loose, and then she pulled the zipper down. Curiosity broke through some of his raging desire, and he looked down as she pushed his underwear away. Without any hesitation, she ran her index finger down the length of him, and his gaze stayed glued to her touch. Then she leaned forward, her mouth taking his again as she wrapped her hand around him.

***

"Why don't you stay here tonight?" Stretched out on the couch, he had his head in her lap as they watched a movie. "Neither of us has work in the morning and Grace won't be home until early evening." He took her hand and kissed it. "You can borrow one of my t-shirts for bed.

Nothing has to happen. I just want to hold you all night."

She didn't have to think about her answer. "I like that idea." Over the course of the evening, their relationship had grown. She knew Mack shared her feelings, and he understood her desire to wait just a little longer before she gave him full access to her body. And while she might not be ready for sex, she'd enjoyed every minute of his hands on her. The only thing she enjoyed more was when she touched him.

A flash of heat went through her as she thought about what she'd done. When she'd taken control of their kiss, it hadn't been her intention to do anything else. Yet, once she had control of the situation, the power had increased her own desire. When she felt him against her, she'd wanted nothing more than to pleasure him.

"Don't ever play poker." Mack smiled.

With her trip down memory lane shattered, she met his eyes. "What?"

"You're as red as a fire truck and I know exactly what you're thinking about."

Another flash of heat scorched her face. "Oh, really?"

Mack sat up. "It's okay. I was thinking about it, too, and how much I'd love to return the pleasure."

Her body still ached in need of the release only his touch could give. It would have to wait, though. As much as she loved him and the way he made her feel, she wanted to wait a little longer. "Soon." She closed the gap between them. "I promise," she whispered, inches from his mouth.

CHAPTER 10

A temporary altar sat at the center of the Town Common along with rows of white chairs filled with wedding guests. If Jessie had to guess, she'd say the entire town had turned out for Maureen O'Brien and Ray Larson's wedding. Not that she expected anything else. Both the bride and groom had grown up in North Salem. High school sweethearts, they'd drifted apart when Ray left for college and had reconnected when he moved back to town.

"Jessie, that color looks fabulous on you. You look beautiful." Mia Troy, Sean's celebrity girlfriend, took the seat in front of her.

Jessie beamed at the compliment. While no one would ever claim she was as beautiful as Mia, she did agree that the deep burgundy dress did look nice on her. "Thanks. When did your flight get in?"

"Around three o'clock this morning and I fly back out tomorrow at ten." Mia's resigned tone spoke volumes. "But in a little more than a month, I'll be done with this movie and back for good."

"Sean mentioned that." He'd also let it slip that he planned on asking Mia to marry him when she returned at Thanksgiving. "How's he doing today anyway?" She'd learned all about Ray and Maureen's involvement and the role it had played in Sean and Charlie's father leaving them. She also knew, in the beginning, Sean had a difficult time accepting his mother's marriage to Ray.

"I think he's put his issues with Ray behind him. When I left him a few minutes ago with Maureen and Charlie, he looked happy."

Jessie saw Grace and Mack approaching and the sunlight got brighter. Never in her entire life had she felt this content and special.

"Jessie, look how Grammy fixed my hair." Grace slid into the seat Jessie had saved for her while Mack stopped and spoke with a friend.

"It's beautiful. Is Brianna's the same way?" Jessie took a moment to examine the intricate braid in the little girl's hair.

Grace nodded, her eyes set on Mia. "You're on television." Grace's strawberry blonde eyebrows scrunched up as she tried to figure out why someone she'd seen on television was sitting in front of her.

Her relationship with Mack and Grace had developed so much that she'd forgotten they'd only been in town since August, after Mia had returned to California. "Grace, this is Mia, Sean's girlfriend. And you're right; she used to be on television."

Grace's mouth dropped open. "Wow!"

"Mia, this cutie pie is Grace Ellsbury, and that's her father Mack." Jessie nodded toward Mack as he headed their way.

Mia leaned back to get a better look. "Sean mentioned you'd started seeing someone. He's handsome."

The seat to Jessie's left moved. "Thanks. My wife thinks so, too."

"Jake." Jessie turned and greeted Charlie's husband.

Jake gave her a quick hug. "Hi, Jessie. Mia." He nodded in the other woman's direction before looking over at Grace who sat staring at him, her mouth still down to her knees.

"Who's the beautiful girl next to you?" he asked, flashing Grace a hundred-watt smile.

"I've seen you on magazine covers," Grace said before Jessie could make introductions.

"Jake, this is Grace, my boyfriend's daughter." Outside of conversations with Mack, she'd never referred to Mack as her boyfriend until now and she liked it.

"It's nice to meet you, Grace." Jake extended his hand. "I'm Jake. Jessie and I are friends."

Sitting up a little straighter in her seat, Grace accepted his hand and mimicked what she'd heard. "It's nice to meet you."

Jake gave Grace another smile and then looked at Jessie. "When Charlie came back yesterday, she said you had a boyfriend."

Charlie and Jake had arrived in town the day before, and she'd stopped at Jessie's apartment while Jake went over to Sean's house. Jessie hadn't even put coffee on the table when Charlie announced she was pregnant. Once Charlie finished sharing her news, Jessie had told her friend about the developments between her and Mack.

"She's my dad's girlfriend, and she helped me pick out this dress." Grace picked up the hem of her dark blue dress.

"And she did an excellent job," Mack said as he took the seat next to his daughter. "Let's try not to ruin it today."

Jessie figured it would survive the ceremony with no problem. Dinner and dancing… well, they were another story. "Jake, this is Mack." By this point, neither man needed a proper introduction. Still, it remained the polite action. "Mack, this is Charlie's husband, Jake."

The two men shook hands. "They should be starting soon. I saw Joseph Bates crossing the grass." In addition to being the Town Administrator, Joseph Bates, Tony's father, was a Justice of the Peace.

Jessie, along with Mack, Mia, and Jake, kept up a steady conversation for the next several minutes. Then, when the music started, silence washed over the crowd and Charlie,

Maureen's matron of honor, started down the aisle toward the altar. Once again, Jessie wished she looked more like her friend. Dressed in an ankle-length dark purple gown, Charlie looked stunning and not at all pregnant. Then again, her friend looked gorgeous in cutoffs.

When Charlie passed by, she smiled at her husband, the one simple gesture telling everyone who saw it how much she loved him. Jessie didn't have to look to know Jake's face reflected a similar smile.

Once Charlie reached the altar, the music changed and the "Wedding March" started. As a whole, the crowd rose, and beaming with joy, Maureen started down the aisle on Sean's arm. For a moment, Jessie gaped at Sean. She'd known him all her life and couldn't remember ever seeing him in a tux.

"He complained all morning about that tux," Mia whispered to her. "But he looks gorgeous in it."

While he didn't hold a candle to Mack, Sean looked handsome today. "He looks great." She watched as Maureen and Sean joined the rest of the wedding party. Then, after a few words between Ray and Sean, Sean took his seat near Mia.

Mack's hand settled on her shoulder while Joseph Bates began the ceremony, and gradually the words faded as her mind wandered. Rather than Ray and Maureen standing up there, she envisioned her and Mack in their place. Before her relationship with Jeremy, she'd dreamed of getting married and having children. After Jeremy, the dream disappeared, but since Mack entered her life, it had emerged again.

In her mind, she saw them saying their vows before family and friends. Afterward, they, along with Grace, would return to his house and begin the rest of their lives. Could it happen? They'd been together a short time, but they loved each other.

Jessie looked away from the ceremony to Mack. Would he want to get married again? For some people, one try at marriage was enough. What about children? He had a happy, healthy little girl; maybe he didn't want to start over. During all their time together, they'd never discussed either subject.

Before Jessie looked away, Mack turned his head and met her eyes. The love she saw reflected there sent her previous thoughts from her head. If he loved her that much, the other stuff didn't matter. Plenty of people spent their entire lives in relationships filled with love and respect without ever exchanging rings. If Mack never wanted to marry again, she'd be okay with that as long as he always looked at her the way he was now.

"I now pronounce you husband and wife," Joseph Bates said after Ray and Maureen exchanged rings. "You may kiss the bride."

Jessie looked back to the couple and watched Ray give Maureen a light kiss before they faced the crowd. Amid the thunderous applause, the couple proceeded down the aisle, followed by Charlie and Ray's best man, his brother, Phil.

"We better join your mom and Charlie so they can finish taking pictures, Sean. Jessie, I'll see you at the reception." Jake extended his hand toward Mack. "Mack, it was nice meeting you, and, Grace, save me a dance."

Grace's face lit up. "Okay."

Throughout the ceremony, Jessie had noticed Grace starring at Jake, something women both young and old did all the time. She suspected Grace had her first crush.

"Jake's right." Sean held out a hand to Mia. "The sooner we get the pictures done, the sooner I can get rid of this tie." He pulled at the offending article of clothing. With that, the three of them disappeared into the crowd.

"Daddy, can I go see Brianna? She's over there." Grace pointed across the aisle to where her cousin sat with her parents.

"Go ahead, but stay with them."

Grace took off as if she wore jeans and sneakers rather

than a nice dress and tights. "It's a good thing her tights are black," Jessie said as Grace slipped, landed on her knees, then bounced back up again.

"Tell me about it. But she does love that dress. She had to try it on again last night." Together, they moved toward where Mack's sister stood with her husband and parents. "My mom asked if Grace could spend the night tonight. Brianna is staying over, too. I told her it was okay."

Jessie had been looking forward to movie night with Mack and Grace tonight. "I don't know how those two don't get sick of each other. They see each other at least five days a week."

Mack put his arm around her waist and anchored her against him. "Since Grace will be gone, I thought maybe you'd want to spend the night."

She'd like nothing better. Actually, since waking up in his arms weeks ago, she'd thought of it often and wondered when she might get a chance to do it again. "I'd love to."

With dinner over and the bride and groom's first dance out of the way, the musicians invited the wedding guests to dance. Couples of all ages took to the dance floor, but Jessie and Mack remained seated while Grace finished her cake. Much to Jessie's amazement, Grace had managed to keep her dress clean thus far. If she got through dessert with no spills, perhaps the dress would remain stain-free.

"Why don't you go dance? I'll sit with Grace while she finishes." Rose Ellsbury took the seat next to Mack. "You know your father hates to dance anyway."

Jessie didn't dance much, but she enjoyed it. "If you don't want to, that's okay," Jessie said, offering Mack a way out. She didn't know if he liked dancing or not.

Even with the music playing, she heard the legs of his chair scratch the floor. "I think we should. Afterward, Grace and I'll have a dance, too." He took her by the hand before she could protest. "We'll be back, Mom."

Gage Larson and his band started another slow ballad,

and Mack locked her in his arms. If there had been anyone left in town who didn't know about their relationship, which seemed impossible, they knew now.

"You look beautiful tonight," he whispered. She had never heard his voice so sensual, and her heart raced. "I'm glad you're staying with me tonight."

Not caring who saw them, she touched her lips to his in a whisper of a kiss. Even though it barely qualified as a kiss, it sent spirals of desire and excitement through her. Earlier in the week, she'd decided that the next time they were alone, she wouldn't hold anything back. The idea of giving in to the passion she experienced with Mack made her eager for the reception to end.

When she ended the kiss, he put his mouth near her ear. "You can do better than that."

She heard the challenge in his voice. Perhaps another woman would've taken the bait, but not her. They were in a room full of family and friends; it wasn't the place for an intense make-out session. "I'll make it up to you later."

His eyebrows arched and a smile played at the corners of his mouth. "I'm going to hold you to that."

They danced to two songs before they returned to the table so Mack and Grace could dance together. As Jessie sat and watched him lift Grace, her heart melted. There weren't many sights sweeter than a father dancing with his little girl.

"Now that's a look of happiness." Jake stopped near her. Since he was looking at her, she guessed he meant her. "Charlie said you were happier than she'd ever seen you."

Just what expression did she have on her face? "Hi, Jake. Where did Charlie disappear to?"

He pointed over his shoulder to the dance floor. "She's dancing with Sean. When she asked him, Mia all but pushed him onto the floor. You should have seen the look he gave her." Jake extended his hand in her direction. "Since we've both been left on our own, how about a dance?"

Since the first day she'd met Jake and he'd comforted her and her grandmother in the hospital waiting room, she'd respected the man. Not many people would go out of their way like that for strangers. Now that she knew him better, she respected him even more and was honored to call him a friend. "Sure. Someone has to make sure you behave until your wife gets back."

Mack dipped Grace, and she rewarded him with a giggle, a sound he never tired of hearing.

"One more time," she said when he brought her upright again.

"Just once." She had eaten a large slice of cake and the last thing he wanted was her getting sick. Adjusting his hold on her, he dipped her back again. This time, when he swung her back up, it wasn't Grace's giggle that caught his attention but Jessie and Jake Sherbrooke dancing. Although they stood an appropriate space apart, the sight of Jessie in another man's arms sent a burning sensation through his chest. For a moment, he considered cutting in. Then the red fog in his head cleared and his common sense returned. He trusted Jessie and knew Jake was a friend. Friends were allowed to dance at weddings. He'd expect the same courtesy if he ever danced with a female friend, not that he expected that to happen anytime soon. His list of female friends was rather slim. Even still, he'd be pissed if Jessie overreacted and dragged him away the way he wanted to snatch her away now. And it wasn't like she was dancing with Tony, North Salem's resident playboy. No, this was Jake, her friend's husband.

Mack clenched his jaw and looked back at Grace's smiling face. Yes, he'd stay focused on his daughter and ignore everything else until the song ended.

"That was fun." Grace held his hand as they walked back to their table and Mack relaxed his jaw when he spotted Jake and Jessie seated with Charlie and Sean. Then, when they got within speaking distance, Grace rushed forward. "Did you see me dancing, Jessie?"

The soft motherly smile she used with Grace formed on Jessie's face. He already realized how much Jessie cared about his daughter, but that smile drove home just how perfect she was for both of them. "I did. You looked beautiful."

Grace's face lit up. "I want to dance with Daddy again."

"Don't forget you owe me a dance, too," Jake said before looking in his direction. "Assuming it's okay with you."

Under normal circumstances, if a stranger ever asked to dance with his daughter, he'd cart the guy off in handcuffs, but since both Jessie and Sean considered the guy a friend, he'd allow it. "Go for it. I'm warning you, though, she likes dips."

"Thanks for the heads-up." Grace and Jake disappeared onto the dance floor while Jessie and Charlie went back to their conversation. Before Mack could start anything with Sean, Mia appeared, and the two walked off together. Left as the third wheel at the table, he zoned out and watched Grace, who had suddenly become the envy of every unmarried female on the dance floor.

"I still can't picture him with a baby. Is he hoping for a girl or a boy?" Jessie's mention of a baby caught his attention.

"You didn't see him with his nephew a few weeks ago." He saw both glance toward Jake and his daughter.

"He says he doesn't care which and I believe him."

The pieces of their conversation came together in his head. "Congratulations. You didn't tell me Charlie was pregnant."

Two sets of eyes turned toward him. "Sorry. I wasn't sure she wanted me telling anyone."

"We just started telling people, Mack."

The two women went back to discussing Jake and how well he'd handled his nephew, leaving Mack to once again zone out. This time, rather than wandering aimlessly, his mind drifted toward children.

He'd become a father a little earlier than planned. When he and Bethany married, they'd decided to wait before starting a family. Bethany had wanted to wait six years before starting and she'd only wanted one or two children. He'd agreed, assuming she'd change her mind and want to start a family after a year or so. Nature had its own plans, however, and three months after getting married, they learned Grace was on the way. From that point forward, their relationship had begun to change.

After Grace's first birthday, he'd brought up trying for a second baby. Bethany had flipped out and they'd never discussed it again as their relationship deteriorated further. Since the divorce, he'd accepted that Grace would remain an only child. The more he saw Jessie with Grace, though, the more he wondered if he'd been wrong. Judging by the way she treated his daughter, he knew she'd make a great mother. Did she want children? She'd never given any indication either way, but his instincts told him she did. A mental image of her holding their baby while she sat and read to Grace warmed his soul.

"What do you think is the hardest part about having a newborn in the house, Mack?" Charlie's question invaded his peaceful image and tugged him back to the present.

***

When he'd asked her to spend the night, he'd assumed her answer could go either way. After her soul-bearing confession, he'd decided to give Jessie control over how fast their relationship progressed. Under no circumstances did he want to make her uncomfortable—or worse—scare her away. He hoped his actions the Sunday she'd spent the night and he'd only held her while she slept, as well as his actions since then, demonstrated he didn't expect anything she wasn't ready to give. Since she'd agreed to spend the night again, he assumed his strategy was working.

Jessie unlocked her apartment door. "Mrs. O'Brien, I mean Mrs. Larson, looked so happy today." She switched on the lights. "It's sounds weird to call her Mrs. Larson. She's been Mrs. O'Brien my entire life."

"You'll get used to it."

"Let me change and grab a few things, then we can go." Jessie went into her bedroom, leaving Mack alone.

She'd told him she'd moved in the previous winter. It had been her final step before leaving therapy for good. Judging by the looks of it, she'd turned the small apartment into her own warm and inviting space, a place that showcased her personality and welcomed visitors.

"I'm shocked Grace's dress survived the entire day." She re-entered the living room as she spoke.

Mack looked away from the family pictures Jessie had on a table. She'd changed from her dress into dark gray leggings and a long, fitted sweater. "She does love it. I told her we could talk about wearing it to school after the wedding."

"Sounds fair. I'm all set if you are."

"One thing first." He crossed the room and pulled her close. In response, Jessie opened her mouth as if to speak, but he didn't give her the opportunity. Bringing his mouth down on hers, he made love to her mouth, his tongue mating with hers. Kissing her like this had invaded his thoughts all day, anticipation building inside him. Now, alone with her, he let the desire loose, drinking his fill as he held her close, throwing more fuel on the constant desire humming in his body.

Her lips left his, her breathing rapid. Rather than say anything, she pressed her forehead against his shoulder, her heartbeat thumping against his chest.

"I've wanted to do that all day." His voice came out ragged. "I wanted to thank you, too."

When she looked up at him, he brushed a soft kiss against her forehead. "For all your help. Grace is crazy about you. After your shopping trip for that dress, all she could talk about was you and how much fun you had together. You really are great with her."

Jessie's lips titled upward in a smile and then she looked down at the floor. "I had just as much fun. When you told me she was spending the night with your parents, I was a little disappointed. I enjoy movie night with you two."

"Next weekend, after Grace's birthday party, we'll all watch a movie together." Mack released her and grabbed the bag she'd dropped to the floor when he'd pulled her into his arms.

Without missing a step, Jessie followed him toward the door, switching off the apartment lights along the way. "I still need to get her a birthday present. Every time I settle on one thing, I think of something else and change my mind."

He preceded her down the stairs. He'd already decided on his own present for Grace and now was as good a time as any to present his idea to Jessie. "Before you do that, I have an idea." He'd wrestled with the decision, but in the end, after a conversation with his daughter, he'd decided to go with his gut on this one. "Grace has been asking for a while to go to the theme parks in Florida, so this year I'm going to surprise her with a week there. Come with us. That can be your present to her. We can get adjoining rooms or maybe one of those family suites with more than one bedroom."

The footsteps behind him stopped. "She'll want to do that just with you."

He retraced his steps up to the landing where she'd stopped. "I already asked her how she'd feel if you came on vacation with us sometime. She loved the idea."

"A vacation sometime maybe, but what you're talking about isn't just some vacation."

Mack touched her cheek. "She won't see it that way. To her, it'll be a vacation to somewhere she's been dying to visit… with the two of us."

Jessie took a deep breath then released it. Maybe he should have waited to ask her. At the time, it hadn't seemed like a bad idea, but then again, he didn't want her to feel pressured into anything. "I don't need an answer tonight."

"Are you sure she won't mind? It does sound like fun. I've never been to Florida." She slipped her hand into his.

They resumed their walk down the stairs. "I wouldn't have asked if I thought she'd mind."

She remained silent as they exited her building. Outside, the temperature had dropped. Although it had stayed in the sixties much of the day, now a cool breeze blew, and he figured the first thing he'd do when they got to his place was start a fire.

"Okay, but under one condition." He opened the car door, but she remained outside. "I help pay for the trip. I don't want you covering everything."

"You got it."

She played with her silver ring while Mack discussed his own memories from the last time he'd visited Florida as a teenager. She'd never gone herself. With her dad on the road so much and her grandparents busy with the hardware store, long family vacations had never happened. Yet, while she found Mack's memories entertaining, she thought about the night ahead. She hadn't announced it, but she had decided tonight they'd take their intimacy to the next level. And while her body zinged with anticipation at finally satisfying the aching need that plagued it, a kernel of worry remained in her head. What if he found their lovemaking a disappointment? She didn't have a lot of experience. What if he saw her naked and decided he wanted someone more like his ex-wife? She knew Bethany had done some modeling in college, and even after having a child, she looked fantastic.

"So I thought we could go to Florida between Thanksgiving and the holiday break. I'd prefer over the break, but Grace is scheduled to spend part of it with Bethany."

Jessie dropped her purse onto Mack's kitchen counter. "Sounds like a good time to go." She heard the kitchen door into the garage squeak as it closed.

"Good. I'll make reservations this week." He took the overnight bag she held. "I need to change. Be right back." He gave her a peck on the cheek and headed out of the room.

Images of Mack in various states of undress formed thanks to his comment, each one increasing her body temperature. "Do you need any help?" she asked before she lost her nerve. The old Jessica, the woman she'd been a few years ago, never would've said such a thing. But that woman no longer existed. Tonight, even if it killed her, she planned to prove that to both Mack and herself.

Mack stopped dead and turned around. "I'd like nothing better."

Like the one time she'd tried singing karaoke, her stomach hit the floor as she crossed the room, but her adrenaline took over when she reached him and led him upstairs.

A soft click signaled he'd closed the door behind them, and she pulled him toward the center of the room. Her hands shook as she reached for his tie, her eyes glued to his. In silence, she undid each button of his shirt, pulling it from his waistband when she reached his belt. Then she pushed the material over his shoulders. The plain white undershirt he wore stretched across his chest, the material unable to hide the strong muscles it covered.

Before she did anything else, Mack grabbed the shirt bottom and pulled it over his head, revealing the strong chest and washboard stomach she'd seen only briefly before. Like a magnet attracted to metal, her hands landed on his pecs and traveled downward. When she hit his belt buckle, she reversed her course, stopping when she felt his heartbeat under her hand.

Her gaze roamed across his upper torso one more time before she looked down at his belt buckle. *The point of no return.*

As she slipped the leather from the buckle, another jolt of excitement rocked her body. There was no mistaking the hard ridge behind his zipper when she pulled it down, and her self-confidence increased ten-fold.

Left in nothing but his boxer briefs, Mack remained still, his hands by his sides, and Jessie took the opportunity presented to her. Her eyes wandered everywhere. Then her hands joined in.

"That made getting undressed much easier. Do I get to repay the favor?" His voice simmered with the same passion that overwhelmed her.

She almost nodded yes, but stopped herself. Tonight, she wanted all the control in her hands. If she allowed Mack to undress her, she'd be handing over some of that control. Not much, but some, and that was something the old Jessica would do. She'd worked hard to get rid of the person she'd become with Jeremy, and taking control tonight with Mack would put the final nail in old Jessica's coffin.

"Not tonight." Jessie kicked off the ballet flats she'd slipped on. Grabbing the bottom of her sweater, she paused and rode the wave of apprehension that swept through her. *He loves me.*

Grabbing onto her self-confidence, she pulled the sweater over her head. *Please don't let me blush.* Although her instincts said to pull her sweater back on, she tossed it away and reached for the waistband of her leggings. With slow movements, she slid them down; all the while her gaze was focused on Mack's chest. When she tossed them away as well, she stood up straight, her hands clasped behind her back, nails digging into her palms.

She watched Mack's hand stroke her shoulder and then continue down her arm. When he took her hand in his and raised it to his lips, she looked at his face. The heat in his gaze made her entire body tingle. Then his eyes left hers and raked over her body, the simple action making her ache for his touch.

After he completed his inspection, he met her eyes again. "Christ, you're sexy. I can't wait to be inside you."

Before he could make the next move, she closed the gap between them. Wrapping her arms around his neck, she stretched up on her tiptoes, crushing her breasts against his chest, and kissed him.

Although he'd let her make the first move, his demanding lips revealed how difficult a task it had been as they moved over hers, ravishing her mouth. His hand slid down her back, his fingers burning her already tingling skin. When they reached her butt, both hands settled on the skin exposed by the lacy thong she'd worn for the first time.

Using her body, she propelled him back toward the bed, coming down on top of him. "You like being in charge, don't you?" He pressed his lips against her neck and made a path toward her bra strap.

"Sometimes." The one word answer came out in a ragged, sensuous voice she didn't recognize.

Mack placed a last kiss on her shoulder and stopped. "You can be in charge whenever you want." His hand closed on her breast, the heat further exciting her already taut nipple. "I have one request for right now." He kissed the skin exposed just above her bra. "Can you get rid of this?" He tugged at a bra strap.

Rather than answer with words, she gripped the clasp between her breasts and released it.

"Damn, they're perfect."

If there had been noise in the room, she would've missed Mack's response, and she had the feeling he didn't even realize he'd spoken aloud. Regardless, his response thrilled her. At a size D, she'd always wished for smaller breasts. Her ex hadn't helped matters by always complaining that other men checked her out because her breasts were so large.

Mack's hand on her waist moved upward, his touch feather-light as his fingers caressed her. Then he dipped his head, taking her nipple in his mouth. An immediate rush of desire and longing shot outward in every direction, and before she could stop herself, she moaned. Then, when he repeated the same thing on the other side, all she could do was grip his shoulders and hold on.

"Tell me what you want, Jessie." His warm breath caressed her breast and she struggled with a coherent answer.

Pulling away just a little, she slipped her hand beneath the waistband of his briefs and touched him. "You."

Mack made no effort to contain his groan. "Be right back." He lifted her off his lap and disappeared into the master bathroom. When he came back, he tossed a box of condoms on the nightstand and stripped off his briefs before he rejoined her.

With him lying there naked and oh so ready, Jessie couldn't look away. After several seconds went by, though, and he didn't reach for her, she tore her gaze away and looked at his face. "What's wrong?" She fought the urge to cover up as she waited for an answer.

His right hand traveled down her arm—more a loving caress than a touch. "Nothing. You're in control now. I'm just along for the ride."

Her eyes flicked toward the condoms. She'd never put one on a man, not to mention, she'd never instigated sex. Then again, that Jessie no longer existed. Grabbing a condom, she tore it open, prepared to show Mack just how much she loved him.

CHAPTER 11

He'd untangled the sheet enough to pull it up and over them, more for Jessie's sake than his when he noticed the goose bumps on her arm. "Can I get you anything?" His own stomach kept rumbling. They'd eaten at the wedding reception, but that had been hours ago. Before he called it a day, he needed one more meal. "I don't know about you, but I'm starved."

Under the sheet, she shifted onto her side, her soft skin rubbing against his, and his body readied for round two. She'd been smooth and silky soft everywhere and he wanted her wrapped around him again very soon.

"I'm a little hungry, too. What time is it?" Her fingers wandered over his chest and down his stomach. Before they could go too low, he covered her hand with his.

"Seven," he answered, checking his watch. "How about I order us a pizza and we can have our own movie night? I picked up *Morning of The Dead* yesterday."

She moved her head back and forth, her hair tickling his shoulder. "The pizza sounds great, but I don't do horror."

"Really? We can find something else then." Climbing out of bed, he grabbed his cell and called the pizza place in town. Halfway though his order, Jessie threw back the sheet and stood, and as the guy on the phone read back his order, he only heard a jumble of words. Never in a million years would he have guessed she had a body like that. Yeah, sure he'd known she'd changed from the way she'd looked before, but nothing prepared him for her tiny waist and cute ass. Then, to top it off, she had breasts to drool over: large, exquisitely shaped, and best of all, real. He'd always gotten hot and bothered by women with large breasts or a cute ass; if they had both, even better. His ex-wife had had both. It had been one of the first things that attracted him to her, but hers hadn't been natural. They'd been well done, but he could still tell her breasts were not real.

He watched Jessie re-clip her bra and almost touched his chin to make sure there was no drool there. After the pizza guy promised to be there in twenty minutes, he tossed the phone aside and watched Jessie collect her pants and sweater.

"Something wrong?" She pressed the sweater against her chest. "You're staring at me."

With a little tug, he pulled the sweater away. "I like what I see." Her uncovered skin called out to him and he ran his fingers down her flat stomach. Her muscles tensed, but he continued downward, only stopping where lace met skin. When she'd stripped off her clothes, her choice of underwear had left him speechless. He'd expected something more along the lines of cotton panties and a plain bra, not the black lacy matching set. "Whenever we're alone, you should go around just like this."

"I only picked up a few sets last week, but the next time I'm at the mall, I'll get a few more."

She'd picked them out for him. Such a simple thing shouldn't mean that much, yet it did. His ex-wife had never done anything with him in mind. If she went shopping for new clothes, it hadn't been because she wanted to look good for him, but because she wanted to impress everyone else around her.

Taking Jessie in his arms, he pulled her against him. "I can't wait for the fashion show. Make sure you get red."

Jessie kissed the skin over his racing heart, then grabbed her sweater back. "Maybe you should consider getting dressed, too, unless you plan on greeting the delivery person like that."

"Good idea, because if I do, he'll never deliver another pizza here again." Mack released Jessie and grabbed a pair of jeans from a drawer.

"And if they send Theresa, we'll never get her to leave," Jessie added, referring to the one female delivery person the restaurant employed.

Disappointment descended on him when she pulled her sweater on, depriving him of the view. No question about it, once the movie was done, the damn thing was history. That, of course, was assuming it even made it that long. There was a good chance he'd rip the thing off again once they'd eaten. "Trust me. There's only one woman in this town I want hanging around, and it is not Theresa O'Leary."

Jessie bent down and grabbed her leggings, and he couldn't deny himself. The skin on her backside screamed *touch me!*

He pressed his palms against the warm flesh and then slid his hands up and over her hips before returning to where he started.

"Mack, stop." Her words came out on a ragged breath. "We don't have time." She straightened, but remained with her back to him.

Ignoring her words, he pulled her back against him as his other hand disappeared under her sweater. "Are you sure?" He teased her nipple with his fingers.

"Positive." Her answer sounded more like a moan than a statement. "Later, I promise." She pulled his hand and he removed it.

Before he let her go, he kissed the side of her neck.

"I'm holding you to that."

***

The pizza box remained open, half of it gone. A raging fire filled the room with heat, and Mack stretched out on the couch with his head in Jessie's lap. On the television screen, the movie's hero shot his way out of captivity and hot-wired a car. Soon, he had half a dozen bad guys chasing him through the streets of New York. While the action scene was designed to build the audience's adrenaline, utter calm radiated inside Mack. He sat in his own home with the woman he loved; not much could make it a better night.

"I'd forgotten about this chase scene." Jessie's fingers ran through his hair, the movements almost hypnotizing. "I haven't been to New York in a long time."

His gaze drifted to her face. "I was there in June when I dropped Grace off to see Bethany. Next time we go, come with us. We can stay and do some sightseeing while Grace visits her mom." At the thought of his ex-wife, he remembered he needed to prepare Jessie. "Bethany might be at Grace's birthday party next weekend." He watched for any sign his news bothered her.

"Makes sense."

He picked up on the disappointment in her voice, but otherwise she took it well.

"It wasn't the original plan. Grace was supposed to spend the following weekend with Bethany, but the school has its annual picnic scheduled for then. Grace doesn't want to miss that."

To the best of his knowledge, the night Bethany had picked Grace up had been the first and only time she and Jessie had met. While Bethany had shared with him her thoughts on Jessie and her friendship with Grace, Jessie had kept her opinions locked away.

"None of the kids ever want to miss that. I remember being disappointed when I started sixth grade and could no longer go."

"It doesn't bother you that Bethany will be around?" In a reverse situation, he'd be less accepting.

Jessie's hand left his hair and her fingertips brushed his cheek over the facial hair that had grown in since the morning. "She is Grace's mother. She has more right than me to be there."

In one motion, he sat up and switched off the television. "You've acted like more of a mother to Grace than Bethany ever does. You belong there just as much because we both love you."

"And I'll be there regardless of who else is because I love both of you." She kissed him, a mere touch of her lips against his.

He knew she loved both him and his daughter. Her actions had told him that a while ago. Still, his heart swelled at her admission. "You make me a happy guy. Do you know that?"

She flashed him a suggestive smile, one he'd never guess she was capable of, and leaned closer. "If you want, I could make you even happier."

Her comment scorched his body from the inside out. Since they'd dressed earlier, he'd wanted nothing more than to strip them both naked and pleasure her until she fell asleep. But now, like before, he held back. Jessie not only wanted, but also *needed* control tonight. She hadn't said that in words, but his gut told him letting her control everything tonight was best for both her emotional state and their relationship as a whole. Besides, he'd enjoyed every second of their time together with her in control.

"Sounds good to me," he answered and then waited, his body growing hard at the thought of making love again.

She didn't keep him waiting long. Standing, she moved in front of the fireplace and pulled off her sweater then slid her leggings down. The flames danced across her skin, making it glow. Then she walked toward him and he took the opportunity to stare at her as his heart hammered away in his chest. When she reached him, she straddled his lap and sat.

His erection jumped against her through his jeans and power surged through her. When she'd arrived here tonight with her mind made up, anxiety had filled her—as had a million questions. Thanks to Mack's love and willingness to relinquish control, none of that remained. Eager for the feel of his skin again, she pulled his t-shirt up. In silence, he took it from her and pulled it off. Jessie ran her hands across his chest. Under her fingertips, she felt his uneven breathing, and she let her hands linger for a few seconds. Then, she removed her hands and reached for the clasp between her breasts. She'd noticed earlier how he'd stared at them, and already her nipples tightened at the mere thought of him touching her again.

When her hands gripped the clasp, he swallowed, his eyes fixed on her fingers. With a simple flick, the bra opened, and she let the material slip away. Mack's hands shot forward, his fingers caressing one breast while he held the other, and then he lowered his mouth to it.

Pleasure flowed through her body as her passion grew. When she thought she'd burst into flames, she pushed on his chest. "Enough."

His lips released her and his eyes met hers. Rather than use words, she slid from his lap, grabbed his hand, and tugged. Before she took another step, he lifted her, and she locked her legs around his waist.

Mack walked toward the stairs. "Damn, you're sexy." His mouth came down on hers only to break away a second later. "What the hell?" He looked down at the floor then kicked aside the pink building block he'd stepped on. "I thought we'd found all of those," he said before his mouth came down on hers again, and this time, he didn't stop moving until they reached his bedroom and he lowered her to her feet.

Much like earlier, he allowed her to lead. "One of us is overdressed," she said.

His gaze swept over her and then he cocked an eyebrow. "I think it might be you."

"I disagree." She undid the button and zipper on his jeans. Then she pushed them and his boxer briefs down, leaving him naked from the knees up.

Mack freed his legs and then closed in on her. "You like taking my clothes off, don't you?" He kissed a path down her neck to where her pulse beat, and words escaped her. Instead, she reveled in the heat building up inside her.

"I like when you do it," he said.

She heard the hunger in his voice, and her need for him exploded. With a step back, she fell onto the bed, taking him down with her. Done with words for the moment, she used her body to convey her intentions, and he moved onto his back. Free from his weight, she grabbed a condom from the nightstand. It took her two tries, but she managed to open the package and roll it on him. Then, after one last passionate kiss, she showed him just how much she loved him.

***

She chopped the mushrooms for omelets and Mack took care of the onions while a fresh pot of coffee brewed. If an outsider viewed the scene, they'd think the two of them prepared breakfast together every morning. "Tomatoes?" he asked as he pushed the plate of chopped onions toward her.

"Let's skip them." She added the mushrooms and onions to the scrambled eggs in the bowl. She'd feared things might be awkward this morning considering the previous night. However, just the opposite was true. Waking up with Mack and cooking breakfast just felt right, as if they did it every day.

Something she could imagine them doing.

"Fine with me. While you take care of that, I'll get us

coffee."

Before he walked away, she touched his hand and kissed him. In return, he smiled and said, "Too bad you're working this afternoon."

As much as she loved spending time with Mack and his daughter, she figured it was a good thing she was scheduled to close the store. Since she and Mack had started their relationship, she'd been taking time from Mack and Grace's alone time. While Grace never showed any signs she resented it, guilt still bothered Jessie. "You and Grace will have fun without me. You two always do."

Mack placed her coffee near the stove while she kept an eye on the omelets. "I know, but we'll still miss you, and next weekend is going to be crazy with the party and everything." He leaned against the counter and crossed his arms. "Especially with Bethany here."

For the most part, he shared little about his ex-wife. While Jessie understood that, she still wondered about the reasons behind their divorce. Mack was everything a woman could want in a husband and Grace was a great little girl. Jessie couldn't understand why anyone would leave them. "Can I ask you something?" In the past, it had never seemed the appropriate time, but now felt right.

"You can ask me anything."

Careful to not break the omelet, she flipped it before she said another word. "Why did you get divorced? Was it because of Bethany's job in New York?" Something like that didn't strike Jessie as enough of a reason, but who knew? Some people got divorced over sillier reasons.

Mack didn't hesitate. "That didn't help, but it wasn't the reason. A bunch of things contributed to our divorce." He accepted the plate she offered him before he continued. "Our relationship changed after she got pregnant. I started to notice things about her I'd either missed or just overlooked before." He took the second plate and carried them over to the table. "Things went downhill after Grace was born. She complained how it was

Grace's fault she now had stretch marks and couldn't shed the last five pounds she'd gained while pregnant. She missed going out with her friends or us just taking off for the weekend at the last minute."

The woman he described sounded more self-absorbed than Jessie had first thought. How had Mack ever fallen for her in the first place? She didn't sound at all like the type of woman he'd want.

"Before we got married, I only saw the fun we had together. Only afterward, when I saw the real her, did I realize we were wrong for each other. We started couples' therapy right before she got the offer for the job in New York. That finally killed our marriage." He stated it as if their breakup was a simple story, without bitterness or disappointment.

"Bethany agreed I could have sole custody before we ever stepped in a courtroom. She'd never wanted to be a mother, so she was content with visitation rights. Then, about six months after we separated, she moved in with someone she met in New York."

A mother who would willing give up custody told her a lot about Mack's ex-wife. "I think Grace is better off without her mom around much."

"I couldn't agree more." Mack reached over and squeezed her hand. "Let's talk about something more enjoyable."

He didn't need to ask twice. With her curiosity satisfied, Jessie squeezed back. "Tell me more about this trip we're going to take. Did I tell you I've never been to Florida? Actually, I've never been any farther south than Virginia."

Mack latched onto the topic and ran with it. Just by the way he discussed the parks and what he remembered as a child, she could tell he was looking forward to the trip and not merely because Grace would enjoy it. The more he told her, the more excited she became as well. In fact, by the time they finished breakfast, she wanted to hop on a plane and fly down that day.

CHAPTER 12

The week dragged on. In fact, Jessie couldn't remember the last time a week took so long to end. Part of it stemmed from issues at work. Two large special orders—one for Phil Larson and another for Brendan Michaels—came in damaged. Thankfully, Phil was a regular customer and easy to work with, but still, dealing with the manufacturers had been a major pain. Brendan, on the other hand, was—and always had been—a jerk, and when he'd discovered the problems, he'd stormed into the store pissed off. Then, on Wednesday, her assistant manager, Ty, had come down with the flu and she'd been forced to cover his hours in addition to her own.

All of that would have been bad enough, but on top of it, she'd seen Mack only once. And it was only for a short time. Tuesday, her only day off, he'd called around six and asked if she could pick Grace up at his sister's house. Some case he was involved in had made it impossible for him to leave work before Erin had to leave for her moms' night out with friends. By the time he arrived home that night around eleven, Grace had been tucked into bed, asleep for hours. She and Mack had talked for a few minutes, but then Jessie had left for her place. Since then,

174

they'd only talked on the phone.

Today, they both had the day off, and in another hour, Grace's birthday party was due to start. As Jessie searched through her closet, her own excitement grew. When Grace found out what they had planned for her, she was going to go crazy. What little girl wouldn't? A whole week in Florida, including lunch with her favorite fairy tale characters. Jessie was ecstatic about the trip herself.

She grabbed the plain yellow top, held it up, and then tossed it back onto her bed. She loved the color, but it didn't love her. Any other day, she might not care how it looked on her, but Mack's ex-wife would be there today. Bethany had called Mack during the week to confirm she'd be at the party. With Bethany there, Jessie wanted to look her best. She skipped over the striped shirt and the bright orange one she'd picked up for Halloween. The last thing she wanted to look like was a giant pumpkin. Then her gaze settled on the dark gray sweater she'd grabbed on clearance at the end of last winter. *This will do.*

Jessie finished dressing and then spent a few extra minutes doing her hair and makeup. Most days, she only wore a touch of eyeliner and lip gloss. Today, she added some blush and eye shadow. When she was satisfied with her appearance, she drove to Peggy Sue's.

Peggy Sue's Coffee Shop and Bakery made the best sweets on the entire North Shore. Everyone in town ordered their cakes for special occasions, and Grace's birthday was no different. "I'm here to pick up a birthday cake," Jessie said when it was her turn. As usual on a Saturday morning, customers sat at every table and a steady line of people remained at the front counter.

"For the Ellsbury party?" Skye Hogan asked. She was Jessie's age, and they'd gone to high school together. Skye worked as an office assistant part-time during the week for a lawyer in Salem and helped her parents out on the weekend.

"That's the one," Jessie answered, not at all surprised

that Skye knew of her and Mack's relationship. By this point, Jessie doubted anyone didn't know.

"Be right back." Skye disappeared into the back room.

While she waited, Jessie looked around the crowded shop until she noticed Tony Bates at the table in the far corner. The fact that Tony was drinking coffee and eating didn't surprise her, but the person with him did. Catrina, Striker's younger sister.

With Skye still in the back room, Jessie crossed to the table more to appease her curiosity than anything else. Sure enough, when she reached them, Tony and Catrina were talking about something as they drank their coffee.

"Hi, Tony. Cat."

They looked at her. "Hey, Jessie. Shouldn't you be at Mack's for his daughter's birthday party?" Tony asked.

"Heading over there now. Just grabbing the cake. You guys have anything special going on today?"

Tony raised his coffee as Cat answered, "I'm meeting Kelsey here. She's late."

"And I was just leaving when Cat walked in. I told her she could have the table." He pushed back his chair. "Have a nice weekend, ladies." And just like that, the town's resident playboy left.

"You're all set, Jessie." Skye appeared at the counter with a large cake box.

"Have a nice day, Cat, and say hello to Kelsey for me."

When Jessie got back outside, she placed the large cake box in her trunk and drove toward Mack's house.

Rose and Matthew Ellsbury's sedan and another car with New York plates were parked in the driveway when Jessie pulled up. She'd hoped to get there before Bethany, but unless Mack had another friend who lived in New York, Bethany had already arrived. Jessie didn't know how that was possible unless Bethany had left her place ridiculously early or driven down yesterday and stayed in a hotel.

With a gift bag hanging from her arm, Jessie carried the

cake up the front walk where purple and pink balloons swayed near the stairs. Resting the cake box on the railing, she managed to ring the bell. Mack had given her a key the previous weekend, but with his parents and ex-wife there, she figured the doorbell was a better option.

"Jessie, come in. Do you need help with that?" Mack's mom opened the door.

"I've got it. Do you know where Mack wants it?" She looked around, but didn't see anyone other than Rose.

"Outside. He has most of the food out there."

That made sense. The weather forecast called for sun and ten kindergarteners were expected today; nobody in their right mind would want that many children running around the house.

Outside, Mack had set up several folding tables. Pink and purple balloons were tethered around the deck and a piñata in the shape of a castle hung from the swing set. Mack's dad worked on filling up a cooler with juice boxes, and when he saw her, he took the cake from her hands.

"Grace has been waiting for you. She's excited to show you what we got her."

Jessie didn't see Grace anywhere, but she did see Mack and Bethany by the swing set. With his back to her, he hadn't yet noticed her arrival.

The clubhouse door attached to the swing set opened, and Grace's head popped out. When she spotted Jessie, she pushed the door all the way open. A furry creature darted out first, followed by Grace.

"Jessie, look what Grammy and Grampa got me!" She ran as fast as her little legs would carry her past her parents, the dog running alongside her.

At Grace's outburst, Mack turned. When he saw her, he smiled then headed her way—with Bethany right behind him.

"They got me a dog!" Grace stopped inches away from her, the dog stopping right next to her. "And they got him some toys and a bed." She paused as if trying to remember if the dog had come with anything else. "And some bowls for food and water. His name is Socks."

Jessie held out her hand for the dog to sniff. "Did you name him?" When the dog approached, she scratched him on the head.

"Nope. He came with that name. Isn't he cute?"

All brown except for his four white paws, the dog was one of the cutest she'd ever seen. On the small side, it reminded her of the fox terrier she'd had growing up, but its ears were a little longer and his snout a little shorter. "He's very cute. Do you know how old he is?"

"Grammy said he's almost three, and he already knows how to do lots of things."

As Grace proceeded to demonstrate, Mack joined them, giving her a hug and a kiss. "I'm glad you're here," he whispered.

Across from them, Bethany gave her a dirty look, but she followed it with a curt *hello* before disappearing into the house. Not long after, the guests arrived, and Grace no longer had time for the adults. Instead, she and her friends set off on a game they concocted with Socks chasing after them, while the rest jumped into the bounce house Mack had rented. While the children did that, the adults congregated on the deck. With the exception of Bethany and two other parents there, everyone had grown up in North Salem and knew each other.

"It must be exciting living in New York City." Jessie heard one parent say to Bethany. She recognized the woman from around town, but until today hadn't known her name.

"There's always something to do," Bethany answered before going into more detail.

So far this afternoon, Bethany had spoken with almost everyone but her. In fact, after that curt *hello*, she'd not said another word to Jessie. While Jessie didn't want a long conversation with the woman, but the fact Bethany ignored her stood out.

Not that Jessie really minded. She wasn't interested in Bethany's stories anyway. Mack on the other hand…

She was definitely interested in him.

She headed toward the grill where Mack was flipping some mean burgers. Without any thought to the people around them, she slipped her arm around his waist. "I've missed you," she said, her voice low.

"I've missed you, too. This week was crazy." Satisfied with the food's progress, he closed the grill cover and turned his attention to her. "Do you need to be anywhere tonight?" He kissed her before she could answer. Not one of the hot passionate kisses like he'd given her the weekend before, but a soft tender one.

"Nope."

"Good. I thought we could give Grace our gift after her friends leave."

"Sounds like a good plan. Did you know about the dog?"

When they'd first moved in, Grace had told her she wanted a dog. She'd mentioned it several times since, but Mack had never hinted at wanting one.

"They checked with me beforehand. I told them it was fine as long as it wasn't a puppy and not over thirty pounds."

Jessie watched Grace scratch the dog's belly. "You're never going to get her into bed tonight. She's going to want to play with him all night."

Mack's cheek brushed against hers as he leaned in to her ear. "I know the feeling. I'd love to play with you all night long."

Heat scorched her face, and she prayed no one had heard him. "Not tonight with Grace around."

He tugged her earlobe. "That doesn't mean I can't wish it." He pulled away then, his attention once again on the food, leaving her to wish for the very same thing.

Although a little chaotic, the party went smoothly considering the children and the dog running around. The only real disaster occurred when Mack left a plate of hot dogs unattended and Socks decided they looked good for lunch. Even with that little mishap, everyone had plenty of food and fun, including Jessie—despite the evil daggers Bethany threw her way all afternoon. Like Mack, though, she silently rejoiced when everyone except his parents and Bethany left. Finally, they could give Grace their birthday gift. Jessie doubted it would trump the dog from her grandparents, but she thought it would earn a close second.

As a team, everyone worked to clean up the backyard. While the children and their parents had been good about throwing away their trash, uneaten food remained out. "If you don't mind bringing in the cake, I'll handle the trash," Mack said. Two large trash bags sat near the deck, overflowing with everything from wrapping paper to unfinished hamburgers.

Jessie grabbed the cake and headed inside while Mack's parents closed up the folding tables.

"Mack mentioned you and he got Grace a joint gift."

Jessie looked up when she heard Bethany. She hadn't realized the other woman had followed her inside, but there stood Grace's mom with extra party plates in her hands.

"We're going to give it to her as soon as we're done with this." Jessie put the cake into its original box and then stored it in the refrigerator.

Stone-faced, Bethany advanced on her. "Word of advice, Jessica. Stay away from my family."

Jessie stared at the woman, shocked by the animosity she heard. "Excuse me?" Had Bethany just told her to stay away from Mack and Grace?

"You heard me just fine." Bethany crossed her arms. "Mack and Grace are not your family. They're mine."

Jessie understood Bethany claiming Grace as her family. Grace was her daughter and Bethany might feel threatened. Mack, however, was not her husband and hadn't been for a while. He could spend time with whomever he wanted.

"Grace is your daughter, I get that." Jessie didn't want a scene in Mack's kitchen, but then again, she didn't want Bethany pushing her around. "I'd never do anything to interfere in your relationship with her. But you and Mack are divorced now. Whether we spend time together or not is none of your business." She managed a calm, cool voice although, inside, her blood boiled with anger. Who did Bethany think she was?

The woman took a step closer. "People make mistakes. We have history together and a child. That supersedes any little fling he's having with you now. Besides, do you really think he'd prefer you to me? Just look at the two of us." A smug, conceited expression settled on Bethany's face and Jessie's hand itched to slap it away.

While she'd never deny that Mack and Bethany would forever be linked because of Grace, Jessie didn't think for a second he'd pick Bethany over her. "Think what you want, but you're wrong."

"He might call you when he needs a babysitter or a night of sex, but he'd never settle for you when he can have me."

Before Jessie could respond, the sliding door into the kitchen opened and Mack appeared with his parents, Grace, and Socks. "We're in good shape out there. It's time to give Grace the rest of her presents."

Without another word, Jessie walked around Bethany. No matter what, she planned to enjoy giving Grace her gift. If Bethany wanted to be a cold bitch, so be it.

"Before we give her the one from both of us, I have a small gift just from me." Remembering how much she'd enjoyed unwrapping presents, she'd picked up a small gift at the mall.

"I have my gift for her, too." Bethany grabbed something from her purse and joined everyone in the living room.

Seated on the floor with Socks next to her, Grace looked between her presents. "I don't know which to open first."

Bethany leaned forward, her breasts almost falling out of the low-cut top she wore. "Why not save the one from Jessie for last since it's the biggest, and open mine first since it is the smallest?"

Jessie had learned enough about Bethany today to know that size had nothing to do with her suggestion. Bethany assumed her gift had the biggest *wow* factor.

Going along with her mom's suggestion, Grace peeled off the paper, letting it fall around her. "They're earrings just like Mom's!" Grace said after she opened up the black jewelry box.

"Now be careful with those. They're real diamonds." Bethany returned the hug her daughter gave her before throwing Jessie a smug smile.

"Look, Jessie." Grace turned toward her.

Stunned, Jessie looked at the earrings. She didn't know a lot about jewelry, but she suspected the diamonds were close to half a carat each. Who gave that kind of gift to a six-year-old?

"You bought her real diamond earrings?" Mack asked, his voice heavy with disbelief. "She still loses her shoes. How do you expect her to keep track of those?"

Bethany gave no outward appearance that Mack's words fazed her. "She doesn't have to wear them now. You can always put them in a safe place until she's older if that makes you feel better."

Her idea held merit, but Jessie kept her mouth closed as the tension in the room grew.

"Why don't you open another present, Grace?" Rose asked from across the room.

Mack's expression said he wanted to say more, but he took his mom's advice and handed Grace the next present. "This one is from Jessie and me."

Oblivious to the tension, Grace ripped off the princess-covered wrapping paper, and opened the box. First, she pulled out the plastic tiara with the fake gemstones. Next, she grabbed a piece of paper with something on it that Mack had made on his computer. Since Grace's reading was limited, he'd included pictures such as an airplane and a castle.

"Get," Grace said. "What's this word?" She pointed to the paper.

"Ready," Mack answered.

"Get ready for," Grace's voice trailed off her eyes taking in the pictures. When she put it all together, her eyes got big. "We're going to Florida!" She leapt to her feet, dancing while wearing the tiara. After a few twirls around the room, she hugged Mack. "This is the best present ever!"

Mack grinned from ear to ear as well. "It's from Jessie, too. She's coming."

Grace launched herself at Jessie—with just enough enthusiasm to set Bethany scowling at her.

"I'm going to Florida!" Grace bounced away toward her grandparents, the last gift still unopened, but Jessie kept silent. After real diamond earrings, a dog, and a trip, the new dollhouse furniture she'd bought would look lame.

***

"What a day." Mack sat next to Jessie and she leaned into him. It was the first chance all day for them to have some alone time. His parents had stuck around for dinner, as had Bethany. While his parents had left not long after, his ex-wife had stayed until Grace's bedtime. "She was fighting it, but I bet she's sound asleep now. Her eyelids were half-closed when we tucked her in."

In the past, they'd tucked Grace in together when she visited. Tonight, with Bethany around, Jessie had hung back and allowed her mother to do it instead, even though seeing Mack and Bethany walk upstairs together had torn her up inside. "She had a busy day with lots of excitement."

Mack pulled her back against him as he reclined. "Did you see her expression when she opened the gift from us? I wish I'd taken a picture."

That expression and the one on Bethany's face were burned into her memory. "I did. I'm not sure which gift she liked best—the dog, the trip, or those earrings."

"What the hell was Bethany thinking, diamond earrings for a six-year-old? I have no problem with her buying Grace some nice jewelry, but those are ridiculous." Mack spat out the words.

Jessie agreed, but rather than further comment on the silly gift, she said, "You'll just have to hold them for now." Then she changed the subject all together. "I enjoyed visiting with your parents. It was too bad Erin and Marcus couldn't stay longer. Brianna didn't want to leave."

Mack's hand snuck under her sweater. His skin was still cold from when he'd taken the dog outside and goose bumps formed on her stomach. "I thought everyone would never leave tonight." His hand continued upward until it reached her bra. Then it pushed the fabric back and caressed her breast. "My parents are crazy about you. They told me on separate occasions how happy they are we're together."

His statement brought to mind someone else's feelings and unease sneaked through her stomach. She didn't blame Bethany for wanting Mack back, if that was, indeed, what she'd meant by her comment, but Jessie didn't have any intention of breaking things off just because his ex-wife wished Mack was still hers.

"You okay?" Mack's hand paused.

Jessie cleared Bethany's expression from her mind. "Yeah, why?" No, she wasn't 100 percent okay, but Mack didn't need to know about her and Bethany's conversation.

Switching his hand to the other breast, he caressed that one too. "You're stiff all of a sudden."

Forget about Bethany. She's just being a bitch.

Determined to enjoy their time together, she inserted her hand between their bodies and ran it down the length of him. "I'm not the only one," she said, her boldness taking her by surprise. In fact, a lot of the things she'd done lately had surprised her, and she loved it. For the first time, she felt not only sexy and desired, but also part of something besides her own immediate family.

He groaned despite his best efforts. All she had to do was touch him and he wanted to carry her upstairs. Who would've thought Jessica Quinn, the skinny girl from high school, would be able to do that? Definitely not him—or any of the other guys in town since she'd stayed single for so long. A fact he'd be forever grateful for. Just thinking about what might have happened if Tony or Striker had asked her out before he'd moved back turned his blood to ice.

"And whose fault is that?" He let his free hand wander down her stomach and inside the front of her jeans, then down more so he could touch her through the cotton panties she wore.

"Mine?" Her voice came out half question/half moan, and he pushed her panties off to the side so he could touch her skin.

"Damn right. Now what should we do about it?" So far, they'd only been intimate when Grace wasn't in the house, but that didn't seem like a permanent solution.

Jessie's breathing became ragged. "We can't do anything, can we?"

"As long we're not too loud and we lock the door, we're good."

She sucked in a deep breath when he touched her again. "Are you sure?" She sounded like she'd run a whole marathon.

"Positive," he said, his lips inches from her ear.

Satisfied with his answer, she wiggled away from him

then stood. Her sweater remained bunched up under her breasts, and her cheeks were flush as her chest rose and fell. Without so much as a single word, she held out her hand.

Unlike in the past, she gave him the control, that one little action signaling just how much she trusted him, whether she realized it or not. In no time, he had them naked and in his bed. But before they could take things any further, his cell phone rang. At first he ignored it. He wasn't expecting any calls, Grace was safely tucked into bed, Jessie was in his arms, and it wasn't the ringtone he'd set for work.

After several rings, it stopped—only to start up again.

"Maybe you should get that."

He tore his mouth away from her neck. "They can leave a message."

Again, the phone stopped and he moved from the sensitive skin on her neck back to her lips, his hands teasing her the way another part of his body wanted to.

The third time the phone rang, she pulled his hand away and broke free from his kiss. "It must be important, Mack."

With a grunt, he grabbed the phone. *Someone better be dying.* "Hello." His voice came out as a growl.

"Hi, Mack. It's Bethany."

His ex-wife's voice sent a litany of curses through his head. "Now's not a good time." He should've turned the ringer off; then she could've called all night and they never would've heard it.

"My car broke down. Can you pick me up at the garage? I wouldn't have called, but they can't fix it tonight."

"I'm with Jessie. Take a bus, Bethany." Bethany was a grown woman. She should be able to handle her current problem.

"I don't think there are any around here."

Mack pinched the bridge of his nose. "What about a

taxi?"

Jessie's hand touched his arm. "What's the matter?"

Mack moved the phone away from his mouth. "Bethany's car broke down, and she wants a ride."

Jessie rolled her lips together. "You should go get her. It is late."

"She can call a taxi."

"Would you want me taking a taxi this late at night?"

No.

"You'd never forgive yourself if something happened to her. Go get her and I'll stay here with Grace." Jessie climbed off the bed and grabbed her clothes.

Fuck, Jessie was right. He put the phone near his mouth again. "What's the damn address?" Mack wrote down the information and ended the call. "This sucks." He tossed the phone onto the nightstand but didn't get dressed.

Instead, he watched Jessie pull on her panties, plain blues ones tonight, nothing like the lacy thong she'd worn for him before. Not that it mattered. His body burned to be joined with her regardless of what she was or wasn't wearing. He contemplated finishing what they'd started and letting Bethany wait.

"The sooner you go, the sooner you'll be back."

"How did you know what I was thinking?"

"I know that expression and how you think," Jessie answered.

With an angry jerk, he picked up his clothes. "I'll be back as soon as I can. Are you sure you don't mind me picking her up? I'm more than happy to call her back and tell her to take a taxi. Trust me, she can afford one." Jessie's thoughtfulness continued to amaze him even now.

"Really. If I was in Bethany's position, I wouldn't want to take a taxi. I'll watch television or something."

***

Several people sat in the twenty-four-hour fast food

restaurant near the garage when Mack walked in. Seated near the far door, Bethany stood out, and not just because many of the customers were twenty-somethings. Even he wouldn't deny she was a beautiful woman. But while many of the men stared at her, drooling and most likely fantasizing about her, he felt nothing. Not a single tingle of desire touched him.

Mack stopped at her table, but didn't sit down. "I'm going to grab a coffee before we go. Do you want anything?" They had an hour and a half drive back, and he could use a caffeine boost.

She joined him at the counter, her arm brushing against his. "A diet soda."

All the way outside, she stayed glued to his side. Every time he moved a few inches away, she closed the gap again.

"Did they say what was wrong with the car?" It would be a long ride back if neither spoke. Since they'd done their usual superficial convo that morning, that didn't leave much now.

"They said some part needed to be replaced. I don't remember what they called it. They closed not long after my car got towed in." She tossed her hair over her shoulder and fluffed it up with her fingers. "Whatever it was, they have, but since they were closing, they didn't have time to work on it until tomorrow."

The way he saw it, she was lucky the guys worked Sundays. Most garages didn't. "Did you call a hotel already? If not, there are a few in Salem." He closed his door and started the car up.

The streetlights provided some illumination—not a lot, but enough to see her face. "I thought maybe I could stay with you and Grace." The beginnings of a smile tipped the corners of her mouth upward. "It'll give me a chance to spend more time with her. Then late tomorrow, you can give me a ride back to the garage."

He did have a spare room he could throw the air

mattress in, and he understood her desire to visit with Grace longer. Plus, it would save him the drive into Salem tonight.

"It'll be like before, with the three of us together." Her fingers touched his arm and slid down to his hand.

With a jerk, he put his free hand on the steering wheel. "You can stay, but you'll have to take the air mattress or the couch."

"An air mattress is fine." She folded her hands together and didn't touch him again, but she shot looks at him the entire ride home.

Jessie and Grace sat at the table when he returned home, a glass of milk and a left over cookie from the party in front of each of them.

A knot of emotion clogged his throat at the sight.

"Mommy, didn't you go home?"

"I left, but got stuck, so I'm staying the night with you, and I'll be here all day tomorrow."

Grace's expression stayed the same. "Okay." She turned her attention to him. "Can I have more milk?"

It didn't escape him that Grace appeared unaffected by Bethany's announcement. Grace had always been closer to him, and since the divorce, their bond had only grown stronger. "You need to go back to bed. What are you doing up anyway?"

"She had a bad dream, so we came in here to talk about it." While Grace hadn't reacted to Bethany's announcement, Jessie had. Even now, her mouth tightened again as she clenched her glass.

After dropping a kiss on his daughter's head, he pulled back her chair. "Do you feel better now, buddy?"

When she nodded, he picked her up. "Then back to bed. Who do you want to tuck you in, me or your mom?"

He expected a plea for just a few more minutes, or even a request to stay in his bed because of the bad dream. "Can Jessie put me back?"

Bethany crossed her arms and sent daggers at Jessie.

"If that's what you want." He thought she'd say him, but if she wanted Jessie, it didn't bother him.

"She's getting too attached to Jessica." Bethany's voice echoed with jealousy after Jessie and Grace left.

Never in all their years together had Bethany acted jealous. Rather, he'd been the one affected by that emotion a time or two. Not that he was proud to admit it.

"I don't think they should spend so much time together."

"Don't go there, Bethany. I don't complain when she visits you and is around Harris, do I? Or any of the other men you've dated."

Bethany's facial expression faltered, and he caught a glimpse of disappointment.

"We're not together anymore. He moved out last month." Her calm collected mask slid back into place. "Besides, that is different. She never acted like he was her father. She treats Jessie as if she's her mother." Despite the calm façade, her voice leaked the anger she carried. "I'm her mother."

Maybe you should act more like a mother. The thought stayed in his head, testing all his willpower. "No one said you weren't, but Jessie's a part of my and Grace's life now. You'll just have to deal with it."

CHAPTER 13

Jealousy kept Jessie awake much of the night. The unfamiliar emotion took root the moment Mack and Bethany walked into his home and grew when she returned home.

At first, Jessie denied it. She told herself her chest and stomach hurt because she'd eaten too much. When she closed her eyes and pictured herself clawing Bethany's beautiful smile off her face, she'd chalked it up to anger. Bethany had been the one to ruin her and Mack's night together. By the time sunlight peeked its way into her room, she gave up and labeled what she felt as plain old jealousy, something she'd never experienced before. Sure, she'd experienced envy, but that was different. She envied people for what they'd accomplished, but did not feel any ill will toward them. But as the room brightened, Jessie wanted to march over to Mack's, pull Bethany out of the house, and drop her somewhere, telling her to find her own way back to the garage.

While she relished the thought, she recognized that particular fantasy would never play out. So rather than sit around and dwell on it, she prepared for the day. The original plan had been for the three of them to go hiking.

With Bethany around, she assumed they'd need to alter their itinerary, but either way, she didn't intend to leave Bethany alone with Mack any longer than necessary. The warning Bethany delivered still echoed in her head. Not to mention, the looks Bethany cast Mack's way throughout the party and dinner spoke loud and clear: Bethany wanted Mack. Whether because she realized what she'd given up or just didn't like seeing someone else in Mack's life, Jessie didn't know. Thankfully, Mack hadn't shown an ounce of interest in his ex-wife, and Jessie trusted him.

The balloons from the party still swayed outside as Jessie climbed the front steps and the heavy door stood open. Through the screen door, she spotted Grace's dollhouse with the furniture and dolls sprawled across the floor, indicating the little girl was up and about.

Jessie opened the screen door without a sound. She assumed the kitchen was the place to stop first, and she was right. Unfortunately, she'd picked the wrong time. At the counter, Mack and Bethany stood together—and Bethany's lips were locked with his.

Jessie watched his hand move toward his ex's shoulder, although Jessie wasn't sure if it was to push her away or pull her closer.

Unable to breathe, Jessie reached for the wall to steady herself then retraced her steps. She made it into the living room when Grace flew down the stairs and skidded to a stop near her.

"Jessie you're here." The little girl's voice forced air back into her lungs. "Daddy's making pancakes for breakfast." She latched onto Jessie's hand. "Come on." Grace pulled her hand. "He's putting chocolate chips in mine."

Back in the kitchen, Bethany and Mack remained near the counter, but they were no longer kissing.

"Daddy, Jessie's here," Grace announced, her cheerful voice breaking through the tension in the room.

Mack's head snapped in her direction, an angry

expression on his face. When their eyes met, the anger disappeared and a forced smile replaced it. "I didn't hear you come in." Mack walked past his ex-wife and embraced her. "I'm making pancakes for breakfast. Do you want some?" He pressed a feather-light kiss on her lips.

No, she didn't want pancakes; she wanted an explanation. And maybe to hit Bethany with the pancake griddle.

"Can we talk in the other room?" She forced a calm voice, no easy task when Bethany stood only feet away in one of Mack's t-shirts. The damn thing only came to mid-thigh.

The anger she'd noticed in him a few minutes earlier returned, and he glared over at Bethany. "Watch the stove so Grace's breakfast doesn't burn. Grace, your milk is on the table."

He knows I saw. Was he mad because she'd caught them or angry because Bethany had made an advance? And why the hell was the woman wearing his clothes? Jessie needed answers, but she didn't want to come across as a jealous shrew either.

"What just happened in there?" she asked as soon as they entered the other room. Despite her best efforts, her words came out as more of an accusation than a mere question. "I walked in and you two were kissing. And she's wearing your clothes."

"It's not what you think." He placed his hands on her shoulders. "She kissed me, not the other way around." The concern and worry in his voice ate away at the anger simmering in her chest. "The only woman I'm interested in kissing is you, and I let her know that. As for the shirt, she needed something to sleep in. She had nothing with her."

When she'd seen Bethany in the shirt, she'd not considered the woman hadn't planned on staying the night. Of course she had no clothes with her.

"Bethany slept on the air mattress in the spare room

upstairs. I stayed in my room alone, thinking about you and what we never finished last night."

The heat in his voice warmed her entire body.

The image of Mack and Bethany kissing stayed in her head, but she didn't call him a liar. So far, he'd never given her any reason to doubt him, and kissing him sounded like something Bethany would do.

"We're good, then." She intended a cheerful tone, but failed, judging by the unconvinced expression on Mack's face. "Really, Mack. Everything is fine." She wrapped her arms around him and took possession of his mouth.

Mack's hands traveled down her back and settled on her butt. Then he pulled her against him. "I wish we were alone right now," he said, his voice low and husky.

The combination of his words and hard body against hers chased away the memory of him and Bethany. "Me, too." She kissed him again.

"Pancakes are done!" Bethany's voice rang out and the heat pulsing through Jessie's body changed to pure ice.

While Grace and Mack worked on eliminating the stack of pancakes, Bethany shot dirty looks in her direction. Rather than retaliate, Jessie ignored her and chose to listen to Grace's constant chatter. Between the forkfuls of food, the little girl jumped from one topic to the next, one minute talking about her birthday party, and the next, about the upcoming trip. When she wasn't talking or eating, she slipped pieces of her breakfast to Socks. The dog hadn't left his spot beside her chair since they all sat down. Mack either hadn't noticed or didn't care because he didn't tell her to stop, but Jessie feared if the dog ate much more he'd get sick.

"Can I wear my new boots for the hike?" Part of her birthday present from her aunt had been a pair of black suede boots.

"Those aren't the type of boots you wear hiking," Mack answered. "Besides, that might not be a great activity for today with your mom here."

"You promised, and Mommy can come, too."

For the moment, Bethany stopped casting the evil eye at her and looked over at Grace. "I thought maybe you, me, and your dad could go to the zoo or maybe the aquarium."

"Daddy and Jessie promised to take me on my first hike today. I want to do that." The same stubborn tone Jessie often heard in Mack's voice resonated in Grace's now.

Bethany's lips pressed together. "You can do that some other time. Don't you want to spend time with just me and your dad?"

Grace's perfectly done braids swung back and forth. "No. Jessie promised she'd help me get pretty leaves and rocks for my fairy village."

"Since she promised, I guess we better all take that hike today." Bethany's mouth twisted in an ugly scowl. "We don't want the village not to have enough leaves and rocks."

"Bethany, you hate hiking. You'll be miserable."

"It's what Grace wants to do." She rubbed her daughter's arm. "I'll survive for one day."

She might survive, but Jessie doubted *she* would. Spending the entire day in the woman's company yesterday had been bad enough. Yet she couldn't leave Bethany alone with Mack either, so that left her no other option than to suck it up for another day.

***

He watched Grace show another leaf first to Jessie and then to her mom before she added it to her collection bag. Then Grace said something to the two women and proceeded forward on the trail. As far as trails went, the one he'd picked was simple. Knowing how much Bethany hated anything to do with nature, and considering this was his daughter's first hike, he'd picked the easiest one he knew.

When Grace paused again, his ex-wife threw an exasperated look in his direction but didn't speak.

"I think you have enough for now," he said as he stopped near the little group. "If we're going to finish the whole trail today, we need to keep moving." What he meant but didn't say was, if they were going to finish and get Bethany to the garage before it closed, they needed to keep moving. No way in hell did he want her spending another night with him. One night had been bad enough. When she'd asked to stay, he'd figured it would be no big deal. He had an extra room and they did maintain a cordial relationship despite their divorce. He'd never imagined she'd kiss him.

What the hell had she been thinking? Not once since their divorce had she tried such a stunt. Of course, Jessie had picked that moment to walk in. He wasn't lucky enough to have her walk in five minutes later.

They started moving again, but didn't make it far when Jessie paused and picked up a bird's nest that had fallen from a tree branch. She showed Grace, who added it to her bag.

"That's going to be one crowded village," he said, coming up next to them.

"Jessie promised to help me make it bigger." Grace looked at him and smiled.

Of course she had. She treated Grace like a daughter, and that was just one of the many reasons he loved her. Damn, he hoped Bethany's little stunt that morning hadn't hurt their relationship. She'd accepted his explanation and said things were good, but she'd remained quieter than usual today.

If he'd walked in on her with an ex who was only half-dressed, the shit would've hit the fan. In fact, he might not have even stuck around long enough to hear an explanation. Thank God Jessie had a more understanding nature. But even though she did, he needed to make sure something like that never happened again—which brought him back to getting their hike done and Bethany on her way.

"Let's keep moving. No more breaks until we're back at the car."

For the most part, Grace did a fantastic job on her first hike. The only reason he carried her on his shoulders the last quarter mile was because she'd slowed down quite a bit. After walking for about three and half miles, he understood her slower pace and would've let her finish on her own if he hadn't been in a rush. The garage closed at four and his watch already read two o'clock.

"That was better than I expected," Bethany said from the backseat.

He'd thought the same thing, but not in terms of the hike. Rather, he'd expected Bethany to bitch and moan the entire time like the one and only time they'd tried camping together. It'd gone so poorly that after the first night, they'd packed up and stayed in a hotel. Today, though, she'd kept any complaints to herself.

"And it tired out *our* daughter. She's already asleep."

Mack cringed at the added emphasis Bethany put on the word *our*. If they'd been alone, he would've said something. Instead, he took Jessie's hand and squeezed it.

The car ride that afternoon would go down as the quietest and most uncomfortable in history. With Grace asleep, she couldn't fill the car with her usual chatter, much to Mack's disappointment. And when they reached their destination, he'd never been so happy to see a garage.

"It's all set. Thanks for the ride today. Tell Grace I love her when she wakes up and I'll see you both next weekend," Bethany said when she returned to the car where he waited.

Next weekend? She'd come this weekend, so Grace could skip the next visit. "Grace has her school picnic next weekend, remember?" Bethany had her faults, but she was an organized woman who didn't forget changes in her schedule.

"I know, but you said it was a family picnic. I *am* Grace's mother, so I thought I'd come, too. It'll give me a chance to meet more of her friends." The cold stare she threw in Jessie's direction canceled out Bethany's smile. The one she'd not intended for him to see, judging by the fact she leaned close to his window, giving him an unobstructed view of her breasts. A view that at one time would've had him ready to go, but now did nothing for him.

The last place he wanted Bethany was in North Salem again next weekend. "It is a family event, but that's a long drive just for a school outing." He couldn't tell her outright not to come. "The kids usually run around. It's a little like a zoo. Maybe you should just wait until Grace's holiday concert to meet her other friends."

She waved a hand in front of her. "I don't mind the drive. I'll call you during the week and let you know where I'm staying. If I can get here early enough on Friday, I'll stop in and see Grace."

Bethany walked away before he could speak again. With any luck, she'd change her mind between now and then. It happened all the time. Maybe if he hoped and prayed enough, it'd happen again.

"Anywhere you want to go on the way home?" He glanced at Jessie, but she didn't notice as she glared after his ex-wife, her expression reeking of jealousy.

Rather than starting the car, he reached for her chin and turned her face toward him. "You have nothing to worry about."

"Who said I was worried?"

You did. "I don't know what she's up to, but it doesn't matter, Jessie. I love you."

Before she said anything, she kissed his cheek. "Really, Mack, I'm not worried. I trust you."

Her tone sounded normal. Her smile looked sincere, yet he doubted her words and didn't blame her for the feelings she had. She'd witnessed Bethany coming on to him all weekend and the kiss that morning. While he knew it had meant nothing and had told her so, he understood how she might have issues with it.

"Good. I'm glad. And I promise to never give you any reason not to." He let the matter go after that. Rehashing that morning's event accomplished nothing.

***

"I'm glad you found the time for dinner with your old man." Her dad sat on the couch while Jessie got them something to drink Monday night. He'd stopped by for their weekly father-daughter dinner, but the roast needed more time in the oven, so he'd taken a seat in the living room while they waited.

Her conscience already bothered her enough without his little reminder that she'd canceled their last few dinners. "Life's been a little crazy, Dad. I'm sorry. But Ty's feeling better and Sue is back from vacation, so my hours at the store should go back to normal."

"Just giving you a hard time. I know you've been busy at work and I'm glad you're seeing Mack."

She'd never come right out and told her dad she and Mack were together. She didn't need to; the town gossip chain had done that for her.

"It would've been nice if you told me. Instead, I heard about how you spent the night from Mrs. Mitchell."

Jessie squirmed in her seat. Having her dad assume she had sex was one thing; having him know it for a fact… well, that was something different.

"You okay with him having an ex-wife and a kid? Raising someone else's kid is different than raising your own. Not everyone can do it."

She loved them both and didn't care that Grace wasn't her daughter. Up until last weekend, she hadn't cared that Mack had an ex-wife either. Since then, her opinion had changed. If Bethany continued her behavior from last weekend, Jessie feared she'd lose it and tell the woman off—or worse.

"No matter what, that little girl will always keep Mack and his ex-wife involved in each others' lives."

Once again, she saw them kissing in his kitchen. Mack insisted she'd come on to him and she believed him. But if Bethany kept doing that, would Mack eventually succumb? A lot of men would take one look at Bethany and fall to their knees, begging for her attention.

"I'm not saying you should stop seeing Mack. He's a good guy from a good family, but children complicate relationships."

Her father spoke from experience and she appreciated his concern. "Things are great between us, Dad." She just hoped they stayed that way. "Maybe Mack and Grace can join us for dinner next week."

Her father nodded. "I was going to suggest that myself."

His words stayed with her all night. About two years after her mother died while giving birth to her, her father had remarried a woman he'd met though a mutual friend. Whether he'd remarried because he loved Sheila or because he wanted a mother for her, Jessie didn't know. She *did* know that Sheila never treated her like a real daughter. Not that she was ever cruel, but she never treated her the same way Maureen O'Brien treated Charlie. When Sheila and her dad divorced around her sixth birthday, Jessie had been sad but not heartbroken. And from what she remembered, her dad hadn't been heartbroken either. Instead, he'd moved them out of their apartment and in with her grandparents. Then he'd gone on with life as if nothing had happened.

In her case, however, she already loved Grace like she would her own biological daughter. Her sticking point was Bethany. Her dad was correct; Bethany would always be in Mack's life. Jessie could handle that. What she didn't know was if she could handle Bethany always throwing herself at him. Mack claimed she'd never done it before and she was only doing it now because she'd recently become single. He reassured her that once Bethany landed another guy, she'd ignore him again. While Jessie agreed Bethany could land any guy she wanted in record time, she believed her recent interest stemmed from more than being single again. In Jessie's opinion, the woman had realized what she'd tossed out and now regretted it.

Whatever the case, Jessie didn't plan on letting Bethany worm her way into Mack's heart again. Both he and Grace deserved better than Bethany.

CHAPTER 14

"I thought you had tomorrow off?" Mack asked Jessie Friday night as they cuddled together on his bed. Earlier that night, Bethany had stopped by and took Grace back to her hotel in Salem for the night, leaving Jessie and Mack alone. Much like the previous week, they'd had little time together since the weekend before. The only day they'd managed to see each other for more than ten minutes had been Wednesday when she'd met him and Grace for dinner at The Jade Orient.

Jessie snuggled closer, absorbing the heat from Mack's naked body. "I did, but then I promised Patti she could have the day off so she can attend the picnic with her husband and son." She hated the idea of Bethany going with Mack and Grace, but she hated disappointing Patti, too. "I'll be here for movie night with you and Grace tomorrow."

Mack's hand drifted upward and he cupped her breast, his fingers fondling her nipple. "People call in sick all the time. There must be someone who could cover for you tomorrow." Pushing her onto her back, he replaced his fingers with his lips while he let his hand travel lower.

Her mind struggled to focus as his lips and tongue

feasted, and his fingers teased between her legs. "People would notice if I called in sick and then showed up at the picnic." She took a deep breath, her body hot everywhere. "You know that." She tried reaching for him, but he pushed her hand away then went back to teasing her again.

He lifted his head and pinned her in place with his heated gaze. "I expect you by my side for the holiday concert in December."

She could only nod once before his mouth came down on hers, his tongue mimicking the actions of his fingers until Jessie exploded. Then, as if satisfied with the accomplishment, he moved his hand away and slid inside.

Her pulse still pounded, but she no longer breathed heavily. Under her hand, Mack's heart continued to race, but his breathing sounded normal once again. He certainly knew how to push her right over the edge. Granted, she'd only had sex with one other man, but it had never been like this even in the very beginning before things turned ugly and Jeremy showed his true self.

"You're quiet. Everything okay?" Mack's question invaded her thoughts.

"Perfect. You?"

"Never better. How could I not be? I've got a beautiful, naked woman in my bed. A guy doesn't need much more than that to be happy."

With no suitable reply, she propped herself up on her elbow and changed the subject. "This week, can you and Grace join my dad and me for dinner?"

"It's time for the 'Are you good enough for my daughter?' test, huh?"

Jessie laughed. "The what?"

"Maybe he called it something different, but he wants to make sure I'm good enough for you. I already have my test prepared for when Grace starts dating," Mack answered with a straight face, and she couldn't tell if he was serious or not. "My test will involve a shovel and a shot gun."

"You're joking, right?"

"No. Any guy who dates Grace will know just what will happen to him if he ever hurts her. The same goes for anyone who tries to hurt you."

Somehow, she had a feeling her father and grandfather would've reacted in a similar manner if they'd known how Jeremy had treated her. Maybe that was why she'd never shared much about their relationship with them or anyone else and why she'd not brought him around her family much. "Okay. Does that mean you'll come?"

"This week might be tight, but I'll try. If not, the week after." Mack became silent and his brows dipped.

"What's the matter?"

Mack shook his head. "Nothing. Just thinking. I don't know if I've ever had a real conversation with your father. I know I haven't seen him since I moved back."

Jessie flopped down onto her pillow. "Trust me, he knows all about you and Grace. Mrs. Mitchell has filled him in— *including* how many times I've spent the night."

"That woman needs a hobby."

She agreed 100 percent. "She does have hobbies, but unfortunately, gossiping tops the list."

***

Preparations for the annual elementary school family picnic were underway when Jessie drove by the Town Common Saturday morning. The two big bounce houses rented by the PTA were spread out on the grass, ready to be inflated. Folding tables decorated with streamers and balloons sat in front of the bandstand. Later, the tables would hold the various gift baskets donated for the afternoon raffle. Inside the bandstand, a local DJ who specialized in children's events set up his equipment. All in all, the entire Common looked like it did every year for this event. In the past, though, she'd had no interest in attending. This year, she'd like nothing more than to join the other families alongside Mack and Grace.

Instead, she'd be at the hardware store all day, mixing paint and selling plywood while Bethany went with them.

She ground her teeth at the thought of Bethany by Mack's side all day. If she believed Bethany would leave him alone and not flirt with him, she'd be fine with the arrangement. Okay, maybe not fine, but better about it.

But after Bethany's warning and behavior the weekend before, she didn't trust the woman for a nanosecond. Mack insisted Bethany would grow bored soon and move on. He didn't know she'd told Jessie to get lost. Jessie had considered telling him, but decided against it. Doing so wouldn't accomplish anything but damage the civil relationship he and Bethany had now, which, in turn, would hurt Grace.

He's not interested in her. He'd both told her and shown her that. Until he did otherwise, she'd trust him around his ex-wife, as well as any other women, even if it killed her.

The morning dragged on. Although a steady stream of customers came and went as they purchased what they needed for their late fall projects, the clock moved in slow motion with no end in sight. Jessie knew it was all in her imagination, but the feeling remained as she glanced at her watch.

"Don't smile too much." Sean dropped two cans of paint onto the counter, and then Taylor added two more.

"Hi, Sean. Sorry. My mind's somewhere else."

"I got that. You okay?" Even though she was now an adult, Sean still treated her like a kid sister. She'd never tell him so, but she loved him for it. As an only child who'd spent much of her time with her grandparents, she'd loved how Charlie and her brother treated her as more than just a friend.

"Fine. It's such a nice day that I'd rather be outside." *In between Mack and Bethany.* "Is this for the new master suite?"

Sean shook his head. "This is for Taylor's room."

That made more sense considering one can of paint

was red and another purple while the other two were primer. She'd noticed Taylor had been around town more and more. Since she now had her own room at Sean's house, she assumed that meant their brother-sister relationship was developing nicely despite Sean's past with his father.

"If you have time, could you help me with something?"

Never in her life had Sean asked her for a favor. Come to think of it, he rarely asked *anyone* for a favor.

"Of course." She rang up his purchase as they spoke.

Sean pulled his wallet from his pocket. "I want to surprise Mia when she comes back. Could you help with some decorating? Nothing crazy, but you know, pick out curtains, get a few rugs. Add some feminine touches."

Ideas formed as she tried to envision what Sean and Mia might like. She loved decorating and changing rooms around. "Sure. When will Mia be home?"

"Thanksgiving."

That gave her a few weeks. "Do you want me to pick out what I like or do you want to come shopping with me?"

Something akin to horror spread across Sean's face and Taylor laughed. "Pick out what you like and I'll pay you for it. I trust you."

"But not me?" Taylor asked, sounding a little hurt.

"Everything you picked out for your room is either purple or red, including the wall paint. I don't think Mia wants an entire house done in those two colors." When the hurt didn't disappear from his sister's face, he dropped an arm over her shoulders and pulled her closer. "You can help with something else, okay?"

The younger girl's expression brightened and Jessie saw the relief on Sean's face.

"Jessica Quinn, why didn't you tell me you had to work today?" a gruff voice called out.

Both Jessie and Sean turned and watched her grandfather approach the register. Since she never ran her schedule past her grandfather, she didn't know what to say.

"Sean, good to see you. This must be your sister. Nice to meet you." He clapped Sean on the back and then came around the counter.

"Mr. Quinn, this is Taylor. She's staying with me for the weekend. Taylor, Mr. Quinn was my boss in high school." Sean picked up two cans of paint and motioned for Taylor to do the same. "I'll call you later so you can get measurements, Jessie. Thanks."

"Off with you, too," her grandfather said when Sean and Taylor left. "You should be over at the picnic with Mack. I'll handle things here."

Jessie took the next customer in silence. Everyone in North Salem might already know her business, but she could at least attempt to keep things private. "It's a family picnic, Gramps, so I'm fine right here. I'll see Mack and Grace tonight."

"Bull. Your grandmother told me how that boy was looking at you when she saw you the other night, and I know how much time you spend together. You two are more than halfway to being a family."

Had her no-nonsense grandfather just insinuated she and Mack would get married? Sure, she'd thought of it a time or two since he told her he loved her, but she'd never mentioned it to anyone.

"I'm serious, Jessica. This is still my store, and I'm telling you to go. I remember how to run this place."

Arguing with her grandfather only achieved two things, a bad headache and a strong desire to scream. "I love you." She kissed his wrinkled cheek. "I'll see you later."

With the weather so nice and winter not far away, Jessie hated driving to the Town Common, but if she walked now, it would mean she'd have to either walk home much later from Mack's or have him drive her. While the crime rate in town remained low, she'd rather not walk home alone at eleven or twelve at night.

Many families, probably wanting to enjoy the beautiful

day, had walked to the Common that afternoon. Those who hadn't walked had parked in the library parking lot. After parking there, as well, she crossed the lot, spotting Amy Osborne, one of the elementary school teachers, walking with her son and daughter.

"Just like when we were in school," Amy commented when they all stepped on the grass.

Jessie glanced around and nodded. Everything looked much as it had when she'd attended the picnics. The only difference now being that the people who had been children back then were now the parents.

"Have fun." Amy and her children headed for the bounce houses.

People were spread out across the Common. Some sat on the blankets they brought with them, while others crowded around the tables that had been set up. Children of various ages danced to the kid-friendly music the DJ played, while the bounce houses swayed from the children jumping inside them.

While she recognized many faces, she didn't see Mack or Grace anywhere yet.

Making her way across the grass, she waved at friends, but kept an eye out. Then she spotted them. Not far from the bandstand where the children danced, Mack sat on a blanket with Bethany next to him. Since they both faced the dancers, she assumed Grace lurked in the group with her friends.

"Hey, Jessie," someone called out. Jessie turned to wave, but whoever it had been disappeared among the crowd. When she turned back, she saw Mack lean closer to Bethany and speak. Bethany said something then moved closer to him, her arm rubbing up against his, a big, fat, Cheshire-cat grin on her face.

Fury started in Jessie's stomach and exploded, almost choking her. The damn woman was at it again. Prepared for battle, Jessie marched in their direction. As she did, Mack said something else, and Bethany laughed and touched his thigh. When she didn't move it, Mack brushed it away, and then put some space between them again. The move should've calmed the anger boiling inside her, but it didn't. It only reinforced how brazen and determined the other woman remained.

When Mack looked in her direction, he smiled and stood, but all she could do was wave. If she even tried a smile it would come out as a grimace.

"I thought you had to work." He met her before she reached the blanket and hugged her.

She'd always found people who practically sucked each other's lips off in public annoying, yet she channeled all her love for Mack and kissed him as if no one was watching, using both her mouth and body.

"Gramps gave me the day off." She mentally patted herself on the back at the heat she saw in Mack's eyes when she pulled away.

He kissed her again, then led her to his blanket. "I'm glad he did. Grace was upset when I told her you couldn't come." Mack sat and pulled her down next to him. "She's in that crowd dancing. I just saw her pigtails fly by."

Jessie didn't even bother with a greeting. Instead, she focused on Mack as if Bethany didn't exist, and Mack never tried to pull his ex into their conversation. And, as they chatted, Bethany sulked. A sight Jessie found amusing.

***

"I'm going to take a break and the lovely president of the PTA is going to start calling numbers for the baskets. So if you bought raffle tickets, now is the time to pull them out." The DJ handed the microphone off to a woman Mack didn't know twenty minutes after Jessie joined him.

Uninterested in the raffle, the crowd of dancers broke up and wandered back to their parents or off to the bounce houses. He expected Grace to head back to them, because before she joined the children dancing, he'd instructed her not to go anywhere else without checking in with him or Bethany first. Grace pouted and whined from time to time, but she was a rule-follower. If he or anyone else in the family or at school told her to do something, she did it. Now though, the dance area was empty and Grace hadn't appeared.

"Did you see Grace?" he asked, scanning for her.

"She probably went with some friends to the bounce houses. She loves those," Bethany answered.

If she spent more time with Grace and paid attention, she'd know Grace wouldn't do that. "I told her not to go anywhere else."

"Maybe she needed the bathroom and couldn't wait to check in. I'll go see." Jessie headed for the temporary bathrooms set up behind the bandstand.

"I'm going to check the bounce houses. Stay here in case she comes back." He couldn't recall a single time Grace had disobeyed him on anything like this, but she was a kid surrounded by her friends. Kids followed their peers all the time.

When a search of both bounce houses and the craft table nearby turned up nothing, he started back for their blanket, hoping Jessie had found her or she'd wandered back. The sight of just Jessie and Bethany standing together froze the blood in his veins. He continued to survey the area as he walked, and he reminded himself this was North Salem not some huge city.

"I checked the bathrooms and asked some parents I passed." Jessie's voice echoed his own worry.

"She has to be here. This town is like Hicksville. Everyone is either related to each other or knows everyone else. Nobody would take her."

While Bethany might be close to the truth, he knew strangers did pass through town all the time, and it only took one messed-up person to snatch a little girl. Hard cold fear knotted inside his chest. As a member of law enforcement, he'd seen what could happen to a little girl like Grace both during his time with the Boston Police and now with the FBI.

He continued sweeping the area as he waited for his father, the police chief, to answer his phone. He might be jumping the gun. She could be playing with friends somewhere, but he wasn't taking any chances.

Every police officer on and off duty descended on the Common and search parties formed, spreading out from the Common in every direction.

"Maybe she walked home," Bethany offered as they crossed onto Fender Drive toward Peggy Sue's coffee shop.

"Why the hell would she do that?" Sure, she could've cut through the church parking lot and made it to the house with no problem, but she had no reason to.

"To see the dog. She was upset when you wouldn't let her bring him today."

Grace had cried a little, and she did love the dog. Still, he didn't picture her doing that.

"It's not a bad idea to check just in case," Bethany said.

Bethany had a point. "I'll call you if I find her." He took off at a dead run and prayed he found Grace inside with Socks. She'd seen him hide the extra key outside the week they'd moved in. If she had gone back to the house, she'd be able to get inside, assuming she remembered where he put the key. Knowing Grace, she remembered. The kid didn't forget anything.

The house remained empty and Socks still sat in his locked crate. The hands around Mack's heart squeezed tighter as he thought about his next move. If anyone hurt his little girl, they'd wish they'd never been born when he got done with them.

CHAPTER 15

Despite her best efforts, Jessie's mind kept bringing up horrific images and headlines from child abduction cases she'd seen on the news. *No, we're going to find her.* Jessie repeated the line in her head for at least the hundredth time. Still, her panic rose.

She reached the corner of Union and Pleasant Streets. When she heard her cell phone ring, hope flared. It had to be Mack saying they'd found her safe and sound. Stopping dead, she pulled the phone out, but the word *Gramps* appeared on the screen instead of *Mack*. Her grandfather didn't know they couldn't find Grace. While it felt like an eternity had passed, it had, in fact, been less than thirty minutes since they'd realized she was missing.

"Hi, Gramps, I can't—"

"Grace Ellsbury is here looking for you."

Had he said what she thought he said? "What?"

"Mack's daughter walked in, looking for you."

Her legs wobbled. "Keep her there. I'll be right there." She flew down Pleasant Street and didn't think to check traffic before she crossed the street and ran into the hardware store.

Jessie's heart stopped and she paused, her brain

processing what she saw. Grace sat in her office next to her grandfather, sucking on a lollipop. She was safe. No one had her.

Once Jessie's brain accepted the sight, she rushed forward and picked her up. "What are you doing here? Why did you leave the picnic?" Frustration slowly ate away at the relief in her chest. Did Grace have any idea of the hell she'd put everyone through?

"I want to come live with you." Tears glistened in Grace's eyes.

Stay calm. Don't shout.

"I don't want to move again." Grace sniffled.

"Grace, who said you're moving?" Jessie asked in a soothing voice as she sat her back down in a chair.

"Mommy did last night."

At the mention of her mom, Jessie realized Mack needed to know Grace was safe. "I'm going to call your dad and let him know where you are. Then you can tell me why you're upset."

Her hands shook when she pulled out her phone. Never in her life had such fear gripped her. Mack's phone rang only once before his anguished voice barked a hello.

She skipped the pleasantries. "I found her. We're at the store."

"Why the— I'll be right there." The line went dead.

"Your dad is on his way." Jessie looked at Grace who sat with her shoulders slumped and tears on her cheeks. "Do you want to tell me why you left without telling anyone? You know better than that." She knelt down and took Grace's hands in hers.

Grace's large sad eyes met hers and she wanted nothing more than to hug her again. "Last night, Mommy said she was going to ask Daddy to move to New York with her. She said she wants us to live together like before."

Jessie bit down on her lip and said, "That doesn't mean you'll move."

"I saw them kissing this morning, and they were sitting

really close at the picnic."

She'd seen them sitting close, too, but she'd chalked that up to Bethany's behavior rather than something Mack wanted. The kiss... How did she explain that one? And this wouldn't be the first time. The image of the last kiss she'd witnessed was burned into her memories.

Grace's bottom lip quivered. Right now, she had to focus on Grace. Everything else could wait. "Don't you want things to be like before?" In her experience, most children wanted their parents together.

Grace shook her head. "I like it here. If we move, I won't see Grammy and Grampa or Brianna or you. I want Daddy to stay here and be with you."

Jessie wanted the same thing, but if Mack wanted his ex-wife back, she wouldn't stand in the way. Grace deserved to have a traditional home with two parents who loved her. Something Jessie had always longed for growing up.

The office door flew open, and Mack rushed into the room. Without a word, he picked Grace up and hugged her as a few tears slid down his cheeks. "Why did you leave? You know never to go anywhere alone." He didn't release Grace as he spoke.

Before Grace said a word, Bethany arrived, her eyes red, and black mascara streaking down her face. "Maybe we should take her home and talk there." Bethany kissed the little girl.

Deciding they needed some privacy no matter what, Jessie stepped out of the office. She'd talk with Mack later about what Grace had said. Right now, they needed some private family time, and while she hated to admit it, Mack and Grace were not her family.

"You holding up okay?" her grandfather asked. He'd left the office when she'd arrived and now stood near the back counter where they always kept coffee for the regular customers.

A turbulent stream of fear, relief, and anger still swirled

around in her body. So far, she'd held it together, but not well enough to share anything with her grandfather. "I'm fine." Or at least, maybe she would be once she could talk to Mack and get some answers. That, of course, assumed she liked the answers she received. Grace wouldn't make up what she'd told her, but she might have misunderstood. And, of course, Jessie didn't know what Mack's reply had been. Grace also wouldn't have lied about them kissing. After all, why would a six-year-old make something like that up? *It could mean nothing.*

Maybe Bethany had come on to him again. Jessie could see her doing that. Yet, it had now happened *twice*. That, combined with how close they'd been at the picnic when she'd first arrived, made her now doubt Mack's explanation the morning she'd caught them kissing. True, she had seen him put space between them, but who knew what prompted that move?

"Why don't you go with Mack and help him sort things out with his little girl?" Her grandfather interrupted her thoughts. "I can stay here until Ty gets here."

Her emotional side said *Great idea.* Her logical self said *No.* Grace had her mom and dad, and right now, that was who she needed, not a third wheel. "Mack needs some time alone with Grace. But if you're sure, I'll head home."

Farther down, the office door opened. Bethany exited first, followed by Mack who carried Grace. For a moment, Jessie thought they were just going to leave, but then Mack headed for her while Bethany waited.

"I'm taking her home. Maybe she'll talk to me then. I'll call you later tonight." He sounded both worried and exasperated, which had her assuming Grace hadn't said much.

A pang of jealousy sliced through her. Bethany was returning home with him and Grace, but he hadn't asked her along. Jessie knew she shouldn't be jealous. Bethany was Grace's mother, but it sill hurt that Mack hadn't asked her to come home with them. "I'm going home, too." She squeezed Mack's forearm. "Talk to you later."

He took a step closer and placed a quick peck on her lips. Then he followed Bethany out.

Not a soul spoke on the short drive from the hardware store to the house. So far, Grace hadn't answered any of his questions. While he wanted to push to get some answers and then fix whatever the problem was, he managed to keep his trap shut. Whatever the problem, it had to be substantial. Grace, like any other little girl, had temper tantrums and the occasional bad day, but she normally wouldn't outright disobey him. He prayed she never did again. He'd never experienced fear like he had today. Even now, with Grace in the backseat, his hands trembled and his heart was up in his throat. When Jessie had called and told him she was with Grace, he'd almost cried.

"Come on, buddy." Mack lifted Grace out of the car. She'd stopped crying, but still looked sadder than he'd ever seen her. "What do you say I get you some milk and then you can tell us why you ran away today?"

Grace's head rubbed against his shoulder, but she still remained tight-lipped.

Mack poured her a glass of her favorite chocolate milk and even added one of the twisty straws she loved. Since he was at it, he poured himself a soda, although at the moment, he would love something stronger. "Okay, buddy, you know you can tell me anything, right?"

Grace nodded, but kept her eyes down.

"It's time to talk. Why did you leave today? You know better than that."

Grace looked at him then her mom before she spoke. "I don't want to move. I left to find Jessie and ask her if I can live with her. She wasn't at the store. Mr. Quinn was there and he called Jessie."

For some reason, he'd thought Jessie had found her and brought her to the store. He'd not entertained the idea she'd made it there herself. "We're not moving again, buddy. Why do you think we're moving?"

"Mommy. She said she was going to ask you ask to move, and this morning you kissed her."

He glared at his ex-wife, several choice words on the tip of his tongue. Did she *ever* think before she spoke? As for the damn kiss, Bethany had kissed him, but Grace had no way of knowing that.

Putting his anger on the back burner for now, he took Grace by the shoulders. "Your mom and I talked about this, Grace. You and I are not moving. North Salem is home now, understand? And your mom is going back to New York today." And if he had it his way, she'd not return anytime soon.

Grace went for her milk, her mouth still in a frown. "But you only kiss people you love like when Uncle Marcus kisses Auntie Erin."

If his daughter believed people only kissed when they loved each other, he was okay with that. She'd grow up soon enough and learn the truth about that and so much more.

"And when you kiss Jessie."

"You're right; people do kiss when they love each other." No good explanation emerged for why Bethany had kissed him.

"Then why did you kiss Mommy?"

He could strangle Bethany for creating this situation. A situation she'd not helped him explain at all.

"Your mom and I are friends, Grace. We'll always be friends, but we don't love each other like Uncle Marcus and Auntie Erin do." It didn't answer her question, but he hoped she'd be satisfied with it.

She took her time processing his response. "Do you promise we're not moving?"

"Promise." He couldn't stop himself from throwing a dirty look in Bethany's direction.

"And I'll visit Mommy in New York?" She looked at

Bethany.

"Either that or she'll come visit you here. Nothing is going to change."

"Good. I like it here. Can I go play with Socks now?" Her frown disappeared and, once again, his happy little girl appeared.

"First, you need to promise you'll never run away like that again. If you get upset like that about something, talk to either your mom or me, okay?" He waited for her answer.

Grace nodded, already half out of her seat.

"No matter what, is that understood?"

Grace nodded again.

"Go play and pick out a movie for tonight."

When Grace raced off toward the dog's crate, he turned to Bethany. Now that his daughter was safe, he let his anger loose. "Did you lose your goddamn mind? Why the hell did you tell her that?"

Bethany's annoyed expression remained the same. In fact, it hadn't changed since they'd walked into the house. "When I told her that, it was my intention to talk to you." She shrugged, her sweater slipping down her shoulder, exposing more skin. "I expected a different answer from you this morning." Long slender fingers with light pink nails curled around his arm. "We were so good together, Mack. If you give us another try, we could make it work. We could hire a part-time nanny and have our weekends to ourselves again. We could go out like we used to before Grace."

She never stopped amazing him. Her take on parenthood and his were polar opposites. Sure, he liked the occasional free Saturday when Grace spent time with her grandparents, but what Bethany proposed sounded awful. Already he felt as if he missed so much of Grace's life because of his job. Nothing in the world could take him away from her any longer than necessary.

"That's not the kind of life I want and not what I want

for Grace."

As if just realizing her top hung off her body, Bethany readjusted her sweater. "If you change your mind, let me know."

***

Jessie chewed her thumbnail until nothing remained, then switched to the nail on her ring finger. In the past few years, she'd stopped biting her nails, a bad habit she'd picked up in high school. Every once in a while, she'd start up again when she was stressed out or upset. The last time had been when her grandfather fell and broke his hip. It had taken months, but she'd broken herself of the habit. Until now.

The short talk with Grace replayed in her head. While she could explain Grace's comments about them moving, she couldn't explain the kiss Grace had seen. Especially since it wasn't the first time they'd been caught kissing. Every time Jessie closed her eyes, she pictured them in Mack's kitchen again, Bethany wearing his t-shirt, her lips locked on his. And Grace was correct: they *had* been sitting close enough to touch at the picnic. Had there been more to that kiss in his kitchen? Mack insisted she'd come on to him, and maybe she had. That didn't mean it hadn't caused him to have second thoughts about their relationship. They had a lot of history together, and at one time, he must have loved her.

Jessie shoved her hand into her pocket before she started on yet another nail. Chewing every nail off accomplished nothing; only talking to Mack would answer her questions.

She'd planned to join them for movie night tonight like she did almost every Saturday night. However, when he'd left the store that afternoon, he said he'd talk to her later, not *see* her later. Did that mean she shouldn't go over? Had Bethany decided to join them instead? Or had he been so relieved over finding Grace that he hadn't even thought of it? She wanted the last one to be true. Still, she remained on the couch.

Usually, they ordered pizza around five and started up the movie while they waited. It was quarter till now. Should she go over and confront Mack with her questions when Grace went to bed? Or should she stay here and let him make the first move?

Stay here, her heart told her. Bethany might still be there, and right now, she couldn't deal with the woman flirting with Mack as if she didn't exist. And besides, Mack might still be working things out with Grace. She could be a stubborn little girl.

Since Jessie was now planning for a night alone, she called for her own pizza and selected a movie—one adapted from her all time favorite book, the narrator had just finished setting up the story about to unfold when her phone rang around five-thirty.

"I thought you were joining us tonight?" Mack asked. His voice no longer shook with fear. "Grace won't let me start the movie until you get here."

Did your ex-wife leave? "I need to skip movie night. My head is about to split open." She experienced a pinch of regret at the lie. "Tell Grace I'm sorry, but all I want is to rest my head and go to bed early."

"I know the feeling." Mack accepted the lie without question, only making her guilt worse. "Do you need anything?"

The concern she heard made her want to slap herself. "No, I took some medicine and now I'm laying down."

"Call me in the morning and let me know if you're up for dinner at my mom's."

She'd not thought of the dinner invitation since Mack had asked her earlier in the week. "I will."

"If you need anything, call me." Once again, she heard concern in his voice. "Get some rest. I love you." He sounded 100 percent sincere, but hadn't Jeremy?

The headache Jessie claimed bothered her hit her not

long after her phone call with Mack, preventing her from finishing the movie. So, after popping some headache medicine, she turned in and decided to figure out what to do about dinner tomorrow when she woke up.

CHAPTER 16

The headache that started Saturday night turned into a full migraine by midnight. Even still, by earlier Sunday afternoon, her body once again felt normal—at least physically. Her head, though, remained a jumble of questions. Was Mack the type of guy who'd cheat on her? And if he was, how would she know for sure? She'd always suspected Jeremy had cheated on her, but she'd never had any concrete evidence, just suspicions and little things that didn't add up. Then, of course, there was Bethany. She'd straight-out told Jessie she wanted Mack back. Did she want to spend her time competing with the other woman? She'd put so much effort into putting herself back together after Jeremy that she didn't want to go backward. She wanted to keep moving forward with her life. A life she wanted with Mack and Grace, but not if it meant lots of drama thanks to Bethany—or any other woman for that matter.

At some point, she and Mack had to talk. It might not guarantee she'd get an answer she liked, but she needed to start somewhere. Today though, wasn't the day to do it.

After skipping dinner on Sunday, Jessie went out of her way to avoid Mack both Monday and Tuesday by covering for an employee who called in sick even though she'd opened the store both days and worked eight hours already each day. At any other time, she would've called the employees with the day off and asked them to come in. Only if she couldn't get anyone to cover would she stay. This time, she didn't even bother calling anyone else. Staying at the store gave her a perfect excuse in case Mack invited her over.

While she avoided seeing him, she still spoke with him on the phone each night. Unlike in the past, she kept their conversations short. Sunday, she claimed her head still bothered her and she couldn't talk. Monday, she told him she had work to complete for an accounting client. Tuesday and Wednesday, she pulled out the "I'm tired card" to end their conversation. Mack never questioned her. Each time, he accepted her excuses at face value. But on Wednesday, his tone insinuated he suspected she was avoiding him, which meant she needed to confront him soon, whether she was ready or not.

"The curtains I ordered for downstairs came in yesterday," Jessie told Sean Thursday afternoon. As promised, she'd started purchasing the necessary items to decorate his house and surprise Mia when she came home at Thanksgiving. "The things for the master bedroom won't be in until next week."

Sean sat on the other side of her desk. He'd stopped in on his way home from work to grab a new saw blade. "That's fine. I'm not done with the master suite anyway."

When she'd stopped for the window measurements, she'd seen what was to become the master suite and she wasn't surprised he still had work left to do. "Do you want me to start downstairs or wait until you're done?"

"Wait. I'm still sleeping in the living room." Sean stood and grabbed the blade he'd purchased. "Tony and Striker are coming over Sunday for the game. Why don't you and Mack come?"

No sooner did Sean mention Mack than her cell phone

rang. She glanced at the number and confirmed what she somehow already knew. "I'll ask him."

"You gonna answer that?"

"I don't recognize the number. If it's important, they can leave a message." She switched the phone to vibrate. "I'll talk to Mack about Sunday and let you know."

***

Something was up. He didn't know what, but since the school picnic and the incident with Grace, Jessie hadn't been herself. At first, he'd accepted her explanation. After all, people suffered from migraines all the time. Her reasons for not being around on Monday and Tuesday were valid, although he found it unlikely she couldn't find another employee to fill in on both days. However, her behavior on Thursday proved his suspicions. When he called and got her voice mail, he'd left a message like he always did. In the past, she'd called him back not long afterward. Yesterday, though, she'd sent him a text and nothing more. Whatever the problem, he needed an answer, and tonight he planned to get it. So, before leaving the office, he made sure Erin knew he'd be late picking up Grace, then headed for Jessie's apartment.

For the most part, she kept a regular schedule at the store unless her assistant manager needed the night off, so she didn't work Friday evenings. Since his suspicions arose, he'd been cognizant of her recent behavior. No matter how hard he tried, nothing jumped out at him as a cause. Yes, she'd appeared a little upset when Bethany showed up the previous Friday night to attend the school picnic, but once she and Grace left, Jessie had acted the same as always. He couldn't count Saturday because of all the stress Grace's actions had caused, and they'd not seen each other since, which brought him back to his original dilemma.

The lights in her apartment window confirmed she was home. Prepared for just about anything, he climbed the stairs and knocked. Right on cue, she answered the door.

"Mack, shouldn't you be picking up Grace?"

His gaze swept over her from head to toe. Other than the dark circles under her eyes, she appeared fine, if not surprised by his unannounced visit. "I asked Erin if she could stay a little longer tonight." He pulled off the tie he'd worn that day. Thankfully, he didn't need one every day, but he'd had an appearance in court that afternoon. "We need to talk, and I figured it would be easier without Grace."

She sighed. "You're right." She closed the door and walked into the living room.

Mack followed her.

Was he right about them needing to talk or about it being easier without Grace around? Did it even matter at this point? He waited for more, but when she stayed silent, he made the first move. "You've been avoiding me. Why?"

She raised her hand as if to bite her nails, then crossed her arms instead. "Are you and Grace moving to New York with Bethany?"

Ah. *Now* things made more sense. Grace had told Jessie why she'd run away. "No. Like I told Grace, this is home now. We're not moving anywhere."

"Then Bethany didn't tell Grace you were moving back with her?" Her words came out as more of an accusation than a question.

"Bethany told Grace she wanted us to move back with her. Grace misunderstood. I explained to both of them why that's never happening. Is that what's been bothering you?"

Jessie unfolded her arms and ran a hand through her hair, then crossed her arms again. "If you two aren't getting back together, why were you kissing her last weekend?" Her voice remained strong, but he noticed the tears in her eyes.

He hadn't realized Grace had shared that, too.

"Listen, Mack. I understand if you want to try things

again with Bethany. You were married and have a daughter together. If that's what you want, then go ahead. Just be honest with me. Don't keep me hanging around in case things don't work out."

Considering all the hell she'd gone through with her last boyfriend, he wanted to strangle Bethany for causing her anxiety now and casting doubts on their relationship.

"She's beautiful. Any man would want a chance with her, but you're the one she wants."

He had a reply prepared until she uttered the last sentence. "Did Bethany say something?"

"You could say that. But you didn't answer my question."

He'd suspected Jessie had a stubborn streak, but she'd never turned it on him until now. "She came on to me Jessie." He saw the conflict in her eyes when he reached for her hands. "She wanted us to give it another try, but I told her no. You're the one I want in my life, no one else." For the first time since he'd walked in, she cracked a smile. Not the one she usually gave him, but he'd take it.

"And I want to be with you and Grace."

He heard the 'but' before she said it.

"But I won't compete with her for you. I can't have her coming on to you or telling me to back off because you and Grace are her family."

Oh, how he'd love to wrap his hands around Bethany's neck at the moment.

"Can you promise she won't be a problem again?"

His instincts said she wouldn't. Since they'd first separated, Bethany had never acted as if she wanted them together again. He suspected she only did so now because she was single and he had Jessie, a situation that had not occurred before. In another month or so, she'd have someone else and not think about him again.

"It doesn't matter if she does; I don't want her. I want you. And, really, she only said that because she's bored and lonely. Bethany doesn't do well on her own. She needs an audience."

Jessie took a step back and his hands fell by his sides. "And what if she wants you to be that audience?"

He understood her concerns, but that didn't make the situation any less frustrating. "Trust me. I made my feelings clear on Saturday, but if they didn't get through to her and she does do something again, you have my permission to deck her. I won't tell anyone." He wanted to lighten the atmosphere.

He didn't get the smile he hoped for. "While that's a tempting idea, I'm serious, Mack."

He wished he could give her a perfect answer. Right now, he just had his gut and what he knew about Bethany to go on. "We'll make it so she can't try anything. If I drive Grace to New York, you'll come with me. When she picks Grace up at my house, you'll be there, too. We'll make it so she's never alone with me. Will that work for you?" He used the first ideas that popped up.

Stunned described her expression. "You'd do that?"

"I love you, remember? But we aren't going to have to worry about it. In another month, she'll introduce Grace to some rich guy she met in the city and all will be right again." He waited for a smile or a nod. When one didn't come, he went on. "Do you trust me, Jessie?" Deep down, he knew she did. If she didn't, she never would have slept with him, not after what her ex-boyfriend put her through. Once she realized how much she trusted him, Jessie would know she had nothing to worry about. She had to reach that conclusion because the idea of Jessie leaving him scared the hell out of him. Somehow, in a short period of time, she'd become an essential part of his and Grace's lives. He couldn't imagine life without her.

The seesaw her emotions sat on leaned in his direction, and she searched her heart. Yes, she trusted him. Throughout their relationship, he'd been understanding and patient. He'd never pushed. He gave her control and let her set the pace of their relationship from the beginning. And she loved Grace. She thought of her more as a daughter than her boyfriend's daughter. She wanted them in her life. If she let Mack go now, not only would she be losing him and Grace, but she'd also be losing some of the new person she'd fought so hard to become.

If Jessie ended things with Mack, Bethany would now have control. That, she couldn't let happen. Whatever else took place between them; it had to be because it was what *they* wanted, not Bethany or anyone else.

"I do trust you." She moved closer. "And I'm sorry about the last few days." Jessie embraced him, managing to hit her arm on the pistol holstered on his side. She'd done it at least a half dozen times since they'd started dating. One of these days, she'd remember he wore the thing to work.

Rather than answer, Mack pressed his lips against hers. When he pulled away, she wanted another kiss.

"As far as I'm concerned, the last few days never happened, Jessie."

He bent his head toward her again, but she beat him to the punch and reclaimed his lips, infusing all the emotion she felt into that single kiss. Somehow, though, he took control of it, and she just hung on and savored every moment.

When they pulled apart, his ragged breathing matched her own, and she suspected the look in her eyes mirrored the hunger in his.

"I wish I could stay, but Grace is waiting for me."

"I know. It's okay."

"Why don't you meet me at my house?" He brushed some stray hairs behind her ear. "She misses you. You can't even imagine how disappointed she was when you skipped movie night."

She'd like nothing more, but she shook her head. "I can't. Maryann is coming over. She's got some big news she wanted to share. When you knocked, I thought it was her." She suspected Gage had proposed. The two of them had been together forever. "I have a few things to do in the morning, but I'll be over afterward. I promise."

Mack's hands brushed the sides of her breasts before traveling lower and around to her butt. "You could always call her and cancel. Tell her something came up." He pressed her against his erection and she considered the suggestion.

"We wouldn't have much time together anyway tonight, and Maryann sounded so excited." She reminded herself how long they'd been friends. It would be wrong to cancel on her.

His mouth came down on hers for one long, drawn-out kiss. "I'll see you tomorrow then. I love you." He released her and took a few steps away.

"I love you, too. Tell Grace I love her."

Mack's smile grew bigger. "Will do." He opened the door as Maryann raised her hand to knock.

***

Everyone expected constant chatter when they walked into Peggy Sue's Coffee Shop in the morning. However, a different noise level greeted Jessie Saturday morning.

With her assistant manager opening the store, she could stop in for a box of her grandfather's favorite lemon pastries. She had a meeting in ten minutes with the owners of The Hair Cottage, one of the businesses she did bookkeeping for. After that, she'd promised to visit with her grandparents, something she hadn't done in a while.

Heading for the long line at the counter, she spotted Sean with Tony and Striker seated together. Not an uncommon sight. All three men lived alone, though that would be changing soon for Sean, and they often met up for breakfast.

"Hey, Jessie," Tony said when she paused at their table. "You just missed Mack."

"I'll see him later. Does it sound louder than usual in

here today or is it me?"

"Everyone's talking about Gage. You heard the news, right?" Striker, the only one without a mouthful of food, answered.

She had from Maryann. While she'd been expecting Maryann to tell her she'd gotten engaged, instead she'd told her how Gage and his band had been offered a recording contract by a big time music company. "Maryann said they were waiting to tell everyone."

"Someone let it slip," Sean answered.

"Maryann told me it wouldn't have happened without Mia's help."

Sean shrugged. "She got the representative out here, but that's it. If he hadn't liked the music, they wouldn't have gotten the offer."

She thought Sean downplayed Mia's role, but that was Sean.

"While you guys gossip, I have work." Striker stood, taking his coffee with him. "See you all at Liam's house-warming party tonight."

"Not me. I'm flying out to see Mia this afternoon."

"Saturday is movie night with Mack and his daughter."

"You in, Bates? I heard the blonde you've been hot for will be there."

"Who is she this time? The secretary from the town hall you told me about or the new bartender at Masterson's who was hitting on you?" Sean asked.

"Neither. Besides, I'm seeing someone."

Jessie hoped the unknown woman didn't expect anything long-term. In every other aspect of his life, Tony was a great guy. He worked hard and helped out his friends and family whenever they asked, including coaching a little league baseball team when his brother in-law needed an assistant coach. When it came to women, though, he drifted from one to the next. He'd been like that for as long as she remembered, and at this point, she assumed he'd never change.

"I'll see you guys later. Tell Mia I said hello," Jessie said before she joined the line.

The meeting with Tina, The Hair Cottage's owner and manager, was brief, and although she couldn't wait to spend time with Grace and Mack, Jessie found herself looking forward to her visit with her grandparents. They'd played a key role in her life, and since moving into her own place, she'd visited them several times a week until Mack entered her life. While she loved the new road her life had turned down, she missed them.

The smell of fresh-baked pumpkin pie filled the old farmhouse. One of her favorite desserts, she hoped her grandmother had baked more than one; otherwise, she'd likely not get a slice to take home. In addition to being her favorite, it also ranked number one on her grandfather's list.

"Don't tell your grandfather, but I baked a pie for you to take with you. I thought maybe you and Mack could enjoy it together," her grandmother said as she gave her a hug. "I hoped he and Grace would be with you today." Her grandmother accepted the bakery box, but before she put it down, her grandfather entered, swiping the box from her hands.

"I'll take those." He walked away remarkably fast considering he used a cane.

"Those are for after lunch."

Her grandfather ignored his wife and kept on walking.

"That man is impossible," her grandmother grumbled with an affectionate smile, which caused Jessie to smile as well.

Even after more than fifty years of marriage, her grandparents still adored each other. The long-lasting love and devotion they had was what *she* wanted. For a while, she'd given up hope of ever finding it, but now, thanks to Mack, she'd changed her mind.

"Do you mind grabbing the sandwiches, Jessie?" A plate covered with roast beef sandwiches sat next to the stove where a pot of beef barley soup simmered.

Grabbing the plate, she carried it to the dining room table, surprised to see her dad seated with her grandfather since he worked most Saturdays. But she was glad he had today off. She'd canceled her last father-daughter meal because she'd wanted to be left alone.

"Did you and Mack sort out whatever problem you had?"

She choked on her water when her father asked his question. She'd expect that question from her grandmother, not her father. "Why do you think there was a problem?" She wiped the water she'd spilled off her chin.

"I drive by that house at least twice a day. Before this past week, your car was there almost every day. It hasn't been there all week."

She'd never guessed her dad was that observant. "Everything's fine, Dad. I just had a crazy week."

"Good, because I want some grandchildren."

Someone had turned the world upside down; that was the only explanation for her father's comments. "We've only been together a few months, Dad." Even before her father's off-the-wall comment, she'd envisioned herself with a baby who looked a lot like Mack.

"Your grandmother told me about the way he looked at you when she ran into the three of you at The Jade Orient. He has no plans of letting you go," her grandfather said, adding his two cents to the conversation.

"And did Jessie tell you she's going on vacation with him and his daughter next month?"

She hadn't told her grandmother not to tell anyone, but she'd hinted in that direction. Both her grandfather and father held somewhat old-fashioned views about sex and marriage.

"Separate hotel rooms, right?" her grandfather asked before reaching for a lemon pastry. He hadn't even finished his lunch, but the temptation proved too much for him.

Her dad grabbed a pastry from the box too. "What did I tell you? A man doesn't invite just anyone on vacation with his daughter. I won't be shocked if next year at this time I have my first grandchild on the way."

Between her father's talk of children and her grandfather's question about separate bedrooms, today ranked as the most uncomfortable lunch ever. "Did you hear about Gage Larson?" If she hoped to survive lunch, another topic of conversation was required.

CHAPTER 17

Jessie had never understood why so many people came to this theme park year after year. She even knew a few people who came more than once a year. Now, she understood. She'd visited theme parks before, but none had prepared her for this place. Here, everything right down to the most miniscule detail was seen to. Heck, yesterday, she'd seen a park employee wiping down the trashcans after a short afternoon rainstorm.

Inside the park wasn't the only place that got special attention. Their hotel rooms were cleaned daily, the sheets changed, and towels shaped like animals or objects left on their beds. So far, she'd found a swan, a butterfly, and a monkey. She couldn't wait to see what showed up tomorrow. Maybe the housekeeper would make an elephant like the one Grace discovered today or a sailboat like they had placed on Mack's bed.

Whatever she found, this vacation would go down as the best ever in her book. In fact, she could say that about the past several months. Ever since Mack and Grace had entered her life, it had been one joyous occasion after another. The only dark spot being the day Grace had run away and the few days that followed. Sometimes, that day seemed like a lifetime ago.

The Sunday after her dad announced his desire for grandchildren, the three of them and Socks had gone hiking together. Later that night, after she'd helped Mack tuck Grace in, the little girl had told her she loved her for the first time. It had taken a lot of willpower to hold back her tears that night.

The weeks between that night and Thanksgiving had flown by in a blur as Jessie had prepared the store for holiday shopping and helped decorate Sean's house for Mia's return. Thanksgiving turned into a huge event, with Mack's parents inviting her grandparents and father over so they could all celebrate together.

Perhaps best of all, Bethany had moved on just like Mack predicted. Not long after the incident with Grace, they drove her up to New York for a weekend visit and met Bethany's new boyfriend, a sportscaster for one of the major networks.

Yup, life doesn't get much better. Jessie checked her reflection in the bathroom mirror. So far, they'd kept to the same schedule: they got up early, grabbed a quick breakfast, and hit one of the parks where they stayed until one or so. Then they'd come back and take a quick swim. The idea of swimming outside in December still boggled her mind, but that was Florida. After their swim, they'd grabbed a quick lunch before going back to another park.

Today, though, Mack insisted on changing the routine. They'd still arrived at the park early, but they stayed through lunch. Around four, they returned to their rooms, but skipped the swim. Instead, he'd ordered Grace to nap before they went back for the fireworks later. Considering everything else she'd seen here, she knew tonight's fireworks would be extraordinary.

"One more minute, I promise," Jessie called through the door that connected their rooms as she picked up her earrings. Tonight, they had dinner reservation at an Italian restaurant, and he'd promised there would be no fairy tale characters joining them. As much as she loved seeing Grace get so excited every time a favorite character passed by, it would be nice to make it through a meal without the little girl needing an autograph.

Anyone who passed them would've thought they were just another family on vacation when they headed out. While they weren't—at least, not officially—in Jessie heart they already were.

***

He watched Grace fidget from one foot to the other. Anyone passing by would assume she was anxious for the parade and fireworks that would start soon. He knew the truth. She knew what he planned to do tonight. Before he'd purchased the ring—now in his pocket—he'd sat Grace down and asked her how she felt about him marrying Jessie. He'd assumed a positive response because the two of them had developed a strong bond over the months. Happy didn't adequately describe Grace's response.

Together, they'd gone ring shopping. He wouldn't trust such a secret with any other six-year-old, but Grace could keep a secret better than anyone he knew when she wanted to. That shopping trip had happened three weeks ago and tonight he and Grace would give it to Jessie. It seemed appropriate to include Grace since, if Jessie agreed to marry him, Grace came along with the package.

"I read online that since it's so close to Christmas, they include Santa in the parade," Jessie said.

From where he stood, he caught a glimpse of the parade coming their way. Hopefully, they'd snagged a great spot close to the park entrance near where the parade ended.

"I hope Santa got my letter with my new address," Grace said. "I don't want him to bring my toys to my old house."

They'd had this conversation several times, and both he

and Jessie had reassured her. "Don't worry, that won't happen," he promised.

As the parade passed in front of them, he heard Jessie reassure her again, too. While his daughter and girlfriend watched the various floats and dancers pass by, he counted the minutes until the fireworks started and he could finally ask Jessie to marry him.

No sooner did Santa Claus pass by in a large sleigh than the first volley of fireworks exploded overhead. A wild mix of blue, purple, and red, the colors lit up the sky and captured everyone's attention.

Everyone's but his.

Between the third and fourth explosions, he squeezed Grace's shoulder and slipped her the ring. Then he grabbed Jessie's hand and turned her toward him.

"Is everything okay?" She looked down at Grace before glancing his way.

"Perfect," he answered. "But Grace and I have something to ask you."

The plan had been for him to ask her and for Grace to hold out the ring, but in true six-year-old fashion, Grace changed things up.

"Will you marry us?" She held up the ring, gripping it as if her life depended on it while, overhead, the fireworks filled the sky with vibrant colors.

Despite the fireworks and various conversations, several people around them heard Grace's question and turned their attention to them.

Jessie's hands flew to her mouth, and she took half a step back. Then she knelt down and reached for Grace, pulling her close while tears streamed down her face. "Yes, I will marry you."

Around them, applause broke out and Grace glanced up at him. "She said yes, Daddy."

"I heard, buddy."

When she heard his voice, she stood and hugged him. "I love you." She kissed him, a soft brush of her lips against his. "And I love Grace, too."

A grand finale of explosions went off in his chest. "I'm ready for that now." He took the ring from Grace and slipped it onto Jessie's finger. "I love you."

"I love you, too," Grace piped up, not about to be forgotten.

Mack let go of Jessie long enough to pick up his daughter so they could have a group hug. Around them, the cheers and applause grew louder, and Mack knew it wasn't for the fireworks in the sky.

And he wholeheartedly agreed.

The End.

Read Cat and Tony's story in *The Playboy Next Door*, book 3 in the series.

***

Hometown Love

Hometown Love

Hometown Love

Hometown Love

Hometown Love

Hometown Love

239

Printed in Great Britain
by Amazon